Proof I Was Here

PROOF
I WAS
HERE

BECKY BLAKE

A Buckrider Book

Buckrider Books is an imprint of Wolsak and Wynn Publishers.

Cover and interior design: Kilby Smith-McGregor
Cover and interior images: iStockphoto
Author photograph: Kara Blake
Typeset in Baskerville, Tibetan Beefgarden AOE, HVD Poster
Printed by Ball Media, Brantford, Canada

10 9 8 7 6 5 4 3 2 1

Canada Council for the Arts   Conseil des Arts du Canada   Canada

ONTARIO ARTS COUNCIL
CONSEIL DES ARTS DE L'ONTARIO
an Ontario government agency
un organisme du gouvernement de l'Ontario

TORONTO ARTS COUNCIL   FUNDED BY THE CITY OF TORONTO

The publisher and author gratefully acknowledge the support of the Toronto Arts Council, the Ontario Arts Council, the Canada Council for the Arts and the Government of Canada.

Buckrider Books
280 James Street North
Hamilton, ON
Canada L8R 2L3

Library and Archives Canada Cataloguing in Publication

Title: Proof I was here / Becky Blake.
Names: Blake, Becky, 1971- author.
Identifiers: Canadiana 20190062061 | ISBN 9781928088776 (softcover)
Classification: LCC PS8603.L3295 P76 2019 | DDC C813/.6—dc23

For my sisters, blood and chosen.

Barcelona. Spring 2010.

PART ONE

1

I pushed out through the front door of the building and walked
away from the apartment that was no longer mine. Barcelona had
turned ugly. The leaves of the palm trees were dead and brown, the
cobblestones of the sidewalk broken and dirty. Even the sunlight
looked damaged – gritty and soot streaked. I brushed away the first
few tears that came, but after a while I didn't bother. Nobody was
paying any attention to me. It was late Saturday afternoon and the
Gothic Quarter was gridlocked with last-minute shoppers: teenagers
with cell phones, parents with strollers, couples holding hands and
taking up way too much space.

The old itch was starting under my skin, but I ignored it. I just
needed to sit down somewhere and collect myself. A bar across the
street looked dim inside and not too busy. I reached into the pocket
of my trench coat for my wallet, then checked my other pocket. For
a second, I thought I'd been robbed. Then I remembered the sign
at the Boqueria market warning about pickpockets; that I'd moved
my wallet into my shopping bag for safekeeping – a bag now sitting

on Peter's kitchen counter. After throwing my keys at him, the only way to retrieve it would require doing things I couldn't face: standing on the wrong side of his locked door, and begging to be let back in.

The itch travelled up my arms and converged in the centre of my chest, a maddening spiky mass that needed to be torn out. I stepped into a souvenir shop and walked up one of the aisles, past the magnets, T-shirts and statuettes: tacky souvenir versions of all the attractions I hadn't had a chance to see yet. At a rack of postcards, I stopped. Slowly, I spun the carousel, reviewing its contents – famous paintings by Velázquez, Miró, Goya, Dalí.

I checked the mirror in the corner of the shop. The sales clerk was busy with a customer at the cash. I slipped a Picasso postcard into my pocket, and the prickling scratch in my chest was soothed for a moment by a warm rush of heat.

Time slowed as I moved toward the exit. I saw the cashier's finger pressing down hard on a ribbon she was tying, the customer shifting his weight from foot to foot. In the front window, the pages of a book had turned yellow from the sun. The bamboo wind chimes jangled like hollow bones as I opened the door to the street.

A block from the shop, I glanced back. No one was following me. In my pocket, the shiny surface of the postcard felt reassuring – I deserved to have at least this tiny thing. I walked for several minutes, feeling buoyant and indestructible. Peter wanted to send me back to Canada, but I wasn't going to go. I had a three-month tourist visa. Maybe by the time it ran out I'd have found some way to belong in this city without needing to be his wife.

"Niki, I can't marry you," he'd said. For a second I'd wondered if he could have found out about what I'd done on my last day back home, but I didn't think that was possible. Something else had happened. An affair with one of his new co-workers maybe, while I was busy packing up our apartment in Toronto. When he'd denied it, I called him a liar. So then he admitted the truth: "I didn't miss you," he'd said. "I didn't miss you when you weren't here."

I pulled the postcard from my pocket. It was a portrait of an asymmetrical woman, the two sides of her face so dissimilar they could belong to different people. I stopped in the middle of the surging crowd on Portal de l'Àngel, unable to take another step. As I looked around, only two people made eye contact: an old woman begging in front of a restaurant and a homeless man sitting on a piece of cardboard beside the Zara entrance. The man had scabby bare feet and long dirty hair. His eyes pinned me in place. He knew what I knew: that in just one moment, everything could change; that the change could leave you invisible, except to others who were unlucky. I had a strong urge to go and sit beside him, to let myself sink down to the ground and then stay there.

Beside me the roll-down door of a dress shop clattered shut. The woman closing up the store clicked a heavy lock in place, then pulled on her motorcycle helmet and hurried to the curb. She had somewhere to go, or someone to see. Those were the reasons that kept people moving – kept them from sinking to the ground. I needed a destination, but the only place I could think of was the Boqueria. I'd been shopping at the market every day – had been there just this morning. I loved the tall pyramids of brightly coloured produce, and the vendors who called out terms of endearment as I passed: *¡Cariño! ¡Querida! ¡Mi amor!* They sounded like a giant family all clamouring to feed me.

I looked around, trying to choose another destination while avoiding the homeless man's eyes. Up ahead was a sign for the metro. As I walked toward it, I folded the postcard down the middle and dropped it in a trash can. At the entrance, I stepped onto a long silver escalator and let it carry me down. I would ride the trains until I figured out some other way to move.

A line of people were waiting to feed their tickets into the auto-mated turnstiles. When it was my turn, I just climbed over. The soles of my boots smacked loudly on the other side. I smoothed my skirt over my leggings, then headed off down a long damp hallway to a set of well-worn stairs. On the platform below, I waited for the train.

There was only one thing in my pocket – a paint chip sample I'd been planning to show Peter. As I touched its edge, I remembered the rush of stupid joy I'd felt holding up the little red square, imagining the white walls of our new home filling up with a colour that I loved.

The tracks of the metro seemed especially close. I turned and placed my hand on the tiled wall, feeling the solid surface beneath my fingers. After a moment, I began to draw with my fingertip, tracing the skyline view from Peter's balcony onto the wall: the Gothic cathe-dral's spiky roofline, and beyond it the wide avenue of art nouveau buildings, then the distant curve of mountains on the horizon.

When the train came, I got on and looked back at the blank stretch of tiles. Maybe if I stayed underground long enough, the city would look beautiful again when I came back up.

2

I rode the trains back and forth for hours, noticing the unloved people. They were suddenly everywhere. A thin woman in a window seat rocked herself back and forth. Quarter-sized bruises lined the inside of her arm. They reminded me of a shirt I'd shoplifted once — when I'd pulled off the security tag, it left splotches of permanent dye all down one sleeve. The thin woman rose and moved toward the exit, rubbing at her arm. People could also be ruined in ways that were impossible to reverse.

A man with a neck brace got on at the next stop and planted himself in the centre of the aisle. He was holding a display box full of small coloured lighters. "My friends, forgive me," he called out. His Spanish was slow and basic like mine. "I am ashamed to be begging for your help. I am a strong man, but I cannot find work. Please, any help at all." He held out a lighter in my direction and flicked it. I had nothing to give him except my attention.

He turned and walked off, starting his speech again from the beginning. At the far end of the car, a group of tall Black men slouched, loose and tired, in their seats. They were speaking French and I guessed they were from somewhere in West Africa. Each man had a large cloth bag between his feet. They were probably illegal street vendors – the kind who sold knock-off purses and sunglasses to tourists. One of the men dug in his pocket for some change and handed it to the guy with the neck brace. No one else gave him anything, and soon he moved on to the next car.

As it got later, the passengers got louder. Groups of teenage boys jostled each other, drinking and spilling cans of San Miguel. On one train a throng of people in Megadeth concert T-shirts crowded around me, smelling of weed and shouting to their friends about epic guitar solos.

Around 3:00 a.m., two security guards in bright orange vests got on at Plaça Catalunya station. They walked the length of the car with wide balanced steps. I sat up straighter as they passed, but they hardly looked at me. I checked my reflection in the window: a skinny tourist with staticky blond hair and a faint half moon of mascara under each of her eyes.

The security guard at the department store in Toronto had taken a lot longer to assess me. A balding man with thick biceps, he had locked the door of the store's security office, then pressed me down hard into a chair and taken my wallet out of my purse. Standing behind me, he tossed pieces of my ID onto the table: my credit card, my bank card, my driver's licence, the art gallery membership Peter had given me for my birthday, the found photographs I'd put into the photo sleeves as a joke to create a fake family for myself.

When he was finished, he bent down and spoke with his mouth so close to my ear that I could feel his breath on my neck.

"Spoiled," he said. "I see women like you all the time."

When I told him he didn't know anything about me, he slammed a hand on the table and pointed to my belongings. "Tidy that up."

I worked to fit the cards and photos back in my wallet, while trying to keep an eye on his hands. "I swear I was going to pay," I said when my wallet was back in my purse. "I was just looking out the window to see if it was raining."

The guard pulled a chair up to the table across from me. "Intent to deprive, that's all I need to prove."

"But I wasn't even outside the store. They're seriously not going to charge me for this. You should just let me go."

"What I *should* do," he countered, pointing his pen at me in a way that made me certain he'd held a weapon before, "is make sure you understand who's in charge here, and what things cost." He shoved the cashmere scarf across the table toward me.

I stared at the scarf as we waited for the police to arrive; I couldn't figure out why I'd taken it. As a kid I'd shoplifted food that my mom and I needed. As a teen I'd boosted clothes and makeup from big chain stores. But it had been years since I'd stolen anything. Plus, this time had felt different – more like the scarf had grabbed onto me instead of the other way around. It had been so soft. The colour so lovely, a perfectly cooked egg yolk. I had brought it to my face, thinking of another scarf I'd stolen. After that, it was in my purse.

When the cops arrived, a female officer greeted the guard by name, then scribbled in her notebook as she listened to his report: how he'd watched me slip the scarf into my purse and then move past the checkout counters to the front door.

"When I grabbed her, she elbowed me in the face." The guard rubbed his chin with a woeful look. "And then, when I let go of her for a second, she turned around and cut me with her key." Gingerly, he began to roll back his sleeve revealing a deep ugly gash on his arm.

"Are you kidding me? I didn't touch him!"

"Mike, you should go to the ER and get that looked at," the policewoman said. She turned to me. "If you assaulted him, that's a much more serious charge."

"But I didn't! If anything, I should be pressing charges against him. I probably have bruises all over me." I could still feel the imprint of his fingers on my shoulders and arm.

The policewoman ignored me and read me my rights while her partner motioned for me to put my hands behind my back. The security guard gave me a small smirk as the cops walked me out.

In the tiny interrogation room at the police station, I waited alone, pacing and trying not to panic. When I asked for a lawyer, the on-duty counsellor called the phone in the room. I told him that the guard hated me for some reason, that he seemed like he might be dangerous, that he'd probably been in a fight; a key couldn't make a gash that big – it must have been a knife or a piece of glass. The counsellor's advice was to say nothing for now. It was the same advice he no doubt gave everyone, no matter what unfair shit they were dealing with.

Finally, a police officer with a crewcut let me out. At his desk, he made me sign a blue sheet of paper with the words *Promise to Appear* at the top. On it was a court date over six weeks away and a list of my charges: theft under five thousand dollars and minor assault.

"And don't even think about not showing up," he said. "Otherwise we'll be adding an extra charge to that list and you'll be spending some time in jail."

The moment I was free to go, I went home to pick up my suitcase, then took a taxi to the airport and checked in early for my flight. I'd already been planning to leave and never come back, so nothing had really changed. I just couldn't believe I'd done something so impulsive and almost ruined everything. I was worried it might happen again.

I was still feeling anxious as I cleared Spanish customs. But then the airport's automatic doors opened, and I smelled a different country's air for the first time, and spotted Peter's face in the crowd of people waiting for their loved ones.

Only a week had passed since then, but now everything was different. I rested my face against the window, letting my cheekbone bounce off the surface each time the train stopped and started, imagining a bruise forming and then spreading, my whole cheek caving in like a rotten apple. I welcomed that level of damage; I deserved it for trusting Peter.

When the train reached the end of the line again, I crossed to the other side of the tracks and settled into a seat on a train that was heading the other way. Travelling back and forth across the city, I was digging a groove, deeper and deeper, into the ground, like an eraser rubbing at the same stubborn mark. There were so many feelings I would need to forget: the rush of pride whenever Peter walked toward me in a room, my gratitude each time his family welcomed me on holidays, the thrill of being Peter's "plus one" at art openings and my secret hope that one of his colleagues might someday want to show my paintings. Love – I'd felt that too. For the first time I'd let it take me over completely.

The view from my window was mostly dirty grey walls punctuated by red plastic tubing. The stations were gaudy baubles strung far apart on a dingy cord of tunnel. After 5:00 a.m. the train slowed down, stopping in each station for longer. I wasn't hungry, felt nothing in my body, and was thankful for that. The metro would shut down for a few hours on Sunday night, but that still gave me almost a whole day to decide where to go next. Eventually I would have to return to the apartment for my wallet and passport. I wondered how long I could survive with nothing in my pockets. Maybe a few days. Maybe longer. A few days of staying away from my mother's apartment had turned into six years. Six years and counting.

The train passed along a brief stretch of aboveground track, and the dawn-diluted sky looked bleached and empty. I'd been thinking about my mother more than usual over the last few weeks – how moving to Spain meant I'd probably never see her again. I'd even sent her a postcard the day after my arrival, the ocean between us making contact feel safe for the first time; there was no chance she could ask to see me. I'd also wanted to show off, let her know that I'd moved into a gorgeous apartment in Barcelona and that I was getting married. Now, if I ever spoke to her again, I'd have to admit that everything I'd been bragging about – all the differences between her life and mine – had disappeared. She might even think I'd been lying. All I could hope for was that maybe she'd moved, and the postcard would end up in the trash.

By 8:00 a.m., the train had picked up speed, and there were people around me again, sitting tall and self-important in their church clothes. The artificial light exposed everyone's flaws: their undyed roots, razor-burned chins and sweat stains. I closed my eyes and didn't bother to open them again, even when passengers sat down beside me. For a long time, there was only the weight of strangers' bodies coming and going.

One particular body eventually caught my attention because it smelled like the outdoors: sea air mixed with soil and exhaust. I shifted slightly away, then thought I felt something touch me. I reached my hand into my pocket before remembering – I had no keys, no money to protect. Instead I felt the brush of retreating fingers. I straightened up and opened my eyes.

Sitting beside me was a young guy with gold-brown skin and dark eyes. He wore a folded bandana over a mess of black hair and a dirty leather cuff around each of his wrists. Both hands were on his knees now where I could see them. He was looking down at his fingers.

"*Mejor quédate despierta,*" he said.

The sense of his words burst in on me without knocking. Growing up, when my mom was working late, our neighbour Rosa had always said the same thing to me if I started to fall asleep on her couch. "It's better if you stay awake."

I took a moment to rearrange my limited Spanish vocabulary, then told him that I didn't need to stay awake; there was nothing in my pockets.

He turned to study me, and the light in the metro flickered. For a second he looked like a small boy, vulnerable, then he was a young man again, a thief. Something raw and open passed between us. It felt like recognition.

He handed me the paint chip he'd taken from my pocket and stood up.

I watched him walk down the length of the train, nobody looking as he passed. A tourist couple was blocking one of the doors, pointing up at a metro map. The woman had a knapsack on her back and the pickpocket stopped behind her. The train made a sudden snaking motion as it entered a new tunnel, and the woman stumbled, then regained her balance. It had happened so fast, I wasn't sure I'd really seen him do it – just a quick flash of motion behind her back. I almost called out to the tourists, but I changed my mind. They were laughing together, the woman holding onto the man's arm. Honeymooners maybe. It was stupid to live like that, like children in adult bodies, so trusting and unprotected.

A recorded voice announced the name of the next station, Urquinaona, and the train began to slow. The pickpocket glanced back at me then disappeared through the open door.

All the blood in my body rushed to my legs as I stood up, propelled by one thought only: I needed to go where he was going. I stepped off the train just as the doors were closing. The pickpocket was already on the escalator, halfway to the top. I squeezed my way around people until I was almost close enough to touch him. Through his thin T-shirt, his shoulder blades looked like handles I could grab.

Outside, the sunlight was blinding. I followed him for a block, keeping a little distance between us. At the corner, he stopped at a red light, and I came up beside him, my heart knocking hard. He turned, and I forced myself to meet his gaze. One of his dark eyes was a little sleepy, and beneath it a constellation of freckles was scattered across his cheek. His nose pointed slightly in the other direction as though it had been badly broken.

When the light changed from red to green, he gave me a small nod, and I felt like we were making a deal; I wasn't sure for what. We began to walk together, first along the top edge of the Gothic Quarter, then into El Raval, the neighbourhood on the opposite side of La Rambla. I'd been to El Raval a few nights before with Peter. We had planned to eat dinner there, but we hadn't really felt safe. There were fewer street lamps, and after taking a wrong turn, we'd ended up in a dark alley full of beggars and junkies that led to a street lined with prostitutes. I'd seen a splash of fresh blood on the cobblestones.

The pickpocket shifted closer to me on the sidewalk as we squeezed by a group of men gathered in front of a butcher shop.

They were talking in a language I didn't recognize, and they watched us as we passed. Above my head, laundry flapped from balconies. I heard babies crying, and somewhere a car alarm was going off.

A tall man in a suit shuffled by. There was something wrong with his feet. When I turned to look, I saw that one of his legs was fake – it had twisted around and was pointing in the wrong direction. The sadness in the city kept creeping up behind me, tapping me on the shoulder. Look, it seemed to be saying. Look here, and here, and here.

I followed the pickpocket through a stone archway. A tarnished plaque said we were entering the grounds of the city's first hospital, no longer in use. There was a damp, hurt smell coming from inside the courtyard. When we walked toward it, I saw a man pulling a needle out of his arm. Another washing his shirt in the fountain. Two others were yelling back and forth, hands in the air. All of them stopped as we entered, and I stopped too.

The pickpocket looked back to see if I was coming, and I searched his face for a promise of safety that wasn't there. When I moved toward him again, he led me into a shadowed corner that smelled like piss and orange blossoms. Behind a pillar he bent down and swung open a metal grate. Inside was a dusty green knapsack. I heard him rummaging through the pockets, and when he turned, he handed me a cream-filled pastry in a plastic wrapper. His fingernails were dirty.

"*Tienes que comer*," he said. "You have to eat."

I took the pastry. "*Gracias.*"

"*De nada.*"

He lifted his T-shirt and pulled the tourist's wallet from the waistband of his jeans. He was very thin, and he had a shiny pink scar snaking across his stomach.

I took a couple small bites of the pastry, then stuck the rest of it back in the wrapper. Eating sweet things always made me feel sick – they weren't really food.

The pickpocket was looking through the wallet and pulling out the money. It was a sensible, beige canvas wallet with snap pockets for change. Empty plastic photo sleeves dangled from its spine. The tourists would be mourning its loss now, their day refocused around cancelling their credit cards, making expensive phone calls, trying not to blame each other.

The pickpocket wrapped the wallet in a piece of newspaper and walked over to stuff it in a trash can. When he returned, he asked for my name.

"Jane," I said. It was an alias I hadn't used since I'd been caught shoplifting as a teen.

He put his hand on his chest. "Manu."

It was either his name, or the name of something that lived inside him. "Manu," I repeated, and he nodded.

As it got dark, more people joined us in the courtyard, flopping down on the grass, tired or drunk, and calling out to each other in loud friendly voices. Manu and I were sitting on his blanket, and he was trying to organize his belongings. He repacked his knapsack, starting with a pair of workboots and a small stack of clothes, then a collection of papers and photos sealed in a Ziploc bag. Into the side pockets, he tucked some items he'd been carrying with him: a pack of cigarettes, some money and a folding knife. We weren't talking too much, but other people kept coming over to visit. Many of them seemed to be missing something: a shoe, an eye, a finger. It was hard not to stare at them, to wonder what Manu might be missing.

A foul-smelling old man in a ripped overcoat stood looking down at us for a moment, then lurched in my direction, laughing and grabbing at his crotch. He didn't have any teeth. As I leaned away from him, my thumb moved instinctively to the band of my engagement ring. It was a gesture of security: I am loved, I am safe. But those things were no longer true.

Manu asked the old pervert to leave me alone, assuring him that we both knew what a ladies' man he must have been in his prime. The old man seemed to like this, and immediately began telling Manu a story about a woman he'd slept with. I waited until neither of them was looking, then slipped off my ring and put it in the inside pocket of my coat. Maybe I could sell it. I wondered how much it was worth.

The old man looked over at me again. "*¿De dónde eres?*" he asked. "*De Canadá.*"

"*¿Y por qué estás aquí?*"

I didn't know if he was asking why I was in Spain, or why I was in the courtyard. Before I could find out, two policemen in black-and-yellow jackets arrived, and the old man grumbled and wandered off, heading toward the exit.

"Mossos," Manu explained, glancing toward the cops. He shoved the rest of his stuff back into his knapsack, and we joined the others who were filing out of the courtyard.

One policeman stared at me as we passed. He probably thought I seemed out of place, but the truth was I'd been around rundown people for most of my life. Growing up, the streets around my apartment building in Parkdale were full of them. At school, I pretended I was from a nicer part of the neighbourhood, making sure I only hung out with girls who lived in the big houses further north, girls who came from proper two-parent/two-job families and had braces and university funds. Brigid was the only one of those girls who knew where I really lived. As teenagers, my apartment was a good place for us to hang out because my mother was hardly ever home. After I got kicked out, Brigid's parents took me in so I could finish high school. Staying in the guest room of their giant house, I had thought maybe the memories of my mother's building and street would fade, but they hadn't.

Manu and I exited through the archway. The others from the courtyard were all heading off in different directions, some of them trailing blankets, like children who were half asleep. Manu looked uncertain, as if he didn't know what to do with me.

"Let's go somewhere else," I said. "I don't care where."

"Okay." He indicated a direction, and we crossed the street, then walked down the same dark alley that I'd stumbled into with Peter — the one that led to a street full of prostitutes. Tonight, I looked at them more closely. They were young mostly, a wide selection of Eastern European and sub-Saharan girls with gold or silver hot pants and dark glossy lips. Unloved and far from home. The city's sadness was heavy now, two hands pressing on my shoulders instead of tapping.

A woman with an orange Afro beckoned to us with a long fingernail as we passed. Manu said something to her that I didn't catch, and she smiled, leaning back against the wall.

At the end of the street we came to a construction site enclosed by a temporary fence of whitewashed boards. One part of the fence featured a picture of how the finished building would look. It was going to be a hotel; tall, black and cylindrical, modern and expensive. Someone had spray-painted the fence with graffiti. Two words jumped out at me: *gentrificación, PIGS*.

Above the fence, the hotel's half-finished skeleton rose into the night sky, its inner workings exposed: iron girders, rusted piping, thick cables. We walked around the perimeter until we came to a gap in the fence. Manu pushed his bag through the opening and squeezed in sideways after it. To follow him I had to suck in my breath, and even still, raw-edged wood scraped me front and back. Inside the fence, I froze. There was a security guard sitting on a chair, listening to a small radio. I was ready to run, but he didn't look up. Manu took two cans of beer from his knapsack and placed them on the ground near the guard, then motioned for me to keep moving. There were wires and broken bricks underfoot. I held out my arms to the sides as we climbed a set of concrete stairs. After being underground the night before, it didn't feel good to be going so high up. I tried to count the floors to distract myself, but I kept losing track.

When we reached the top, maybe the tenth or twelfth floor, Manu walked straight to the unfinished edge of one of the rooms and sat down with his legs dangling out into the open air. I could see the lights of Montjuïc beyond him; we were as high up as the mountain. Some of those lights were coming from the art museum where Peter now worked. I wondered if he was looking for me some-where in the city down below, wishing maybe that he'd bought me a cell phone that worked here.

Manu turned. *"Venga."*

I shook my head. I was too dizzy to join him at the edge. Instead, I sat down on the dusty floor, but I couldn't escape the view. I'd never been afraid of heights before, but now the open space was pulling me like a magnet while sadness pushed me from behind. There was a cemetery on the other side of Montjuïc – it was one of the first things I'd seen driving in from the airport – and I thought about how easy it would be to stand up and walk toward it. Five seconds to the edge, then five seconds of falling, maybe ten. I hugged my knees to my chest. I needed to contain those thoughts.

Manu got up and came over to where I was sitting. He took the thin blanket out of his pack and spread it on the ground. I shifted over and he sat beside me. From down below, the shouts of the prostitutes, beer sellers and drunken tourists rose up. Distorted and tangled by the distance, they combined into a racket that spiked and dropped in unpredictable patterns, impossible to block out. I was grateful for the noise; I didn't want to fall asleep. I had a sudden urge to reach out my hand and slip it under the edge of Manu's T-shirt. I wanted to trace the pink line of his scar, but that was just another thought I needed to contain.

I stared down at my empty hands, at the thin white tan line on my ring finger that looked like a scar of my own. "I don't know what I'm doing here," I said.

Manu picked up some pebbles from the floor and tossed them toward the edge of the room. A few of them skittered over the side and fell. "We're looking at the city," he said in Spanish.

Then we sat beside each other for a long time, breathing all the emptiness in and out.

3

When I woke, there was an absence of noise, and for a few seconds I didn't know where I was. Then I saw Manu standing at the unfinished edge of the room, the sky a deep pre-morning blue beyond him. The smoke from his cigarette spiralled into the open space.

I sat up slowly. Every part of my body felt stiff and cold. I couldn't believe I'd spent the night more or less outside.

Manu flicked his cigarette butt out into the air, and I remembered we were at least ten floors up. *Not yet,* I thought. *It hasn't hit the ground yet.*

Manu turned. He was probably only a few years younger than me, maybe twenty or so, but his bandana made him look younger – like one of the teenage boys who hung out on the steps of the community centre in my old neighbourhood back home.

Now. Now it's hit the ground.

I assumed the workmen would be arriving soon, so I stood and began to fold the blanket. Manu came over to help me, and our fingers touched when we came together with the corners. It was strange to have slept beside him. During the night I'd woken to find his hands clutching at me, but it had only been a nightmare he was having. When I'd asked if he was okay, he'd apologized, his voice travelling up from under something heavy. Neither of us had gone back to sleep for quite a while.

We finished packing up, and Manu shouldered the knapsack. At the top of the stairs, he turned and waited for me to pass. I shook my head. I wanted him to go first so I'd have something to focus on, rather than looking down. There was a sheer drop to the ground floor on the left side of the stairs and no handrail to steady myself.

When we reached the bottom, Manu led me back toward the fence. The security guard and the cans of beer were gone. We squeezed out through the gap, then stood for a moment on the other side, looking around. There wasn't a single person on the street.

"*¿Vamos a la playa?*" Manu asked.

"Sure." I had wanted to see the Mediterranean ever since my arrival, but I'd been holding off until Peter had time to join me. There was no longer any reason to wait.

Manu and I walked down to the port, then followed the line of coast around until we hit sand. I stopped for a moment to scan the Mediterranean's curving length and took my first breath of sea air. Despite everything, I felt a surge of joy. I was finally here. In high school, Europe had seemed like a different world, a kind of utopia where people sat around all day in cafés talking about painting and architecture. For months, I'd saved up any money my mother left for me on the kitchen counter, eating only stolen food, and hiding her ten-dollar bills in an overdue library book called *Europe on a Shoestring*. My bedroom walls had been covered with the pages I'd torn out: the Eiffel Tower, the Colosseum, the canals of Venice, the Louvre. I'd often wondered if those pages were still stuck to my old walls, if the money was still in the guidebook, if my mother even lived in the same apartment.

The Mediterranean looked less inviting in person than it had in pictures. Tall whitecapped waves smacked over and over against the breakwall, and a strong wind raced across the sand. Manu led me to an open-air shower and we took turns washing up a bit, splashing cold water on our faces and hands, our arms and feet. When we were finished, we sat down on his blanket to wait until we were dry. Nearby a tall sculpture towered above us: a stack of four rusted cubes with a window in each. The cubes sat atop each other at slightly off angles, like a four-storey apartment building in danger of toppling over.

A man in a windbreaker was coming toward us, a plastic bag of canned beverages swinging from one hand. He was one of the beer sellers. There seemed to be an army of them working the city, day and night. Most were South Asian, newcomers to Barcelona who were trying to make a bit of money by selling beer without a licence. Peter said the beer sellers stashed their bags in the sewer whenever police approached. Because of that, he never bought beer from any of them.

The man called out a greeting, then came over and sat beside us, hiding his bag under the corner of our blanket. I looked around. The beach was deserted, but I guessed you could never be too careful if you were living in Spain illegally, like he probably was.

The beer seller was speaking quickly to Manu in heavily accented Spanish. I thought I heard something about money, the word *marijuana* maybe. After a few minutes, he turned to me, smoothing down his mustache. "Where are you from?" he asked in English.

"Canada."

"Canada?"

"Yes."

"My cousin lives in Canada!" He put his hand over his heart. "Céline Dion! Niagara Falls!" He started to sing "My Heart Will Go On." He had a good voice. After a few bars he stopped. "What city?"

"Toronto."

"Toronto! My cousin lives in Toronto! Kipling and 401! Do you know where this is?"

"Yes." The trade school where I'd studied graphic design was out there. It was an ugly part of the city – just a bunch of highways and industrial strip malls near the airport, noisy airplanes flying overhead.

"It's very nice – my cousin told me." The beer seller looked out to sea. "Someday I will go there. Maybe to live."

I recognized the expression on his face – I'd felt the same way about moving to Spain – but it was hard for me to imagine that someone's dream could be to go to Highway 401 and Kipling Avenue in Toronto.

Down the boardwalk, people were beginning to arrive, most of them with jackets and scarves, walking little dogs. The beer seller stood up. It was time for him to go to work. He shook hands with Manu, then rummaged through his bag for a can of soda to display. "Goodbye, Canada!" he said. "Have a good day!"

I watched him walk off, then turned to Manu. I wasn't sure how much he'd understood, so I tried to explain the conversation to him in Spanish. I was surprised at the number of words and expressions that were coming back to me from the time I'd spent with Rosa and her family growing up. The only thing I was having trouble with was conjugating the past, but maybe that didn't matter. Sticking to the present with Manu would keep things very simple between us. It would be like nothing important had happened before we met – like everything that mattered started now.

Manu took a battered-looking apple out of his knapsack and cut it into pieces with his knife, handing me slices one by one and choosing the bruised parts for himself. We ate without talking, staring out at the endless procession of waves crashing into the shore. When the apple was finished, Manu wiped his knife clean, then used the blade to smooth flat an area of the sand.

"Do you know Jaume I metro station on the yellow line?" he asked.

"Yes." It was the metro station closest to Peter's apartment.

"Good. So this is the entrance," Manu continued in Spanish, but slowed his words to make sure I could follow. He drew two sets of stripes with the tip of his knife, then pointed from one to the other. "Stairs. Escalator."

"Okay."

"And here, by the ticket machines" – he cut an *X* below the stripes – "would be the best place for you to stand." He stopped and looked at me, reading back and forth across my face.

I studied the drawing again, and then I understood. He wanted me to help him rob someone. My face flushed as I realized I'd been waiting for him to ask me, hoping that he would.

"What would I have to do?"

"Just distract someone. Talk to him, keep him busy."

"Would I have a disguise?"

"No. He'll think you're a tourist, and if you do it right, he won't remember you at all."

That sounded like a perfect job for me – to be there one moment and then forgotten.

Manu retraced the *X* in the sand. The wind was flapping the sleeves of his ratty T-shirt against his thin arms. "I have to send money to my family," he said. "But whatever we get, I'll share it with you."

I took the knife from him and drew a circle around the *X*. "This is where you want me to wait?"

He nodded.

"Okay, I'll be there."

The yellow line of the metro made stops at the beach, the cathedral and the most expensive shopping street, so the trains were always packed with tourists. I hoped I'd understood Manu's instructions. *Espera*. He'd said the word a number of times, but it was a verb that meant both to wait and to hope. In any case, I was doing both of those things: waiting for him by the ticket machines inside the Jaume I entrance, and hoping he was going to appear. It had been at least twenty minutes, but I didn't think he'd abandoned me – he'd stashed my boots in his knapsack and loaned me a pair of his shoes to wear instead. I looked down at my feet, winter pale and too small against the rubber frame of his dirty white flip-flops. The shoes seemed like an obvious prop, a glaring indicator that something wasn't right. To steady my nerves, I pretended to be waiting for a friend, pretended so hard I could almost picture her, another tourist who I'd greet with a hug before we smacked up the stairs in our unseasonal sandals, talking loudly in English.

I asked someone for the time. Ten fifteen. Peter would be at work already, no chance of running into him. Beside me on the wall there was a map of the city, sprawling and complex. At the top the streets were organized into a grid, but in the centre there was no pattern – just a broken plate that someone had tried to glue together. Superimposed over the city, the lines of the metro looked like a small child had drawn them with crayons: red, yellow, green, purple and blue.

I turned from the map just in time to see Manu coming down the corridor from the tunnel. He touched the leather cuff on his left wrist. I glanced at the man to his left and did a quick assessment: he was wearing a *Pac-Man* T-shirt and cargo pants, he didn't look very fit. I watched him from the corner of my eye as he pushed through the turnstile. I guessed he would take the escalator instead of the stairs. Just before he passed, I turned and stepped on ahead of him, a shiver racing up my spine. I could feel the man at my back.

As we approached the top, I pretended my flip-flop was caught in the moving stairs. I hopped around, causing a minor traffic jam as the man reversed as far as he could on the escalator to avoid running into me. Manu was behind him.

"Sorry," I said in English, turning and smiling. I was playing a clumsy tourist – a carefree girl backpacking around Europe on her parents' money. I saw him glance down the front of my shirt as I bent to adjust my shoe. Then I walked off down the street, the finer details of the city leaping out at me for a moment: the lacy edge of a red fan in a shop window, the sweet smoky smell of hot chocolate and cigarettes as a café door opened and closed. After a block, I turned to look back. Both Manu and the escalator man were out of sight. I'd thought standing on Manu's *X* might change me in some way, but I still felt almost the same. The only difference now was a new itch, just beginning: the question of what else I might do, how far I might go.

When I met Manu back in the courtyard, he pulled the wallet from the waistband of his jeans and handed it to me like a gift. I tore open the Velcro flap. Inside was the man's face, an old picture on a gym membership. In just one moment, his entire day had changed. Manu and I had made that happen.

Manu frowned; I was taking too long. I dipped my fingers into the billfold and slid up the edges of the money. The colour was orange, fifty euros. I spread the bills with my fingers: one, two, three. Each of them was crisp and new, straight out of the bank machine.

Manu's jaw relaxed. "You have good luck."

It was funny he thought that; I wasn't a lucky person at all. I slipped the gym membership out of its plastic sleeve to keep as a souvenir, then handed the wallet back to Manu. He held out one of the bills toward me.

I didn't want to have a fifty-euro bill in my pocket when there were so many thieves around. "Can you keep it with yours?" I asked. "I'll get it from you later."

Manu reunited the three bills and stashed them in his knapsack. "Let's go have lunch," he said. He wrapped the wallet in a piece of newspaper and tossed it in a trash can as we exited the courtyard. Back on the street, he stopped a passerby to ask her for a light. I watched the position of his hands to see if one would slip into her pocket, but they both stayed cupped around the tip of his cigarette. The woman tucked her lighter back in her purse, then continued up the street. She had no idea how close to a thief she'd just been. I wondered how Manu decided who to rob.

"What do you feel like eating?" he asked.

I shrugged. There was something else I needed now much more than food. We walked in silence for a moment before I could bring myself to ask.

"Hey, Manu? If we do it again —"

The corner of his mouth lifted into a half-smile; he'd been expecting me to want this. It was a relief to have someone finally know what I was really like.

"Could you show me how you choose a mark?"

He studied my face. "If that's what you want," he said, "we can go to La Rambla after lunch and I'll show you some things."

4

La Rambla was the pedestrian street that split the city down the middle. After stuffing ourselves with giant empanadas from a stall in the market, Manu and I started at the bottom of the street, down near the port where the cruise ships came in. The passengers surging from the boats looked anxious but determined: they had four hours of freedom to squeeze in as much sightseeing and shopping as possible. As we followed them around the statue of Columbus, they were all holding tightly to their purses or camera straps – they must have been given a warning on the ship – but by the second block they were already distracted. We watched a man buy a bottle of water, then absently stuff his change into his fanny pack without zipping it closed. A woman at a café set her purse on the ground beside her chair rather than holding it in her lap.

"Stupid," I said, and Manu agreed.

We continued to follow the pack of tourists as they fanned out moving northward. La Rambla was so busy it forced people to stroll whether they wanted to or not. There were caricature artists and kiosks with exotic pets and flowers. There were men selling bird whistles or toys that lit up and went zinging into the sky. Attractive young couples handed out flyers for clubs and flamenco shows. Some of them did demonstrations, pulling the tourists into a dance.

"Anyone who touches you on La Rambla is trying to rob you," Manu said, and after that, I looked at everyone more closely.

In between the kiosks, buskers were performing, some doing tricks, others frozen in place like statues while tourists posed beside them for photographs. As we walked by, one of the human statues jumped down off his crate. "Boo!" he said. He was spray-painted gold from head to foot and was holding an inflatable globe.

Manu introduced us: Atlas from Australia, Jane from Canada. He seemed to think we would feel some kind of connection as English speakers.

"How's it going?" I asked.

"Good." Atlas took a swig of water from a bottle. "You on vacation?"

"No, I live here now." For the first time that actually felt true.

"Cool." Atlas turned to Manu and switched to Spanish. Language between people was fluid in Barcelona. Catalan was the region's official language but not everyone spoke it. This divided the city into a hierarchy of comprehension: locals from Catalan-speaking families were at the top, then Spaniards from other regions, followed by new immigrants who could speak Spanish, then those who couldn't. Tourists were at the bottom.

The tourists passing by us now were slowing down to stare at Atlas. A couple days earlier, I would have done the same. Atlas sighed and cracked his neck. "Three more hours. Then I'm getting blitzed." He climbed onto his crate and looked over at me. "I guess I'll see you around."

He froze in position, and Manu and I continued up the street. A block further along, we stopped in front of an antique-looking fountain. It was shaped like a giant urn, and it had an ornate black lamppost perched on top. When Manu twisted one of the gold taps, a gush of water came out. He bent down and turned his face skyward to drink, then stood back so I could do the same. The water was very cold, and it tasted like something metallic that had come from the sea: a moss-covered anchor, or a fish pierced by a hook. When I was finished, I stood up and wiped my chin.

Manu nodded in the direction of a passing man. "Guess," he said.

"Guess what?"

"Tourist, local or thief?"

I looked at the man again. He was moving quickly through the crowd. "Thief?"

Manu shook his head. "Local. What about those ones?"

I followed his gaze to a pair of men holding matching tote bags. "Tourists?"

He shook his head again. "Thieves. You have to look at their eyes."

I guessed wrong a couple more times, then I started to feel like Manu was messing with me — there was no way he could know for sure.

"I don't get it." A space became free on a bench and I plopped down to rest. Manu squeezed himself into the half-space beside me, and the woman on his other side got up and left. He smelled like he'd been setting off firecrackers in a damp sandbox. I wondered what I smelled like to him.

He pointed at a woman whose eyes were fixed on the scalloped roofline of a building. "Tourists: They're looking at things to take pictures of, things to buy. Looking left, looking right, looking up."

"Okay."

"Locals." He pointed again, this time to a man moving fast and focused along the edge of La Rambla, trying to avoid the crowd. "Looking straight ahead."

I nodded. "And thieves?"

He scanned the crowd. "Do you see those two guys over by the metro entrance?"

"Yes." I watched them for a moment. They were leaning casually against the wall, looking down into the metro stairwell as if waiting for someone to arrive. As people exited the station, the two men followed them with their eyes, assessing.

"Except for the vendors and the Mossos, thieves are the only ones on La Rambla who are looking at other people," Manu said. "And there are almost always two of them."

I thought about this. "Do you work with someone else?"

"Not anymore." Manu picked up a longish cigarette butt from under the bench, straightened it out, then slid it into his almost empty pack.

It was obvious he didn't want to tell me what had happened, but suddenly I had a lot of other questions. "Have you been doing this for a long time?"

"Not too long. Five months or so."

Five months. That wasn't long at all. For some reason, I'd been picturing him picking pockets since childhood, like Oliver Twist. "So before" – I was struggling with my Spanish; I moved my hand backward to indicate time reversing – "what are you doing for money?"

"What *were* you doing for money," Manu corrected me. "I was working in construction."

I thought about the security guard who'd ignored us sneaking in through the fence the night before. "At the hotel?"

"Yes." Manu looked down and pressed the toe of his sneaker into one of the raised cobblestones. "The company brought a lot of workers from Ecuador. So they could pay us less."

"Is that where you're from?"

He nodded.

"And what happened to your job?"

"The financial crisis started. Now the Spaniards have to take the jobs they didn't want before." Manu stood. He was finished answering questions.

I jumped up to join him, reminding myself that from now on I should just stick to the present tense the way I'd planned.

Manu pointed with his chin at a man who was searching for a street sign.

"Tourist?" I guessed.

"Good. Now you pick one."

I looked around, the crowd splitting into three loosely braided strands. It was like a trick of the eye: once I saw the street divided, I couldn't unsee it. I turned back to Manu. There were two of us and we were watching other people.

"Thieves," I said. "We look like thieves."

When we were finished with the guessing game, Manu gave me some tips on how to pick out a good mark. He explained that tourists were the safest bet because they were already distracted, and then instructed me on how to assess people for value. Older tourists were more likely to be carrying cash. Tourists wearing certain brands of watches and shoes were the ones whose wallets might be fullest.

It seemed like there were lots of potential marks, so I still didn't really know how Manu chose one person over another – why one tourist's vulnerability made her a target, and another's didn't. If he ever let me choose, I decided I would add another element. I'd try to pick a person who deserved it. To make my selection, I would have to get very close to people – close enough to see all of their flaws.

"Are you ready to try this for real?" I asked.

Manu shook his head. "Working on La Rambla is too dangerous. There are a lot of Mossos and too many other *carteristas*."

I'd never heard the Spanish word for *pickpocket* before. It sounded like a combination of the words for *wallet* — *cartera* — and *terrorist*.

"What if we went somewhere else?" I asked.

"We can go back to the metro tomorrow, if you want. Today, we've already had our luck."

Tomorrow. The word rippled through me in two directions. On one hand, it was disappointing to have to wait, but on the other hand, I was happy that Manu assumed we would still be together the next day. It wouldn't hurt to stay with him for another night. I wondered if Peter had found my wallet in the kitchen yet — if he was worried about me.

"I should check my email," I said.

"There's a locutorio over there." Manu pointed to an Internet café across the street. The front window was covered with flag-studded posters showing the long-distance rates for every country in the world. Inside, Manu told the woman at the counter that I needed to use a computer, and that he was going to wire some money to Ecuador. He took out two of the fifty-euro bills and passed them across the counter. I didn't know whether the third bill was mine still, or if maybe it was ours now.

I went to the back of the shop and sat down at a computer. When I signed in to my email, there were three messages from Peter. I read them fast, almost without breathing. The first was an apology, the second a statement of concern, the third a warning that he was going to notify the police if he didn't hear from me soon. He was definitely worried. I felt a dizzying pressure drop, and then an unstable relief wobbling wide and uncertain around a tiny pinprick of hope.

I wiped my palms against my leggings, and looked toward the cashier's desk where Manu was filling out a form. If he and I hung out together much longer, we were going to start to feel responsible for each other, but so far we hadn't crossed that line. I could still walk away and pretend that the last day had never happened. I could go back to the apartment and ring the intercom buzzer and Peter would let me in. I could look him straight in the face and find out if maybe he'd made a mistake, if he might lift me up and squeeze me close like a very precious thing he thought he'd lost. I hit Reply on the third message and began to type: *I need to come and get my things.*

I stopped. Everything I owned in the world was still travelling across the ocean by slow boat. I pictured the shipping crates I'd packed arriving in the weeks ahead, Peter separating our belongings into two piles, and then sending my things back. I bit at a loose piece of skin on my bottom lip, then tore it off between my teeth. There was a little burst of blood, and I sucked it into my mouth as I reread Peter's emails. For two years he'd been signing-off with *love* and then his initial, but now there was only a blank line and then his name spelled out in full. He hadn't made a mistake. He was worried about me, but that wasn't the same as wanting me back. I didn't need his charity. In just one day I'd made fifty euros. If I worked with Manu a while longer maybe I could earn enough to survive without ever going back to the apartment, without ever finding out what I might say or do to be allowed to stay there.

I deleted my first message and started over: *I'm staying with a friend. Please don't contact me again. I'll email you when I'm ready to get my things.* The *staying with a friend* part would bother him. He'd assume I'd met some guy, which I had, but not in the way he'd think. I left a blank line, then typed my name. Without an endearment, it looked like an island, a lost crate afloat in the middle of the ocean.

I hit the Send button before I could change my mind, then skimmed the other messages in my inbox. There was one from my old boss, and one from Brigid, asking if Peter and I had booked our appointment at the courthouse to get married. She and I had run into each other on the streetcar the day before I left, and we'd talked about what a coincidence it was that we were both engaged, and about how fast time had flown in the six years since I'd lived with her family. I could tell Brigid was impressed at how well I was doing – that she was happy to see we were on the same path. If I wrote and told her my wedding was cancelled, we'd have nothing in common again.

I logged off the computer and stood. The other Internet customers were all staring at their screens with their backs to me. It gave me the same invisible feeling I'd had while standing in the middle of the surging crowd on Portal de l'Àngel when only the beggars had returned my gaze. This time, it was Manu who was watching me.

I joined him at the cashier's desk, and he pushed a few coins across the counter to pay for my time.

"Thank you," I said.

He shrugged. "It's nothing."

He opened the door for me, and together we stepped into the street.

5

Over the next week, Manu taught me a lot of things, like how to distract a mark on the metro and how to dumpster dive outside of the Carrefour. He showed me where to exchange foreign money from the wallets we stole, and introduced me to Yaya, one of the illegal purse sellers who'd buy foreign coins from us that the exchange kiosks wouldn't take.

Manu was giving me a portion of the money from each of the wallets, and I kept these funds in an empty bread bag, stashed in the bottom of our knapsack. Someday I would have enough money to start a new life here – to rent a small apartment, then buy some new clothes and a cell phone so I could find a job. In the meantime, it just made me feel better knowing the money was there, watching it accumulate day by day. I allowed myself to spend a small amount on basics – food, toiletries, underwear – but whenever I had the impulse to buy something non-essential, like a pillow or a sketchbook, I pushed the thought away. It wasn't hard to do; I didn't want to acquire belongings that I might get accustomed to having, and then lose. Living with Peter, I'd been completely surrounded by possessions. There were so many things to miss that sometimes I didn't know where to start.

Walking empty-handed around the city, my biggest fear was running into Peter – bumping into him as we rounded a corner, or having him tap me on the shoulder from behind. I was dirtier than I'd ever been. My clothes were wrinkled, and there was a tear in the bottom of my skirt where I'd ripped it on the fence at the unfinished hotel. I was sure I must smell like the construction site or worse, despite washing off at the beach each morning. In the Gothic Quarter, I always found excuses to draw a wide circle around Peter's street, and everywhere we went I scanned above the crowds at just his height.

Manu never asked me why I didn't like the Gothic Quarter, or who I was trying to avoid. He often seemed nervous himself and was constantly on the lookout for Mossos. In the city centre we saw them everywhere, and more than once I'd observed them listening with bored expressions while a tourist complained about being robbed. The Mossos' indifference had given me the impression they were slow-moving, but I was wrong.

One afternoon, two of them ran by us on La Rambla chasing a pickpocket. When they caught him, they threw him to the ground, pushed his face into the cobblestones, then yanked him up and shook him hard before forcing him into a police car. I recognized the awkward angle he was sitting at – I'd been forced to lean forward the same way when my hands were cuffed behind my back.

"You see?" Manu said. "That's why we work in the metro. The Mossos almost never go down there."

The thief in the police car was bleeding from his forehead. He peered out from the back-seat window, searching for someone. I surveyed the group of onlookers who'd gathered. If his partner was in the crowd, he was putting on a good show. More likely he'd run off, or maybe *she'd* run off. Manu had told me there were lots of female thieves, but so far I'd only seen one example: a gang of women in head scarves swarming around a tourist at a bank machine. Their approach had seemed crude and aggressive compared to the technique Manu used. He had a delicate touch that no one ever seemed to feel. I guessed he was more skilled than the thief in the police car, but maybe it was only a matter of time before we got caught. If that ever happened, it was Manu who would have the stolen goods in his hands, his hands in the pockets. I could just deny my involvement, and the police would have no proof. That was assuming they would listen to me, of course.

When the car moved off down La Rambla, Manu and I walked up to Ronda Sant Pere, a street that curved around the top edge of the Gothic Quarter. Outside of a tobacco shop, Manu shaded his eyes and looked through the window at the clock behind the counter. "Quarter past six." Most of Barcelona would be heading home from work now, which meant it was time for our second shift to begin.

We entered the metro at Arc de Triomf, feeding our tickets through the machines at the turnstiles. On the platform below we stood separately, waiting for the train. After a few days of practice with the escalator routine, we'd come up with a new plan for working together underground. Twice a day at rush hour, we stepped onto a crowded train pretending not to know each other. If we had the knapsack with us, I wore it to look like a tourist. I also carried a map, or a large shopping bag from El Corte Inglés. Both items worked well to camouflage Manu's fingers as they slipped into a purse or a pocket and slid out a wallet.

The train pulled into the station with a gust of hot air and my pulse quickened; each moment needed my attention now. I stepped aside for the throng of people getting off, most of them wearing business suits, or skirts and heels. The Catalans dressed conservatively for work. That was one of the ways to guess who the locals were and avoid targeting them.

I boarded the train and squeezed into a central position in the middle of the car where I could look in all directions. Even though there weren't usually Mossos underground, we still had to watch out for metro security. I scanned the car for their bright orange vests, then began to assess the passengers around me. All of Manu's tips about picking out a mark on the metro were based on circumstantial details: positioning, clothing, timing. Now that it was my job to choose, I tried to select marks who also caught my attention because of a flaw, a mistake or a misstep. Each time I picked out a deserving target, it felt like I was righting something that had tipped over in me. It was such an intense feeling that it blocked out most of my guilt. To get rid of the rest, all I had to do was remind myself that I wasn't actually stealing. I was only assisting Manu with something he was going to do anyway, a petty crime he needed to commit so he could send money back home to help his family: his mother and three younger brothers, and his older sister who had twins and no husband.

I counted the stops as they went by, biding my time. Manu was superstitious about robbing anyone before we'd travelled at least five stops, and he had another rule about not robbing anyone near Plaça Catalunya. He wouldn't tell me why, but I figured it must be because there was a police station inside the metro there. Manu had a lot of superstitions. Aboveground he always pulled me off the sidewalk and into the street if he could feel the metro rumbling underneath his feet. He wouldn't tell me the reason for that either.

After six stops had passed, I checked to make sure Manu was in place. There was a tourist with a sunburn and an expensive polo shirt standing close to me. I'd selected him because he was smug-looking and seemed bloated with good fortune, the type of guy who always ate before he was hungry and never thought about feeding anyone else.

I studied his body language, waiting for him to pat or cradle a pocket, pointing out the most valuable thing he was carrying. Manu had taught me to watch for this movement, and the predictability of the behaviour always gave me a brief pang of empathy. I felt it now as the guy clutched and released at something in the side pocket of his jacket. It was almost as if he was expecting to be robbed. As if he wanted, or needed, it to happen.

"Excuse me," I said. "Do you speak English?"

"I'm British," the guy said.

"Oh good!" I smiled, but he didn't smile back. The train entered the next station and the people around us jostled into different positions. I knew Manu was behind me.

"I'm just trying to get to the Sagrada Família." I unfolded a city map, positioning myself so that the side pocket of the guy's jacket was concealed from view by the cascading sections. "Do you happen to know how to get there? I'm not even sure if I'm on the right line!" I smiled again, blinking. Lost blond. Bewildered.

The guy squinted at me. Something was wrong. Maybe he'd been robbed before and was extra suspicious of strangers. I dipped my head lower so I was looking up at him. "Sorry, I'm really terrible with maps."

He pointed with a stubby finger at a little picture of the church. Then he gave me a scornful look and walked away.

I got off the train at the next stop, glancing back along the platform to make sure no one was following me. As usual, Manu was walking toward the opposite exit. The stairs at my end of the tunnel seemed to take forever to reach. Outside, I let out a long breath.

When I arrived back at the courtyard, I found Manu already there, stretched out on his back in the grass, one arm shading his eyes from the sun. I stood looking down at him.

"How much?" I asked.

He uncovered his eyes. "Forty."

Forty euros was slightly better than average. Manu had been right about my luck on our first day working together. The 150 euros in the escalator guy's wallet had been an extremely good take. Most days we were happy to get half that, even when we managed to swipe two wallets.

"That guy almost seemed like he knew what I was doing," I said.

"I don't think he was a tourist. Probably an expat." Manu sat up and looked at my feet. "Can you run in those?" Now that the weather was starting to get warmer, I'd bought myself a pair of dollar-store flip-flops.

"Sure. I guess so."

"Show me." He pointed to a tree at the end of a pathway.

I didn't feel like running.

"Come on," he said.

I rolled my eyes, then started off in the direction he was pointing. The movement felt unnatural, like going for a first jog after a long winter indoors. I did a small loop and came back.

"That's not running," Manu said. "Imagine that someone's chasing you." He jumped up and hopped over the back of a bench, then ran with his whole body. He was even using his arms to move forward like he was swimming through air.

When I tried it again, I lost one of my flip-flops and stumbled, landing on my knees in the grass. I flipped over and brushed myself off, embarrassed.

Manu came over and held my bare foot against his palm. His fingers were warm, and they just capped my toes. "Sit here and rest for a bit," he said. "I'll be back." He tossed me the British guy's wallet and walked off.

I lay in the grass and thought about being chased, maybe being caught and punished. Until today, the passengers on the trains had always trusted me, even the first few times when my hands had been shaking so much I'd had trouble unfolding the map.

I opened the British guy's wallet and took out an ID card; he was some kind of diplomat. Maybe that explained his caution: he'd been everywhere and seen everything. A world-weary cynic, he'd built up an immunity to bewildered blonds, or maybe he'd never been susceptible to begin with. I pictured him at home with a husband. Classical music on the stereo, sipping Scotch from a rock glass that reflected the light. On their walls, they'd have expensive artwork: two large abstract pieces that spoke to each other across a long dining-room table.

I pulled the stack of ID cards from my pocket. My collection was growing with each day that passed. I had flipped through the cards so many times I knew each mark's details by heart – their names, birthdates and heights. I'd also invented a story for each of them, bios that stretched from the distant past right up until the moment our paths had crossed. Most of the IDs had pictures on them, but even for the ones that didn't, I could still remember the person's face, and also the reason I'd chosen them: obnoxiously large purse, loud voice, fake laugh, ignoring her kid, not giving up his seat, being too fit, too rich, too vain, too stupid, too smug. That last one was the diplomat. I added his ID to my pack. Maybe he'd been distrustful because I was too dirty to pass for a tourist. It was probably time to buy myself a new outfit, something clean and pressed.

When Manu returned a quarter of an hour later he handed me a pair of unfashionable white sneakers. "Try these."

"Thanks." I wondered if he'd stolen the shoes or bought them. He knew I didn't like to buy things for myself. I pulled them on, then sat looking at my feet.

"What's the problem?"

"No problem. They're great." I tied a double knot in one of the shoes' laces, then the other. When I was finished, I looked up. I couldn't wait any longer to ask. "What happened to the partner you had before?"

Manu sighed.

"Did he get caught?"

"It's bad luck to talk about that."

"Sorry," I said. "I just want to know." If I was going to keep us safe, I needed to have the threat confirmed.

"Yes," Manu said. "He got caught."

"At Plaça Catalunya?"

"Yes." Manu pulled me to my feet, then pointed at the tree again. "Now go."

This time I ran as fast as I could, maybe faster than I ever had in my life. "He got caught." I recalled how it felt to have a pair of strong hands grab me by the shoulders. It could easily happen again. I was not invisible. Not innocent.

"Better," Manu said when I returned. "And if you act like you're chasing someone instead of being chased, people will get out of your way. No one will try to stop you." He was staring off into the distance, remembering something. "And don't look back. It only slows you down."

I nodded. If someone chased me now, I'd think of Manu's partner and run like my life depended on it. I'd seen lots of people in Barcelona run that fast: the other thieves, the purse sellers and the beer sellers. Many of their lives really did depend on not getting caught. I had to learn to run as fast as them.

46

6

The knock-off purse sellers travelled in packs, always four or five of them together with another standing lookout. Yaya's crew worked a high-traffic area on Passeig de Gràcia using a complicated system of whistles to warn each other when the Mossos were coming. At a high-pitched double signal, the whole group would move in unison, pulling on the drawstrings that closed their display blankets over the fake Prada and Gucci bags. Then they'd take off fast, sprinting out into traffic where the Mossos didn't dare to follow.

Yaya had been in Barcelona for over a year, but he was still working to pay off the money he owed to the mob for transporting him to Spain. In Senegal, he'd studied to be an economics professor, but couldn't find a teaching job. Some afternoons, Manu and I sat with him in the park, and he tried to explain complicated theories to us in a combination of French, Spanish and English. The Prisoner's Dilemma seemed to be his favourite. As far as I could understand, it was about two criminals who were being asked to rat on each other for a chance at a lower jail sentence. According to Yaya, they almost always did it.

"Every man for himself, *non? C'est la vie,*" he said. "Nobody wants to go in the cage." He looked toward the entrance of the zoo. The night before, one of the guys in his crew had been arrested and was now in jail. Without papers he'd be deported for sure.

I took a wallet from our knapsack and tossed it to Yaya to cheer him up. The change pocket was filled with British pounds we'd been saving. Yaya knew a guy who would buy them. He tipped the money into his hand, then flipped through the cards in the wallet. I'd already removed the woman's driver's licence for my collection. Yaya stopped at another piece of photo ID, an employee access pass for her office.

"Suzanne Tom-kin-son," he read. He held the picture level with my face and pretended to be doing a comparison. I swatted away his hand.

"*Guiris*," he said, smiling.

"Hey." *Guiri* was one of the first new Spanish words I'd learned in Barcelona. It was a derogatory word for *tourist.*

"*Guiris* like *guiris*," Yaya said. He took a stubby pencil from his shirt pocket, and held it in the air like a piece of chalk. "I have an idea."

A crease of worry appeared between Manu's eyebrows as we listened to Yaya's plan; he was suggesting we sell the stolen wallets back to their owners after we removed the money.

"It will be better than just stealing," he said. "You will have more cash, and the people will get their cards back." He held up Suzanne Tomkinson's ID. "Everybody laughs."

"It's too risky," Manu said. He glanced over to see what I thought.

I shrugged. Something about the idea appealed to me. In the metro, we were always long gone before our marks realized what they'd lost. Yaya's plan meant I would have the chance to finally see someone's reaction.

"Come on, man!" Yaya squeezed Manu's shoulder. "It will be a gentleman's crime, instead of a coward's. And if it works, you can buy me lunch someday."

I saw Manu's lips set tight, and I knew he'd accepted the challenge.
Yaya released his grip. "You'll see," he said. "There will be more
money for you, plus you'll sleep better at night."

Manu shot me an annoyed look; he thought I'd told Yaya about
his nightmares. He pushed himself to standing, suddenly ready to go.

We said goodbye to Yaya and his crew, then started along the
path toward the park exit.

"I didn't tell Yaya," I said. "Seriously. I wouldn't."

Manu nodded, but remained quiet. We'd never talked about his
bad dreams before, and it was obvious he didn't want to talk about
them now.

His nightmares seemed to fall on him like heavy stones. Each
night I felt his hands clenching and releasing in startled pulses as if
he was bracing for their impact. When the clenching sped up, I had
to wake him, and the fear in his eyes always made me think of horses
trapped in a burning barn. Sometimes the afterimage kept me awake,
and I wondered whether sleeping so close to him was a good idea.
Our proximity helped us to keep warm, but maybe it also trapped
the dreams between us, forced them to pass back and forth with no
chance of escape. My own nightmares were different than Manu's,
simple but cruel dreams that were mostly about Peter. In one, a new
woman's name had been poorly dubbed over my own. In another, I
got injured and he didn't come to help.

"Do you want to go check out that grocery store?" Manu asked.

"Sure." A Dutch squatter named Annika had told us about a
supermarket on Via Laietana that was under renovation. She'd said
they were planning to throw out everything that was close to its
expiry date.

When we reached the store, we found a small crowd of people
filling their purses and bags. We pushed in toward the boxes on the
sidewalk and began to stuff our knapsack with dented cans, small

wedges of cheese, bags of broken breadsticks. I was trying to squeeze in a last carton of yogurt when I froze. Peter was standing with his back to me in front of a store across the street. He was typing a message on his phone, looking up periodically as if waiting for someone to come out.

"What's happening?" Manu asked.

I didn't answer. A blond woman in a trench coat exited the store holding up a bottle of wine like a trophy. She called to Peter in a language that sounded Polish or Russian. When Peter turned, his profile was wrong: the nose too long, the chin too weak. It wasn't Peter after all, just another tall, middle-aged man with the same dark wavy hair, and the same busy distracted manner: an almost-Peter who'd been waiting for an almost-me.

"It's nothing," I said. I shoved the yogurt into the top of our knapsack and pulled the drawstring tight. Manu was studying the couple across the street, trying to figure out what had bothered me about them. I knew he wouldn't ask, but maybe he could guess. It had been nine or ten days since we started sleeping so close to each other's dreams. There was no way to know what secrets I'd shared in my sleep.

We dropped off our bulging knapsack at the courtyard, hiding it inside the wall, behind the metal grate where it was cool. It was almost rush hour so we needed to go back to the metro, but after that, we were planning to have a feast.

By the time I emerged from the underground an hour later, the sky looked as if a piece of charcoal had been dragged very lightly across its surface. I missed the drawing and sketching I'd been doing at the apartment in the Gothic Quarter. Even more, I missed the painting I'd been doing in Toronto. The wives of Peter's friends had never liked me much – I was younger than most of them, and I didn't know anything about real estate or organic food, or even how to hold their babies right – but once I'd started giving them portraits as gifts, one by one they'd warmed to me, pulling me by the hand to show me the special location they'd found to hang my work. The fourth portrait I'd done had turned out so well that Peter had tried to stop me from giving it away. "It's really, really good, Niki," he'd said, his words filling me with pride.

There was no point in remembering that now – no point in having "a good eye for colour" when its only use was to notice the shade of a strangely darkening sky.

Back at the courtyard I walked along one of the paths toward Manu. He'd already pulled our knapsack from its hiding place and chosen a patch of grass where we could sit. Dusk was the time of day when the courtyard was busiest, filling up with street people and addicts. It coincided with the time of day when people outside of the courtyard – people with jobs and families – were just getting home, greeting their loved ones and washing their hands before dinner.

Manu began to lay out some food, picnic-style, on our blanket. As I watched him, I thought about the almost-Peter and the almost-me – how the real-Peter and the real-me had almost gotten married. When Peter had proposed I'd jumped up, spilling a glass of red wine across the restaurant tablecloth. One of the waiters had shouted "Opa!" and the other diners had laughed. Then I'd thrown my arms around Peter's neck and hung there for a moment, time halted by joy. I'd really thought he was mine.

"Almost ready," Manu said. He pushed himself to standing and headed off to fill our water bottles at a tap near the corner.

The old toothless man approached as soon as he saw I was alone. He liked to proposition me when he was drunk.

"Lucky," he said, pointing at Manu's back.

I didn't respond. I figured he was going to say something crude about my relationship with Manu. Something untrue.

The old man leaned down. "He's lucky to be alive."

The tone of his voice gave me a chill. Everyone in the courtyard had a story, but I'd noticed that the worst tales were often shared when the main character was not around.

Manu was chatting to someone over near the tap. "What happened?" I asked.

"He was buried. For two days."

"What do you mean 'buried'?"

The old man vibrated his hands in front of my face. "*Terremoto.*"

The unfamiliar word sounded like *earth* and *motion* – he meant an earthquake.

"In Ecuador?" I asked.

The old man nodded. "A building came down on top of him. Killed his father, just like that." He made a sudden smacking noise with his hands and I jumped.

From across the courtyard, Manu looked over.

"Lucky," the old man said. "Lucky to be alive."

Manu was heading back toward us now. I thought about his scar, and how he hated the feeling of the metro rumbling underneath his feet. I had a sudden urge to take care of him, but I knew he wouldn't like that, and besides, I didn't know how.

"Everything okay?" he asked.

"Yes."

He flicked his fingers in my direction, splashing water droplets in my face.

"Hey!" I grabbed his legs and he tumbled down beside me. He reached across my lap and pulled a bag of cookies from our pack. He had a crazy sweet tooth.

Manu took out four cookies, then offered the bag to the old man.

"Poison." The old man spat on the ground. I gave him some bread and cheese instead, and he wandered off, muttering a phrase that didn't quite make sense – something about unstitched things matching up with broken things.

When I glanced over at Manu, he looked different somehow, older maybe, and I didn't know if it was because of the twilight or because of what the toothless man had told me.

Fatherless and two days buried. I'd been underground when Manu and I met, and I'd never had a father to begin with. I shook off the comparison – those things meant nothing. I scuffed my sneakers against each other, trying to mark them up a little. They were so white they were almost glowing.

"Hey." Manu stuck one of his feet between mine like he was breaking up a fight. "Why do you want them to be dirty?"

"I dunno." I kicked his foot away.

He kicked me back. "Well, stop," he said. "They'll be dirty soon enough."

We smiled at each other. Beneath us, I could smell the soil, above us the orange blossoms. Older. He definitely seemed older, more like a man.

We ate until we were full, trying to focus our appetites on the food that wouldn't keep.

"Do you have the room key?" I asked, when we were finished.

Manu pulled an invisible key from his pocket, then placed it in my palm. It was just a dumb joke, but we did it every night.

"Ready?" he asked. He stood, then turned and pulled me to my feet.

After a second, he let go of my hands, readjusting the space between us to arm's length. Maybe one day that space would disappear – we'd bump into each other by accident, then just stay close. It was the first time I'd ever really considered it.

We walked toward the hotel through the hectic evening noise of El Raval. A beer seller was working on the corner, and we bought six beers from him for five euros: four for us, and two for the security guard. The guard at the construction site was Bolivian, and Manu said the only reason he'd gotten to keep his job was because it paid almost nothing. What little money he did make, he seemed to spend on prostitutes. His favourite was a girl who everyone called Fanta because of her orange hair. Sometimes she came to visit us after they were finished, and later that night, we heard her climbing the stairs in her high heels, whistling for us on every floor until we whistled back.

"What's wrong with the rooms downstairs?" Fanta asked when she found us. Manu liked to stay in a different room every night, and this time he'd picked a room high up. He smiled and passed her a can of beer.

She opened the tab with a long fingernail, warm foam spraying outward. "Shit!" She bent over into a curved shape and brushed a hand down her body to wipe away any drops that had landed on her tank top or jean skirt. After a moment, she stood upright and took a long sip, then set her beer on the edge of a crate. The can looked like it was going to fall, and I watched it, waiting.

"Hey, Jane," Fanta said.

"Yes?" A split-second delay. I was still getting used to the name. Manu didn't use it much.

"Did I ever show you the picture of my son?"

"I think so." She'd shown it to me three or four times. "But I'd love to see it again."

She dug for the photo in her purse. "He's a very good boy. He hardly ever cries."

I held out my hand and she laid the picture in my palm, keeping hold of a corner. Her fingernails were decorated with heart-shaped decals. "He looks very sweet," I said. "When do you think you'll see him again?" Her son lived with her mother back in Nigeria.

Fanta sighed. "Not until all of the money is paid off."

Manu had told me she owed money to the mob, the same way Yaya did. With interest, it was probably an amount that would be impossible to repay.

She put the picture away. "Hey, Manu, do you have a smoke?"

Manu took a half-cigarette from behind his ear and handed it to her.

Fanta smiled. Her lips were shiny. "You're a good boy too." She winked at him, and he looked away, embarrassed. I wondered if Manu and Fanta had ever had sex.

Fanta walked to the edge of the room and peered down at the street. "It's busy tonight."

She was right. There must have been thirty girls working when we'd walked by, and at least that many men. I didn't think the rich tourists would put up with having so many prostitutes outside the front entrance of the new hotel, not if they were paying five hundred euros a night for a king-sized bed and a view of the Mediterranean.

"What's going to happen when the hotel opens?" I asked.

Fanta frowned. "The cops will probably make us go. That's what they do with the Gypsies – they take them away in trucks. Put them outside the city, somewhere nobody sees."

"That doesn't seem right."

Fanta shrugged. "We'll come back. Maybe one street over." She took a final drag from her cigarette, then ground it out with the toe of her shiny yellow shoe. The shoe had a black smudge on one side like it had been pressed up hard against something greased. She retrieved her beer from the edge of the crate and finished it in two long swigs. "I have to go."

Manu was watching her. "Take care of yourself."

Fanta laughed and shook her head as if he was crazy. "Who else is going to take care of me?" She started down the stairs.

I looked over at Manu. I might not know how to take care of him, but at least there were two of us. The phrase the old man had muttered came back to me — the one about unstitched and broken things finding their way to each other. Maybe it did make sense.

Manu handed me the can of beer we'd been sharing, and I tipped the last warm sip into my mouth.

7

The next morning, there were loads of extra people on the metro. At first, it seemed like we were going to have an easy day – lots of marks to choose from – but then I realized that the people were all local, or almost local: Catalan families streaming in from around the region for a protest. They all had red-and-yellow striped flags with a blue triangle on one end. Their picket signs tangled at the exits, and their voices joined in a chant I could feel buzzing through me: "InDUH- inDUH-inDUHpendència!"

I caught Manu's eye, then pushed through the crowd toward him. "What's going on?" I asked.

He shrugged. "A *manifestación* at Plaça Catalunya. They have them all the time."

"Do you want to get off the train? Maybe try out Yaya's plan?" We'd practised several times at the beach that morning and I thought we were ready.

"I don't know." Manu still wasn't convinced it was a good idea.

A toddler with a flag painted on his face was staring at us, sitting astride his mother's hip. She lifted his hand and waved it in our direction. Manu smiled and waved back.

"Okay. Let's try it," he said. "My nephews have their birthday soon. It'd be good to send my sister some extra money."

We decided to get off the train at the bottom of the green line, down near the port where the tourists would be shopping at the mall, oblivious to the giant rally. I needed to do some shopping myself before we put our plan in action. I wanted to look as much as possible like a tourist – one who'd just arrived in the city – and I couldn't do that in a ripped and dirty outfit.

Manu said he also needed to buy something and would meet me on a bench by the exit in a half hour or so. He took the knapsack from me and handed me the bread bag with my money in it before he walked off.

I tucked the money in the pocket of my trench coat. At the H&M, a barrel-chested guard sat perched on a tiny stool. As I passed, I knew he was sizing me up, imagining a history for me, the same way I did for the people whose IDs I kept. Whatever he was thinking, I didn't care. I wasn't going to shoplift today. With money in my pocket, there was no need to take the risk.

I browsed through the racks of clothes, eventually picking out a pair of navy capri pants and a blue-and-white striped shirt. At the cash, my total came to €22,65, and as I counted out the money, I remembered my first days in Barcelona – how I'd paid for everything with euro bills because I hadn't learned the denominations of the heavy change that filled my pockets. Now, I was an expert on the colour and size of every bill and coin.

The cashier handed me a plastic bag with my new clothes folded inside. As I exited the store, I had to pass the guard again, and my stomach tensed even though I hadn't done anything wrong. He gave me a long look. Security guards who worked in Loss Prevention were like dogs – they could smell fear – but the anxiety he was sensing was weeks old. The other guard had grabbed me so hard it'd felt like his fingers were made of steel. They had dug into my shoulders with an inescapable grip and stopped me in my tracks.

I took my new clothes into a bathroom near the food court to change, then sat on the bench waiting for Manu. When he reappeared, I stood up, and he smirked at my outfit. I knew I looked stupid, but that was the whole point – to look like the *guiris* we'd be interacting with.

I passed him my old clothes and my money to put back in our knapsack. After storing them away, he handed me Suzanne Tomkinson's wallet, which I needed as a prop for the scam. We left the mall and walked along the boardwalk.

"Are you ready?" I asked.

Manu nodded. He wasn't used to being seen by his marks, and I could tell he was nervous. He'd bought himself a cheap wristwatch that he said would make him look more professional and trustworthy. I understood the impulse. It was always easier for me to talk to our marks if I pretended to be someone else.

I checked my image in a shop window. With my white sneakers and new outfit, I looked vaguely nautical, like a young woman who ate dinner at her father's sailing club on Fridays. A woman who wore comfortable shoes for sightseeing – that's who I was today.

Near the statue of Columbus, a row of artisan stalls was swarming with tourists who hadn't figured out yet that pan flutes and sombreros were actually souvenirs from other countries. I slowed my pace and fell back as Manu began to wander through the crowd toward the city centre, keeping to the smaller streets and scouting for a target.

Up ahead, I saw him pause behind a couple on a park bench, then disappear. The woman was eating an ice cream cone, holding it away from her body and licking at the messy drips. It wasn't until she finished and reached to get a tissue that she noticed her bag was missing. At first she didn't believe it. She stood up. She looked around.

Then it landed on her: the full weight of her mistake. Her carelessness. Her stupidity. She'd thought that nothing bad could happen to her in a place so warm and beautiful, but she should never have let down her guard.

Yaya had called it the Everybody Laughs Scam, but as I approached the couple, I found that prospect hard to imagine. The woman was teary-eyed now, and the man had the strap of his camera bag wrapped three times around his fist.

"Excuse me," I said. "Do you speak English?"

"Uh huh," said the man. He sounded American.

"Sorry. I don't want to interrupt. I just – I got robbed here a couple of days ago and, well, did you just get robbed?"

"Yes." The woman was wringing her thin hands. "They took my purse."

"Oh, I'm so sorry." I felt like a bad actor reading from a script. There was no way this was going to work.

Her husband was staring at me, angry and distrustful. A few minutes ago, someone invisible had taken his wife's bag and there was never going to be an opportunity for him to punch that person in the face.

"Apparently, this neighbourhood is really bad for thieves," I said. "They got my wallet. All my money. My credit cards, my licence. Everything. I felt so stupid."

"Did you go to the police?" asked the woman. I could tell she was hoping there was still some way to fix things – a way to reverse her misfortune.

"I did go to the police," I said. "But it's hard. They don't really speak English and I don't think they care. They basically just told me I should come back and look in the garbage cans."

The woman nodded at the ground and the man sighed. "Her pills were in there," he said. "Now we have to go to a doctor, get a new prescription."

The woman wiped away a tear that had escaped, smudging her mascara into her sunscreen. "We were just about to go to the Gaudí buildings. Take some pictures."

I nodded. One minute you had plans for the future, the next minute you had only the present. "I don't know if I should tell you this, but I actually got my wallet back."

"How?" The woman's eyes widened. Her hope was a fragile thing she was trusting me not to drop. I felt an unexpected twinge of sympathy and then another of guilt; two separate sharp pangs, like a knife being plunged into my guts, and then pulled back out. She didn't deserve this – no one did.

I forced myself to stay on script. "There's this guy who works at the reception desk at my hostel. He's really nice – we went out dancing the other night – and anyway, when I told him my wallet had been stolen, he said he'd call this guy, some guy who knows all the thieves in the neighbourhood, and he might be able to get it back for me. Not with the money – obviously – but with everything else. And he did. Look, he got it back!" I showed them Suzanne Tomkinson's wallet. "Anyway, I don't know if he'd be willing to do it again, but this is pretty much the exact same spot where I got robbed."

The man was still looking suspicious, and I felt a flush intensifying on my face, spreading toward my ears. "Don't give them time to think," that's what Yaya had said.

"Anyway, I've got to head back to the hostel now. I just thought I'd mention it. It's called Casa Central, if you ever want to go and try to talk to the guy at the desk."

"Wait," said the woman. "Are you going there now?"

"Yeah. A friend of mine's waiting. I should really go."

Her husband was puzzling something out. "Where are you from?" he asked.

"Canada."

"Oh!" The woman turned her whole body to face me. "Would you mind if we came with you to the hostel?"

"Linda," her husband said, "I think we should just forget it."

"I don't want to forget it. Do you think we could talk to the desk clerk?"

"Yeah, if you want. I'm not sure if he'll do it for you. And if he does, you'll have to give him a little money. It's not for him. But he has to pay the other guy. The guy who goes to talk to the pickpockets."

The man shot his wife a look but she ignored it. "How much?" she asked.

"Not much. I think it was forty. For me, it was totally worth it." I flashed them the wallet again. "My life is in here."

I waited while they gathered up their things, then the three of us walked in the direction of the hostel. When we came around the corner Manu was standing outside smoking a cigarette. He'd stashed our knapsack somewhere.

"Hey, that's him." I waved. "He doesn't speak much English. *¡Hola! ¿Qué tal?*" I kissed him on both cheeks, taking a second's comfort from the familiar smell of his sun-warmed skin. "*Estos turistas son víctimas de un robo.*" I turned back to the couple. "I'm just telling him that you were robbed."

Manu scowled.

"Sorry. I know you told me not to tell anybody. But I felt really bad for them. You know, *super mal. Ella necesita sus medicinas.* Her pills. *¿Entiendes?*"

He looked backward through the glass doors and up the stairs to the hostel reception, then returned his gaze to the couple. "*¿Qué perdieron?*"

"A purse," I said. I was glad he'd remembered to ask that. When we'd been practising, we'd both kept forgetting to ask what had been stolen.

"Yes," said the woman, speaking slowly, "it was my purse." Her earnestness and desperation were too intense. I had to look away for a moment.

"It was blue," she said. "About this big. With a zippy part on the front."

"*Azul*," I told him. "*Con un bolsillo.*"

He nodded. "*Los veo en media hora. Que me esperen en la terraza. Nada de policías. Que no entren al hostal.*" He looked at his wristwatch. ·

"He says he needs half an hour. You should wait on the terrace of the restaurant around the corner. He says don't go into the hostel. He'll get in trouble. And no police." I turned back to Manu. "You'll bring it to them, right? *¿Vas a traerla?*"

He nodded. "*Dame el dinero. Cuarenta.*"

"Okay. You just have to give him the forty euros."

"Now?" asked the man. He looked like his head was going to blow up.

"Yes, he needs to give it to the guy."

"And what happens if they can't find it? Do we get our money back?"

"Mmm ... I'm not sure. *¿Qué pasa si no la encuentras?*" I asked Manu. "*Nada*," he said, shaking his head.

"You just have to keep your fingers crossed," I told the couple.

The man expelled a snort of disgust and opened his wallet. He took out two twenty-euro bills, folded them together, then passed them to Manu with a menacing look. Manu walked into the building, and I took the couple around the corner and pointed out the restaurant terrace. "I really hope it works out for you."

"Thank you," said the woman. "Thank you so much."

I walked back to the hostel and up to the second floor where Manu was waiting on the landing. My legs were trembling. I couldn't believe it had actually worked. We looked at each other for several seconds. Then Manu furrowed his brow like the woman's husband had done and passed me the twenty-euro bills with a grunt. We both cracked up. I'd never seen Manu laugh before and he looked pretty funny, his shoulders bouncing up and down as he held a finger to his lips. We were both trying to be quiet, our eyes glistening with the effort. A moment later, my laughter rolled over and there were tears underneath. I turned away and placed my hands on the wall, pulling in long deep breaths of humid hallway air. The purse woman was lucky. Most of us didn't get a chance to recover the things we'd lost.

Manu touched my shoulder, and I wiped my eyes and turned. The smile on his face disappeared when he saw my expression. I waved away his concern. "It's nothing." I handed him the forty euros, and he grabbed our knapsack from behind a plant in the corner to put the money away. The blue purse was hidden behind the plant as well.

"How much was in her wallet?" I asked.

"Thirty-five."

"Not bad."

We sat down on the stairs to wait. "I don't think I can do that again," I said.

A leftover giggle escaped from Manu, and we almost started up again.

I regained my composure. "Are you really going to give it back to her?" That final step suddenly seemed too dangerous. The couple would have had time to process our interaction. The woman's husband was big, and we had nothing else to gain.

"Yeah, I think so," Manu said. "She's going to be so happy."

He was right. She'd be overwhelmed with relief and feel incredibly lucky for a long time to come.

"Everybody laughs," I said.

8

Down at the beach the next morning, I took off my leggings and washed myself in sections under the open-air shower: first my hair and my face, then under my shirt and under my skirt. My fingernails seemed to have stopped growing and so had the hair on my legs. In a way, this made sense. Most days it felt like Manu and I were stuck in a tight loop of the present, each moment erasing the previous one. It was only at night that I could really be sure time was passing. That's when I sifted through my growing stack of ID cards and counted the money accumulating in my bread bag – almost three hundred euros now. It was probably enough to rent a small room for myself – and for Manu if he wanted to join me – but each morning down at the beach, I thought, *We'll just do this for one more day*. I didn't want everything to change again.

Overnight, I'd stored my new clothes in their plastic bag to keep them clean. I went behind the tall sculpture of stacked rusty cubes so I could have some privacy to change. When I was finished, I shoved my other clothes into the bag, then circled the sculpture, peeking into its windows and trying to figure out how it had been made. There was a little placard on one corner of the base that read: *L'Estel Ferit* (*The Wounded Star*). The artist was a woman. Rebecca Horn.

I walked over to where Manu was lying on his stomach and sat down beside him on our blanket. He had poured some water onto the sand and was making an elaborate sketch with his knife in the damp area. He often did this, and today it was a futuristic city: domed buildings, spaceships, other planets. He seemed to have a real talent for drawing, and I considered again whether we might be able to earn some money by making art instead of stealing. I had wondered the same thing a couple days earlier when we'd seen three hippie guys creating a sand sculpture further down the beach: a faithful rendition of *The Last Supper* they'd been working on for days. Tourists had been throwing the occasional coin into a straw basket beside them, and I'd asked Manu if he thought we might be able to do something similar. He'd watched the basket closely for a few minutes before shaking his head. He didn't think we'd make enough. Lately his mother had been asking him to send more money. No matter how much he gave her, it never seemed to be enough. Last night, he'd been so stressed after talking to her that I'd let him keep all the money from the Everybody Laughs scam, and had even given him an extra hundred euros to send. He hadn't wanted to take it, but I'd insisted. I would have given Manu all my money if he'd asked.

When the sun was higher than the breakwall, it was time for us to go to work. Manu's futuristic city formed almost a complete ring around us. I stood up and jumped over his artwork, then reached back and lifted our blanket out of the circle by one corner. Manu started to smooth down the sand with long sweeps of his blade.

"Wait." I grabbed his shoulder. "Why are you erasing it?"

He looked up at me. "Why not?"

I didn't have a good answer. If we left his drawing behind, it'd just be blown away, kicked through by joggers or trampled by children; there was no way to save it. "I guess I just like it."

Manu shrugged as if liking something didn't matter. He finished flattening the sand, then flicked his knife closed and stood up.

I picked up our knapsack, and we followed the boardwalk to Port Olímpic, then brushed the sand from our feet and put on our shoes. As we veered north toward the metro, Manu began to walk further ahead of me, and by the time we reached the entrance it was as if we were strangers. Inside the station, we stood separately on the crowded platform, waiting for the train.

I had a bit of a cold and had been sniffling all morning. When I sneezed, a nearby woman smiled at me and for a second I felt like I was just one of the other regular passengers. I wondered if that would ever be true again – if I'd ever be taking transit to go to work the way she was, using the metro to draw a line from where I lived to where I made my money. I looked away from her and down the track.

When the train arrived, I tried to focus, but nothing was going our way. The first car we stepped onto already had thieves on it: a Roma family with an adorable child who was trying to sit on a passenger's lap. The next car we chose had pickpockets on it as well: an accordion player who was working with a partner, serenading people to distract them.

By the time we got off that car and switched trains, the work crowd was thinning. This made things harder for Manu. There was less camouflage, and within a few more stops it would be too risky. I kept looking around for a promising mark, but for the first time, no one seemed to deserve my attention. The woman with the blue purse from the day before had been so hopeful that her lost item would be found. I wondered if all the people we'd robbed had felt the same.

Maybe for some that hope never really went away, and they'd catch themselves, a month or a year from now, still dreaming that their lost possessions had been found.

Manu was at the edge of my vision, his proximity a sign that he was getting anxious. I didn't want to just choose someone at random, but Manu needed the money, and it would be a long time before he'd agree to take any of mine again. I approached a man standing beside a large suitcase and struck up a conversation. He was on his way to the airport – he'd had a good trip.

"There's a really nice park up here you should visit next time." I pointed to a patch of green on my map. "It has a labyrinth. Not too many people know about it." This piqued the man's interest; he seemed like an off-the-beaten-path type of guy. For Manu's sake, I hoped he was also the type of guy who paid for things with wads of cash. As it turned out, he wasn't.

"Ten euros," Manu said when we met up at the ornate old fountain at the top of La Rambla.

"Shit." I bent down and took a drink. "Should we try again?" I didn't want to, but it felt like a safe question. On unlucky days, Manu always said it was better to stop. Frustration could make you do stupid things, and stupid things could get you caught.

"No, let's go see Atlas," he said.

For a couple of slow blocks, we manoeuvred around kiosk lines and tour group clusters. I tried to guess the languages of the people we passed: French, German, Italian, Japanese.

When we got near Atlas's spot, we sat down on the ground to watch him. As usual, he was frozen in place, the weight of the world balanced on his gold spray-painted back. He had a pretty good crowd around him, better than the giant tree woman on his left, not quite as good as the acrobats on his right.

We tried to catch his eye, but for some reason he was ignoring us, even when we threw a coin into his hat and he was supposed to heft the weight of the world up high over his head. We'd been hoping he might buy us lunch at the Black Sheep, the way he'd done a couple of times when he was having a good day. He'd never tell us how much he made, just say things like, "A hundred thousand tourists walk by me every day. You do the math." Then he'd peel off some money from a thick wad of bills, throw it onto the table with the flourish of a toreador. There was always a little bit of gold under his fingernails.

Manu searched one more time through the almost empty wallet we'd stolen. He took out a metro ticket and some coins. When he was done, he handed me the wallet, and I flipped through the cards inside, selecting a gym membership for my collection. I studied the photo of the man who'd belonged to the wallet. He might be at an airport restaurant now, trying to pay his bill. I pictured him standing up and kicking his metal chair, the scraping sound of it clattering across the floor like the keys I'd thrown at Peter. For some reason, I couldn't imagine what he would do next. There was just a blank, as if he'd disappeared into his shock and anger, and never emerged.

Tourists were stepping over my outstretched legs. I pulled up my knees. I'd seen how the woman with the blue purse had reacted after being robbed, but she'd been a special case; she'd recovered her lost item in less than an hour. Now I wanted to know what happened to our other victims, what they did to make themselves feel better and how long it took. "One time, I want to see what happens after," I said.

"What do you mean?" Manu asked.

"I want to follow one of them."

He threw another coin toward Atlas. "Definitely not in the metro."

"Okay," I said. "But maybe somewhere else?"

Tourists were staring at us as they walked by like they were expecting us to do a trick. I scratched at a mosquito bite on my ankle. We had no plans, nothing to eat, nowhere to be.

Manu looked across the street toward the entrance of the Boqueria. "Somewhere like the market maybe?"

"Sure."

He sighed. "I'll meet you back here afterwards." He stood up and took off, skirting the traffic and then entering the crowd.

I stepped up onto the base of a lamppost so I could track his progress. When I saw him bump into someone and apologize, I knew he'd done it. The girl was a tall blond, Scandinavian maybe. She hardly looked at him; just flicked her long hair, then turned away. I crossed the street and followed her into the market, watched her join her friends, a group of girls. Next to the sweaty hard-working fruit sellers, the girls looked like royalty. I trailed behind them as they went out through the back exit of the market and into El Raval. They were probably staying at a cheap hostel there and hadn't stopped to consider that it might be dangerous.

They walked into a convenience store and I watched them through the window. The shopkeeper was frowning at their bare shoulders as they approached the counter with a bottle of cheap cava. I watched the tall blond as she dipped her hands in and out of her purse, shuffling and rearranging things, laying out her possessions on the counter. I watched her movements begin to loop and backtrack, gradually becoming more urgent. I watched her friends trying to be helpful, the shopkeeper giving up hope before the others. Then I watched her become still for a moment, the shock of what had happened freezing her in place. It only takes a second for things to be lost, even things you thought were yours to keep. Then she was moving again, her eyes reaching to the ceiling, remembering in detail what was in her wallet: her money and credit card, her ID that she needed to get home. Maybe a little pouch with every fortune she'd ever gotten from a cookie. Or an old photograph of her grandfather that she loved. All of it was gone now. Someone had taken those things from her. She'd been wearing her purse across her body the whole time, just like the guidebook said, so why did this have to happen?

Outside of the store, a three-legged dog sniffed at my ankles and made me jump. I pushed him aside with my foot, then turned back to the window. The girl's friends were looking uneasy now. There was nothing for them to say, no way for them to comfort her. They seemed to be wondering how they could step back from the situation, continue on without the wounded one, get back to the hostel and try on their new clothes. But of course they couldn't do that. Not just yet. One by one, I watched them shift into postures of sympathy. Their friend had been careless, more careless than themselves – the lucky ones were tossing this thought between them with their eyes.

I crossed to the other side of the street as the girls emerged from the store. The young woman who'd lost her wallet took a deep breath, pulled a clip from her bag and began to wind her long hair up and out of her face. This was no longer the time for having hair that men wanted to touch. The girls conferred for a moment, then hugged each other, the wounded one heading back toward the market, alone.

I stayed where I was in the shadows, still as a human statue. She was going back to make sure it was really gone. I'd been planning to follow her for longer, but now I didn't need to. I already knew what she'd be doing: slowly retracing her steps, studying the gutters and doorways, wondering what she'd done wrong. When she reached the market, she'd approach the sun-hardened vendors, asking each of them a single question in her fragile broken Spanish: My wallet, have you seen it? The vendors would shrug their shoulders.

Becky Blake

I wished I hadn't followed her. I'd wanted to see what happened
next – how she made herself feel better – but now I was wondering
if it might be time for me to go back to Peter's. The idea made my
chest hurt and the itch start under my skin. My voice would sound
so tiny, cracked and broken, climbing up through the intercom from
the street. It would feel like begging. It would feel like – something
shifted inside me and I was outside my mother's front door, knocking
and knocking. I squeezed my hands into fists. I didn't need to go back
to Peter's; I already knew that the things I'd lost there were gone.

Across the street, the three-legged dog was making its way from
store to store, looking for a handout. Eventually someone would give
him something, but so far he wasn't having any luck. I whistled at him,
and the dog hopped toward me, then sat at my feet, waiting to be fed.

"You shouldn't beg," I told him. I had a packet of crackers in my
pocket. I ripped it open and bent down so he could eat them out of
my hand.

When the last one was gone, I headed back to La Rambla to
meet up with Manu. I was curious to find out how much money the
tall blond woman had lost.

9

Manu hadn't told his mother about the layoffs at the construction site because he didn't want her to worry. If he could manage to survive in Spain for another year, he'd finally be allowed to apply for his permanent residency. Then he'd be able to get a real job again and bring over his relatives, one by one, reassembling his family like a jigsaw puzzle.

At the locutorio the next day we went into side-by-side phone booths, and after a moment, I could hear him talking to his mother, smoothing down the edges of the truth. In my own booth, I studied the number I'd written on my hand. Brigid had emailed again, and this time she wanted me to call her – she said she had something to tell me. It was probably just some news about her wedding, or maybe she was pregnant. If she *was* pregnant, then she'd officially have everything: a good job, a handsome fiancé, a rich family, a perfect life. When I'd lived at her parents' house, the wooden bannister of their staircase had always been polished and gleaming, the sheets in their guest bedroom scented with lavender.

I pressed the buttons on the phone, watching as Brigid's number appeared on a little screen. After a suspended silence her phone began to ring. Once, twice. Maybe she wouldn't answer.

"Hello?"

Hearing a voice from back home felt like a scab coming off too soon. I had to stop myself from hanging up. "Hey, Brigid."

"Niki! Oh my god! I didn't recognize this number."

"Yeah, my phone doesn't work here and I haven't got a new one yet. I'm just calling from an Internet café."

"Oh, wow. I hope it's not too expensive."

"No, it's fine." On the little screen, the price of the call was rising in steady five-cent increments.

"So? Is it beautiful there? It is, isn't it?"

"It's pretty nice."

"I love Spain," she said. "You're so lucky to be living there! How's Peter doing? Is he liking his new job?"

Those things were connected in her mind: my luck and Peter. If I told her about the breakup, I knew she'd say all the right things, but inside, she'd be judging me – trying to guess what I'd done wrong.

"Yeah, I think he likes it," I said. "The people he works with are really talented." I suddenly remembered him telling me how there were five different Marias in the restoration department. Even if I'd been wrong about him cheating, one of them was probably sleeping in our bed by now.

"He must be busy," Brigid said.

Crimson lipstick. Black lace panties. "Yes."

"You know" – Brigid's voice brightened – "one of the girls at my office told me she hides a candy in her husband's pocket every morning before he goes to work. That way, he thinks of her at least once a day, while he's sucking on something sweet."

I waited to see if she was joking. She wasn't. "That's very 1950s."

Brigid snorted. "Yeah, I guess you're right. It *is* kind of old-fashioned. Still, I might try it. Or maybe I'll ask Charlie to do it for me." I pictured her drawing loopy hearts on the corner of a fresh sheet of paper.

"Are you guys doing okay?" I asked. In her email she'd mentioned they were arguing a lot, although it didn't sound serious, just some minor disagreements about wedding-planning stuff.

"I think so. Sometimes I just feel like I'm going to freak out on him, and then the whole wedding will be cancelled. It'd be like forty thousand dollars down the drain."

"I'm sure everything will be fine." Brigid always mentioned the price of things.

"I know. But you guys are so smart! No wedding. No guests. Just put the ring on your finger, say the vows. Who cares who else is there?"

"Yeah, I guess it's better that way." She seemed to have forgotten that I didn't have any family to invite anyway.

"Hey, how's your painting coming?" she asked.

"Not too good. I haven't really had a chance to start yet. I still need to buy some canvases, find a class to take." I wondered if that would ever happen now – if I might someday find myself standing in front of a blank canvas again, a million possibilities surging through me. I pulled the red paint chip from my coat pocket. For some reason, I hadn't thrown it away yet.

"You were always so good at that stuff," Brigid said. "Almost every class Mr. B was dragging us over to look at your work." She mimicked Mr. B's pensive voice. "You see this line? *This line* has motion. It's going somewhere."

I smiled. "Mr. B was the best." I'd had an intense crush on him all through grade twelve. I still thought of him every time I opened a new tube of paint.

"So, have you and Peter set a date yet?" Brigid was back on-point.

"Yeah. We made some arrangements at the courthouse for June eleventh." This was actually true, although Peter had probably called to cancel our appointment by now.

"Wow, that's only a couple weeks away. I really wish I could be there."

I heard static on the line, another voice coming through faintly, like a conscience. I should just tell her the truth. A handful of words – that's all it would take. I dared myself to do it. "Actually, Brigid –"

"Wait. Hold on a sec. My phone's doing something strange. Let me take you off headset and see if that helps."

I listened to her fumbling around. In the booth next door, Manu was agreeing to something with a long slow string of yeses. I touched the wall between us.

"Does that sound better?" Brigid asked.

"Maybe a little." The voice was still there, an urgent whispered warning. Telling Brigid what had happened was going to make the breakup feel more real – like it was permanent in some new or sadder way. The thought disturbed me. It meant I was still carrying a little bit of hope inside, a dangerous useless spark that refused to go out. I didn't know where it was coming from.

"What were you going to say?" Brigid asked.

"Oh, I don't know. I can't remember; it was probably nothing."

She paused for a second – a hiccup in time, a skipped heart-beat. If she knew something was wrong, she didn't ask. "Well, we'll have to celebrate the next time you're in Canada. I'll get you a cake. A big floofy one with five layers and those disgusting sugar rosettes."

I sighed. "You know I hate cake." When I'd stayed with her family, I hadn't been able to eat even one piece of the birthday cake they'd made me.

"Yes, I *know* you hate cake," Brigid said. "But *wedding* cake is not optional."

"Cake is always optional. Maybe you can get me something that doesn't come from a bakery."

"Oh, that reminds me!" she said. "That's actually what I wanted to tell you: I saw your mom a week or so ago."

Sugar rosettes – I could suddenly taste them; feel the sharp edges of cheap icing against my tongue. "Where?"

"I had to get my driver's licence renewed and she was at the office. She was taking her test."

"My mother's learning how to drive?"

"I guess so."

"That's weird." I'd just gotten a driver's licence myself – less than a year ago with Peter's help.

"Have you talked to her?" Brigid asked.

"No."

"Hmm." I could tell Brigid thought that was a mistake. "Well. I didn't know if you had or you hadn't, so I didn't say too much. She was asking me a million questions. I wasn't going to tell her about you getting married, but then she brought it up. She said she already knew. That you'd sent her a postcard."

I let out a long breath. "I guess she's in the same apartment."

"Yep, she's still there."

"Great." I picked at the edge of one of the little coloured stickers that were covering the wall of the phone booth. Most of them were ads for locksmiths: *Cerrajero rápido. Servicio 24 horas. Especialistas.* The stickers were all over the city for some reason: stuck like handfuls of adhesive confetti onto doors, street lamps and mailboxes.

"Anyway, I just wanted to tell you," Brigid said. "Maybe you should call her. She seemed like she really wanted to talk to you. I know it's none of my business though."

"Was Max with her?"

"No. She was by herself."

It had been so long since I'd seen my mother that I could only picture her in fragments: the soft curve of her upper arm, her smudged glasses, the chemical smell of her hair dye, the crumbs she left behind on the table – the only proof I'd had sometimes that she'd been home.

"Are you okay?" Brigid asked.

"I'm fine." After six years, my mother knew something about me. And I knew something about her. A loose thread had been pulled, and I didn't know how much damage would result.

"I miss you," Brigid said.

"I miss you too." Especially when she'd gone off to university. I'd missed her like crazy back then.

"Are you sure you won't be able to come home for my wedding in August?" she asked.

"I don't think so."

"Well, let me know if you change your mind, and I'll put you guys on the list. Two extra guests, one with no cake."

"Thanks."

"Hey, can we talk again soon? I want to know how the wedding ceremony goes!"

"Yeah, sure. I'll give you a call in a couple of weeks."

After saying goodbye, I hung up the phone and touched my forehead to the wall. The booth next door was quiet. When I exited, I found Manu waiting for me in a chair by the window. His bandana was in his lap and his hair was covering his face. From his slumped posture, it seemed like his mother had asked him for more money.

I unzipped the inside pocket of my coat and took out the ring I'd been keeping in there. It was a white gold band with a sprinkling of small diamonds embedded in it like imprisoned stars. In the centre of my palm, it looked like a hole that a promise had fallen into. Maybe the last bit of hope I was feeling about Peter was coming from the ring. I didn't want to carry it close to my body anymore.

"Here." I held out the ring to Manu and he looked up. "Take it. For your family." I figured he could get a couple hundred euros for it. Then maybe his mother would leave him alone for a while.

I was expecting him to protest, but he just looked tired, like he'd given up on something. "Are you sure?" he asked.

I nodded and handed him the ring.

"Thank you," he said.

Outside the front window a couple walked by, their hands shoved deep into each other's pockets. When I glanced back at Manu, he'd already stashed the ring away.

"Let's get out of here," he said. He stood up and took my hand by mistake. As we walked to the counter to pay, I could feel him letting me go in tiny self-conscious increments, and I imagined how sweet he must have been a couple years earlier, with a first girlfriend maybe.

Out on the street there was a vendor selling flowers, his stall lined with deep buckets of freshly cut blooms. Manu went over and picked out a rose, a red one with its petals still tightly closed. "Do you like roses?" he asked.

"Yes."

He passed the rose to the vendor, a large man in a blue apron, who stuck the stem into a little vial of water.

"A special occasion?" the man asked me as Manu paid.

I shook my head.

"A flower just for today, then. The best kind."

I carried the rose around all afternoon, smelling it from time to time, and wishing I could paint it: a splash of vermilion on a white canvas. After a few hours the rose was drooping, and I considered trying to save it somehow: hanging it to dry, or pulling off the petals and storing them in my pocket. I let each plan pass through me and move away. Living on the street, there was no real way to keep things, no way to mark them as yours. You just had to enjoy them while they were there. At dusk, before leaving the courtyard, I wove the stem of the rose through the wooden slats of a park bench and left it behind. Manu had bought me a rose. I no longer had any proof, but that didn't mean it hadn't been a very lovely thing.

Manu was quieter than usual as we walked to the hotel site. When we got there, we climbed up and down the stairs for a long time before he picked out a room. On our first night together, he'd taken me straight to the top floor, but every night since he'd been having more and more trouble deciding which room to stay in. Lately, I'd been wondering where he and his father had been on the night of the earthquake, if maybe they'd had a choice to be somewhere else and had made the wrong decision.

I followed Manu up another floor and waited at the stairwell as he walked the length of the building, slipping in and out of rooms, moving forward, moving back. At the far end, he walked into a room and didn't come out again. I waited another minute, then went to join him. He'd already laid out our blanket in a corner and was sitting on it with our knapsack open in front of him. "I have to go back out for a while," he said.

"Really?" We didn't usually leave the hotel after we'd set up for the night, so I was curious where he was going.

"Don't worry," he said. "I won't be gone long."

He seemed embarrassed, so I didn't ask for details. Maybe he was working with the beer sellers who also sold drugs to tourists.

When his footsteps had faded down the stairs, I walked over to the edge of the room. It was my first time alone at the construction site. I forced myself to sit down with my legs dangling out into the empty space. At first I felt a swoop of dizziness, but I ignored it. After a few minutes my vertigo faded, and I was able to appreciate the view. It was a powerful feeling to be balanced above the city with no barrier between us.

I sat there for a long time, feeling like a god or a queen, and thinking of all the things I might change if I had the power. I would make sure Manu's family had enough money so he didn't have to steal. I would find Yaya a teaching job, and maybe even sign up for his class. Fanta would get her debt paid off and be able to bring her mother and son to Spain. For me, all I wanted was a way to start a new life here – a little apartment where maybe Manu would keep me company, a place where he could draw and I could paint. Once we had a home base, I could look for a job – one that might provide me with a work visa so I could legally stay. Renting a small apartment was something I could do any time with the money I'd saved. I decided to ask Manu what he thought of moving indoors as soon as he got back.

I stood up and got ready for bed, changing into my old clothes again, then putting my coat back on. Even though it was the end of May, it still got chilly at night. I heard Fanta coming up the stairs. Her whistle sounded more urgent than usual. I whistled back until she found me.

"Where's Manu?" she asked, jutting out her chin. Someone had left a bloody scratch on her face and she was sparking mad.

"He just went to the store," I said. I had no idea how long he'd be gone, but I wanted her to think he'd be coming back soon. Even though Fanta was friendly with us, I didn't fully trust her. The interest on her debt was probably rising each day at a slightly greater rate than what she could earn. People without hope were unpredictable. "Are you okay?" I asked.

She didn't answer.

I offered her a towel from our pack so she could clean up her face, but she waved it away.

"Evidence," she said, pointing at the blood. The heart-shaped decals on her fingernails had been replaced by little palm trees.

I opened a can of beer and held it out toward her. She snatched it from my hand on one of her trips pacing back and forth. After some time, she tossed a plastic baggie into my lap.

"How much do you think I can get for that?" she asked.

I picked it up. It was heavy, and it looked like cocaine. "I have no idea."

"A thousand?"

"Maybe." I shrugged and handed back the baggie.

Fanta let out a breath, then started to laugh, deep from the belly. "That man is going to be mad!" she said.

I watched as she emptied out her tiny purse and stuffed the drugs inside. I was worried that maybe she'd taken too big of a risk and might be in danger. But there was no point in saying that. What's done was done. She'd stolen something with enough value to maybe tip the scales in her favour for once. It was a bigger score than any-thing I'd ever stolen, and I figured it must have been triggered by a bigger need than any itch I'd ever felt.

She gave me her cell phone and some makeup to hold onto because they wouldn't fit back in her purse. Her pimp was whistling for her down below on the other side of the fence.

"Keep those for me until I come back," she said. "And tell Manu I need to talk to him." She tugged her skirt into place and was gone.

Something was going on that she and Manu didn't want me to know about. I wondered if Manu was trying to protect me. I scooped Fanta's things toward me and curled up beside them in the darkness. Her phone was flashing like a tiny lighthouse, and I dozed off waiting for either her or Manu to return.

I awoke to a man's voice shouting up the stairs in a language I didn't understand. I lay very still. There were so many rooms that he wasn't going to find me as long as I stayed quiet. I heard his heavy steps pass by my floor and keep on going. Then he stopped on the stairs and a few seconds later, the phone beside me started ringing. The ringtone was a Bob Marley song, the one about how everything was going to be all right. I jumped up and grabbed the phone, but I couldn't see how to shut it off. Then the angry man was there, and Manu was still gone, and there was no way to prove I was a person who anyone might miss.

Manu's knife was probably in his pocket, and I couldn't think of anything else to use as a weapon. The man was shouting a bunch of words, his spit flying into my face, his lips the colour of bruises. I started toward the stairs, but he grabbed my arm and yanked me back. I held out my hands, showing that they were empty, showing that I didn't understand. A heavy gold ring with a square blue stone flashed in front of my eyes, then cut through my cheek as he backhanded me across the face. Little chips of light framed the man's silhouette.

I wiped my cheek and looked at the blood on my fingers. The man picked up our knapsack and dumped its contents onto the floor. He squatted down and began pawing through our things, throwing them around. When he found the bread bag with my money in it, he put it into his pocket without even checking the amount, without being impressed at all by how far I'd come from nothing. Suddenly I was on top of him, hitting at his broad back, pulling at his thick hair with my bloody fingers. I didn't try to get the money – I already knew he was going to take it from me – but I wanted him to know I was angry, just like him.

He stood to shake me off, and I landed hard on my shoulder. Before I could get up, he started kicking at my ribs. Each time his foot made contact, my body curved a little more. The taste of dusty floor filled my mouth. Eventually I heard a pair of voices above me. Everything was going to be all right now. Manu was having another nightmare. We were having it together. I wrapped my arms around his neck and closed my eyes. When I opened them again, I realized it was the security guard who was holding onto me, swearing a bit under his boozy breath as he stumbled with me down the stairs. *Don't worry*, I wanted to tell him, *I won't say anything*. But I couldn't think of the words in Spanish. Couldn't think of any words in Spanish.

When we reached the ground floor, he opened a gate in the fence and tipped me out of his arms and onto the sidewalk. "*No te quedes aquí. Él va a regresar.*" Then he closed the gate and left me lying there, alone.

I repeated his words in my head until the translation came to me in slow motion. "Don't stay here. He's coming back." The cobblestones were cool against my face. I remembered my first night at the hotel, how I'd imagined walking to the edge of the room and beyond: five seconds of falling, maybe ten. It had taken a lot longer than that, but finally I'd hit.

I tried to get up but something in my chest had come unhinged. It was broken, and it hurt to breathe. Also I was shaking. At first I thought it was from the cold, but no – it was from fear.

"Please." I sent the word up into the air, followed by a bunch of promises: I'd go back to Peter's, go back even further if I needed to, all the way back to the beginning, to the very start of having nothing if I could just get up and get away.

My words fell back to the ground, uncaught, unheard. No one but me would know if I kept my promises.

Get up, I told myself. *Get off the ground.*

I tried once again to rise.

PART TWO

10

The sheet under my fingertips was cool and crisply pressed. I blinked several times, my eyes adjusting to a strong light streaming in from a large window. The door of the room was ajar, and from the hallway I could hear the murmur of voices and beeping machines. The air smelled of fake lemons. In the corner, a chair was angled attentively toward my bed, and for a second I wondered why Peter wasn't in it. Then I remembered, and I wondered where Manu was.

The contents of my coat pockets were laid out on the bedside table in a patch of sunlight: the red paint chip, a handful of coins, a metro ticket and my collection of stolen IDs. Someone was going to want an explanation for those.

I tried to push myself to sitting, but a sharp pain tore through my left side. I eased myself back down. Other parts of my body were hurting as well: my elbow and shoulder, my knee and my face. I touched the gauze patch that was taped to my cheek. The angry man's eyes had been the darkest I'd ever looked into, all compassion extinguished. I didn't think he would be able to find me here, but just in case, I reached for the call-button cord beside my bed and held it in my hand.

Becky Blake

There seemed to be a backward drag on each of my thoughts –
the effect of painkillers maybe. I studied the low ceiling, trying to
piece together what had happened. Manu had left me alone, and
then Fanta had come looking for him, possibly to help her sell the
drugs she'd stolen. For some reason, Manu hadn't told me what was
going on. I knew he wouldn't have put me in danger on purpose, but
I wasn't sure about Fanta. Maybe she'd robbed the angry man and
then blamed me. The man had definitely lost something. And when
he couldn't find it, he'd taken something of mine.

The ache in my left ribs was spreading through my body. I lay
a hand on my chest and felt my heart beating underneath. It was a
gesture of Rosa's, something she'd done when I'd gotten hurt as a
child. "Still alive?" she'd ask, teasing a little, but holding her hand
there for as long as it took until I felt better.

I closed my eyes, and all the sounds of her apartment came
rushing back: the chaotic chatter of her kids and grandkids when
they came to visit on weekends, the music on her radio, the telenove-
las and soccer games on her television. A large pink seashell in her
bathroom whispered when I held it to my ear. In her tiled kitchen,
Rosa's slippers made a swishing sound while she cooked, and then
no sound at all as she walked me back across the carpeted hall when
it was time for me to go home. In my apartment, it was always quiet,
my mother either sleeping or at work. Except on our balcony. Out
there, I could hear the rumble of streetcars, ambulance sirens, the
hum of the expressway. People on the street below came and went in
different coats depending on the season. There was a rusty ashtray
filled with rain-bloated cigarette butts in the corner, sharp flakes of
peeling paint on the railing under my fingers. In the distance, Lake
Ontario was a thin static line. Compared to the lusty roll of the
Mediterranean's waves, it would now look like the line of a heart
monitor gone suddenly flat and lifeless.

In the hospital room next door, a bare voice was climbing up and down the ladder of a flamenco song, the emotion spilling over and creeping through the hallways, under doors and into cracks. I didn't want to live outside anymore, or spend time in places where sadness and danger seemed to collect. The angry man had taken my savings, but I wasn't going to wait any longer before moving indoors. I had to get some money another way.

I rolled the call-button cord between my fingers. If I asked the nurses to contact Peter, I knew he'd come within the hour. I pictured him sitting by my bed, reaching for my hand and then breaking down – admitting that sometimes he missed me so much he felt like dying. But no, that wasn't right; that's not what he would say. There was definitely a drug in my system, pulling my thoughts backward to times that were gone. For the last two years, I'd thought that Peter would know if I was hurt, but the chair in the corner was empty. He had unattached himself from me, and the next time I saw him, I needed to be standing up, not helpless in a bed as if the damage he'd done had broken me.

The singing voice next door was swelling, breath by breath, toward a wet and ragged protest: life was unfair and it hurt each time we remembered that. The many points of injury in my body joined together until they were all connected. Tears slid sideways into my hair, and I allowed them to fall, but just until the song was finished. Then I made sure the call-button cord was still in my hand and let myself drift back toward the cloudiness of sleep. The next time I woke up in this clean white room, I would see if I was strong enough to stand.

I stayed in the hospital for another night. Whenever the nurses came to check on me or give me some pills, I pretended not to understand the questions they asked in Spanish – questions about what had happened to me, and where I felt the pain the most. All I wanted was to rest for as long as possible; I couldn't seem to get enough sleep.

The next morning one of the nurses brought in a doctor who spoke slowly and clearly to me in English. "What is your name?" he asked.

I blinked.

"Your *name*," he said, tapping his name tag.

I picked up Suzanne Tomkinson's licence from the bedside table and handed it to him. When the cleaners had been in my room the day before, I'd slipped the other ID cards into their garbage bin. I knew the cards' disappearance was suspicious, but at least the most blatant proof of my criminal activity was gone.

The doctor studied the licence, then said something to the nurse in Catalan. I heard the word *policia*. He turned back to me. "How do you feel today?"

If he was going to call the police, I had to sneak out of the hospital before they arrived. "Tired," I said. "Like I need to go back to sleep."

The doctor frowned. "We'll come back in one hour."

"Thank you." I closed my eyes.

I heard the click of his pen, then the soft squeak of the nurse's shoes following his brisk footsteps out the door and down the hall.

I waited for a few minutes to make sure they were really gone. Then I got out of bed and dressed as quickly as I could. The bruises on my body ranged from purplish red to yellowish green. In front of the mirror over the sink I removed the gauze patch from my cheek. The cut underneath was smaller than I'd imagined, but uglier: a half-inch smile of black wiry stitches crusted over with dried blood. When I pulled on my coat, the pain in my ribs spiked. It was going to be hard to deal with once the painkillers wore off.

I collected my things from the bedside table, then looked out into the hallway. There was an exit sign at the end, no hospital staff in sight. I stepped from the room and walked down the corridor at an even pace, then rode the elevator to the ground floor. The lobby was crowded with a mix of slow- and fast-moving people: the sick and the well. I increased my speed and headed for the sliding front doors.

Outside, a garbage truck was blocking the street, traffic piling up behind it. Motorcycles squeezed by me on the narrow sidewalk, their drivers honking out quick insistent messages. My hospital room had been safe and quiet. Now that I was back on the other side of the sliding doors, it was time to start taking care of myself again – time to go back to Peter's for my wallet.

I didn't know what day it was, or if he would even be home. All I could do was go ring his buzzer and find out. I crossed through the gridlocked traffic to the shady side of the street and looked up to the thin scraps of skyline for a clue to my location. There were no mountains, no churches. I guessed at a downhill direction, hoped I was heading toward the sea.

Each step I took seemed to hurt a little more, as if my body was trying to prevent me from reaching my destination. I reminded myself that I was strong enough to survive an attack; going back to the apartment wouldn't kill me. All I had to do was go upstairs and pack some things in a bag. I'd spend as little time as possible there – say as little as possible to Peter – and then I'd be able to go find Manu. Together we could decide what to do next, whether to stay at a hostel or to find a room to rent for longer. Once I had my credit card and bank card, we'd have lots of options, at least for a while.

I was a little surprised that Manu hadn't come looking for me, but that was probably unfair. Even if the security guard had told him what had happened, Manu still would've had to find the right hospital, describe who I was and then somehow prove that he knew me. I wondered what he was going to say when I invited him to come and stay with me indoors. When I thought about cooking at a stove and eating at a table, it was hard to picture the two of us together in the frame.

Suddenly I wanted to see Manu right away, to find out what had happened on the night I was attacked and to close the gap of days that was opening up between us. Looking for him before going to Peter's was a kind of delay tactic – I knew that – but it also made sense. Once I'd found Manu, he could come with me. He could wait outside the apartment, and that way I'd be sure to come back out.

At the first major intersection, I spotted a sign for the metro in the distance: Sant Antoni station. After that I knew where I was; the metro system was more familiar to me than the streets. I considered going underground, but there was no way I'd find Manu on the trains. It was better to stay aboveground and look for him in places where he might be stationary for a while.

I walked to the courtyard to check for him there. Inside, the old toothless man was circling a broken bench mumbling to himself. The three-legged dog was lying on a dirt path nearby. It was the first time I'd seen them together. They seemed like a good match.

I went behind one of the pillars and pried open the grate to see if our knapsack was inside. It wasn't.

"*Oye*," the old man called over. "Why did you come to this fucking country?"

He'd asked me the same question several times, and nothing I came up with ever seemed like a good enough reason for him. For a second, I considered telling him the truth: that I'd moved to Barcelona with a man who didn't love me anymore. Someday I might say those words out loud and maybe a spell would be broken.

"I guess I just wanted to see what Spain was like," I said. I walked over and bent down to pet the dog. His fur was twisted and waxy, sour-smelling. The dog made a sneezing sound, then laid his head in the dirt. When I stood up the old man was beside me.

"You should go home," he said.

He was standing so close that for a second his certainty felt like my own. But no, I didn't want to leave. "I'm not going home."

The old man shook his head. "If I had a country like yours . . ."

I shrugged. "It's not so great. Not nearly as beautiful as here. And besides, if I go back, I'll have to go to court. I got into some trouble before I left."

The old man didn't ask what kind of trouble I meant. "You should still go home," he said. "Believe me. It will only get worse if you wait."

I knew the old man wasn't from Barcelona – that he'd come to Catalonia from some province in the South. Maybe he'd done something illegal there too, made a mistake that had compounded over the years. Possibly over many, many years.

"How old do you think I am?" he asked. It was like he'd read my mind.

He had deep creases in his forehead and drooping pouches beneath his eyes. Apparently he'd been some kind of athlete in his day, had even done the Tour de France on an empty stomach once just after the Spanish Civil War. Manu had told me that.

I started to do the math, then gave up. "Mmm … seventy?" It was better to start low, just in case.

"More!"

"Seventy-five?"

"Ha! I'm eighty-nine years old." He was talking loudly now, and the dog's ears stood up. "And every year of my life this fucking country has gotten worse."

I made a sympathetic noise and looked back over my shoulder. I wanted to leave before he launched into his usual tirade about the government and corruption, about the immigrants who spoiled everything. "I'm sorry," I said. "I have to go look for Manu."

The old man pointed a bent finger at the cut on my cheek. "Everything is shit these days."

I nodded and took a step back.

"Too many immigrants." He was talking to the dog now. "Eating out of the garbage. Getting sick. What do they expect?"

I turned and moved toward the archway. The dog was in for an earful.

Outside the courtyard, the sun was high overhead. I went to the fountain at the top of La Rambla and looked around at the sea of people. Someone touched my shoulder, and I turned, relieved, but it wasn't Manu. Instead, it was a woman with a guidebook.

Anyone who touches you on La Rambla, I thought. I looked at her more closely, but she didn't seem to be a thief.

"Excuse me," she said. "Do you know if this is the special fountain?"

"The special fountain?"

"Yes." Her eyes darted to the cut on my face and she hesitated. Then she decided to trust me: I was blond like her; I spoke English. She showed me a picture in the book, pointing her finger at the caption she wanted me to read:

A MEETING PLACE FOR THOUSANDS OF BARÇA FANS EACH TIME THE TEAM WINS A MATCH, THE CANALETES FOUNTAIN ON LA RAMBLA IS ALSO SPECIAL FOR ANOTHER REASON. TRADITION SAYS THAT IF YOU DRINK FROM THIS FOUNTAIN, YOU ARE GUARANTEED TO RETURN TO THE CITY AGAIN AND AGAIN.

"Huh. I've never heard that," I said. "But this is definitely the fountain in the picture."

"Great! Thanks!"

She shoved the guidebook into her open purse, then pulled back her hair and took a tentative drink. She stood up. "It tastes a bit funny."

"It's probably dirty." When I'd first arrived in Barcelona, drinking unfiltered water had made me feel sick. Now I was used to it.

A tiny frown flashed across her face, then disappeared. "Oh well. I totally love it here. I definitely want to come back!" She retrieved the guidebook from her purse and flipped to the next page. I watched as she began to meander into the crowd. If she kept walking down La Rambla with her bag open like that, she wasn't going to love it here for long.

I followed her for a block, wondering if maybe I should warn her, but I didn't see the point. If a hand was going to slip into her bag, lock onto the beating heart of her vacation and steal it away, there was nothing I could do to prevent it. It would either happen or it wouldn't. It could happen to anybody. Even someone who was holding her purse with the utmost care. Maybe especially to her.

Further down La Rambla Atlas was sitting on the edge of a crate, talking on his cell phone, the world at his feet. His hand was resting on Australia like he was homesick. He held up a gold finger. I walked a few steps away to give him some privacy. There was a blind woman selling lottery tickets from a kiosk. Above her head a sign read: *Is Today Your Lucky Day?* Five or six people were waiting in line to buy tickets, and the beer seller with the mustache from down at the beach was one of them. He gave me a thumbs-up. Maybe today was his lucky day.

When I looked back at Atlas, he motioned for me to come over.

"What happened to your cheek?" he asked.

"Nothing. Just some bad luck."

He squinted at me, trying to see behind my words. "You should be more careful."

"I know. I will."

He handed me a can of gold spray paint and pointed to a faded spot on the back of his costume. "Do you mind? A big cruise ship just came in."

"Sure." I shook the can. "Hey, have you seen Manu?"

"Nah. Not for a while."

To Atlas, "a while" probably meant only a day, or a couple of days at most. We usually passed by him several times each afternoon. I turned my head away and sprayed, then handed back the can.

"Thanks." Atlas lifted a corner of his crate and tucked the can underneath. "How did you end up hanging out with that guy anyway?"

I shrugged.

"You must have better things to do."

"Not really."

Atlas got up on his crate. He pointed to the world and I handed it to him.

"Well, if you can't find him, come to the Black Sheep later and we can get something to eat. I'll be there after nine." He bent over and froze in place. Just like that our conversation was over, and I felt like I'd been talking to myself.

I crossed La Rambla, then skirted around the edge of the Gothic Quarter. All the shops were closed, except for the bakeries, which meant it had to be Sunday. I was starting to get hungry, but I folded the feeling in half and kneaded it down. At 3:00 p.m. the bakeries would close, and the staff would throw out bags of day-old bread. Until then, I'd go to the park. Even if Manu wasn't there, it was a good place to rest for a while. If I hadn't found him by nightfall, I'd go to Peter's on my own. There was no way I was looking for Manu at the construction site; I didn't want to ever go back there.

The park was Sunday-busy, every path and patch of grass occupied by people having picnics, playing guitar, blowing bubbles, eating ice cream. The fake lake was full to the brim with paddleboaters bumping into each other and making clumsy turns. I walked to the end of one of the paths and found Yaya's crew sleeping on the grass.

Yaya himself was sitting on a bench with a newspaper. He looked up at me as I approached. I waited for him to ask what had happened to my cheek but he didn't, which meant he must already know. The idea made my heart speed up. "Have you seen Manu?" I asked.

Yaya closed his newspaper. "His *maman* is sick," he said. "He had to go home."

"Home?"

"Yes."

"When?"

"Yesterday."

I nodded, kept nodding. So that's why he hadn't come looking for me. I remembered the long slow string of yeses coming from his phone booth on the last day I'd seen him, and how quiet he'd been afterwards. Maybe he'd already known he was leaving on the night I was attacked. If so, he would have wanted to pull together as much money as possible to take home with him. Probably he'd gone out to pawn the ring, or sell some drugs, or both. I wondered when he'd been planning to tell me. Maybe he'd bought me the rose as a goodbye gift.

Yaya bent over and began rooting around in his bag. After a moment, he pulled out something long and thin, wrapped up in an orange piece of paper. "Manu asked me to give this to you."

The paper was a locksmith flyer, an advertisement that Manu had probably ripped down from one of the bulletin boards at the locutorio. When I unfolded the page, Manu's wristwatch slid out – the one he'd thought made him look professional, like someone who had a job and appointments to keep. On the back of the flyer, he'd written a short note: *I'm sorry. I had to go. Please! Don't forget to eat!* There was a drawing at the bottom of the page: a smiling woman with a clock for a belly. Her arms were pointing to the two and the nine – Spanish lunchtime and dinnertime.

I folded the note back up and put it in my pocket, then lay the watch across my wrist. One hole on the band was bigger than the others, and I used that hole to fasten the clasp. When I dropped my arm to the side, the Manu-sized watch slid down halfway over my hand.

Yaya was observing me. "He won't be allowed to come back."

"I know." Manu's work visa had expired when he lost his job so now he was gone for good. I thought about the drawing he'd made in the sand at the beach; how he'd wiped it away, smoothing it back to nothing as if it hadn't ever been there. I tried to wipe away my disappointment the same way, but it kept reappearing. I was so stupid: getting attached to people, trying to hold things in place. I opened my hands and lay them flat against my thighs.

"Do you need some money?" Yaya asked.

His generosity made my throat tighten. "No, that's okay. I can get some."

Two children ran by us squealing, their dad squirting them with water from a plastic bottle. On the other side of the bushes, a dog was barking, protective and alert.

"Malik can help with *les points de suture.*" Yaya pointed at my stitches. "He was a nurse before he came here." Malik was sleeping in the grass, his head propped up against a sack of knock-off purses. He was holding the ties of the sack in his hand. It made me think of the way I'd held onto the call-button cord in my hospital room, ready to pull it at the first sign of danger.

Yaya turned my face so he could look at the cut more closely. "Two days more maybe. I think it will be a small scar for you, *non?*"

"Probably." If so, then I'd have a permanent reminder of the damage a ring could do. "I think I'm going to lie down for a minute."

Yaya nodded, shook out his newspaper.

In the grass nearby, I lay down on my back. It was the only position that didn't hurt my ribs.

"Jane," Yaya said.

"Yes?" Above me the sky was empty. No birds. No clouds.

"That ring – is it true you gave it to Manu as a gift?"

"Yes." I closed my eyes. There was no need to worry about thieves. I had absolutely nothing left to steal.

11

When I woke the park was still busy, but Yaya's crew had disappeared. For a while I couldn't get up — just lay there listening to the sounds: a bicycle bell, a crying child, faint guitar music mixed with laughter. I lifted my wrist in the air and looked at Manu's watch. Four thirty-four. Each tick was another second we were further apart. My belly felt like an empty bowl.

Slowly, I pushed myself to standing and walked toward the park exit. The garbage cans along the path were overflowing with picnic remnants. I stopped at one of them and picked through the topmost refuse: sticky pop cans, ice cream wrappers, bags of sweating cheese rinds, apple cores. I'd have to go to Peter's on my own now, and I didn't want to be hungry when I saw him. I pulled out a paper bag that was see-through with grease stains. Empanadas maybe, or fried chicken. A family was sitting on the grass nearby and their little kid was staring at me. I wished he would mind his own business.

There was no food in the bag, just some balled-up dirty napkins. *Don't forget to eat!* I couldn't believe that's all Manu's note had said — that he hadn't left any way for me to contact him. Probably he wouldn't even miss me. The cut on my cheek was throbbing like there was something behind it trying to escape. I brought my hand to my face and pressed it against the wiry stitches until the pain made my vision sharpen.

Up ahead, a couple was kissing on a blanket. The woman's purse lay unattended behind her. The sun felt hotter on the left side of my face as I started toward it. Her purse would fit perfectly over my shoulder – would immediately be mine. In just a few minutes, I'd be out of the park, using her wallet to buy myself something to eat. And then I'd be her for a while. Peter wouldn't be able to feel sorry for me when I saw him; I'd be a woman with a purse again. A switch would be flipped.

I was two steps away when the couple stopped kissing and lay back on their blanket. The woman looked over at me, and the distance between her life and mine expanded again. There was no switch to flip – just a long ladder I'd have to climb if I ever wanted my life to be like hers again.

I exited the park, then walked along the top edge of the Gothic Quarter in search of a bakery. I just had to stick to my plan: Eat something and then go back to Peter's for my wallet. Try to forget that once again everything had changed, that instead of finding a place to stay with Manu, I was going to be staying in a hostel alone. For some reason, it had been easier to care about protecting the two of us than it was to care about protecting only me.

Beside one of the bakeries, I saw a bicycle with a front basket covered in plastic flowers. Annika's bicycle. That was a good sign. Annika was the tall Dutch squatter who'd given us the tip about the supermarket renovation. We'd run into her a couple of times since, and she always seemed to know where there was food.

Annika was bent down over a pile of clear plastic garbage bags. She was wearing a sundress with army boots and knee socks of two different colours. Her red hair was tied in a thick braid that hung down her back.

"The bread's good today," she said when she saw me. She picked up a baguette and broke it in half, pressing into the soft centre with her finger. There was already a crushed box with some kind of tarts inside her basket. She saw me looking at them. "Do you want one?"

"No, that's okay." I was hoping to find something that wasn't sweet.

Annika used her toe to turn over a bag full of paper plates. "Where's your friend?"

"Manu?" His name felt like sand in my mouth. "He's gone."

I bent down and untied a bag that was full of crusty rolls and coffee grounds. I picked out one of the rolls and brushed it off. Annika tied the bag back up for me.

"Thanks." I could feel her looking at the cut on my face.

"Where are you sleeping these days?" she asked.

"We were staying at a construction site, but now ..." If Peter wasn't home when I rang his buzzer, I'd go to meet Atlas at the Black Sheep, and maybe afterwards we'd end up at his apartment. If he didn't invite me, and Peter still wasn't home, I didn't know where I'd spend the night. "I might stay down at the beach."

"It's cold down there," Annika said. "Also, it can be dangerous."

Dangerous. The rough hand with the gold ring swooped again toward my face. "Maybe I'll just walk around," I said. I could always sleep tomorrow during the day. Worst-case scenario, if my plans with both Peter and Atlas failed, that was probably the safest.

I took a bite of the roll and discovered a pocket of sugary almond paste hidden inside. If Manu had been there, I would have given the roll to him. I couldn't believe I was never going to touch his scar.

Annika was arranging the baguettes in her basket. They looked like arms without hands reaching up for help. She glanced over. "If you want, you could come back to the squat with me. Maybe for dinner? Maybe to stay for one night?"

"Are you serious?" Her offer seemed too good to be true – staying at the squat would mean I could rest for another night before I had to go back to Peter's.

"Sure. Why not?"

"Where is it?" I asked.

"In Gracia." The way she pronounced Gràcia with a *th* sound over the *c* meant she'd learned her Spanish in Spain. I still spoke Spanish with a Colombian accent, the way I'd learned from Rosa growing up. Manu had always found that amusing.

I tried out Annika's pronunciation: "In Gracia?" Using the lisping sound felt pretentious.

"Yes. I'll have to double-check with the others, of course, but I'm sure it will be fine."

Her kindness was making me nervous. I scanned her face. If she wanted something from me, I couldn't tell what it was.

Annika smiled. Her teeth looked strong and even like in a milk commercial. "Come on," she said. "It's no problem. I can double you." She pointed at the rack on the back of her bike. "We just need to make a few more stops. Sylvain's making dinner tonight and he wants some vegetables. Sundays are hard, but I think I know a place."

She held the bike upright while I climbed on behind her. The pain in my ribs spiked, and I sucked in my breath.

"Are you okay?" she asked.

"Yeah. I'm just a bit sore."

"Alright, we'll take it slow," she promised. "You just tell me if you need a break."

Gràcia was a little outside of the centre. To get there we had to go uphill, away from the sea. Annika was pedalling hard, the back of her neck red and splotchy with exertion. We rode through a square where a group of teenagers was playing Ping-Pong, yelling at each other and laughing. I could tell they were speaking Catalan because it sounded like a tug-of-war between Spanish and French.

I held on tight as Annika turned the wrong way onto a one-way street. All the shops were closed, metal shutters pulled down over the front windows. It made it hard to get my bearings. In the morning, the shutters would all be rolled up and the neighbourhood would be populated again: with pharmacies, hardware stores and fruit markets.

On the corner, one tiny shop was open. An oscillating fan blocked the doorway, blowing back and forth across a wet floor.

"*Hola!*" Annika called into the shop. An old woman with thick ankles turned from her mopping and waved.

Out front on the curb she'd left a waxed box of damaged produce, a sort of cardboard cornucopia that reminded me of the Old Master still-life paintings that Peter had always joked made him hungry – the kind with rotting figs, orange peels and rabbit carcasses strewn across a table.

Annika got off her bike and examined some bruised tomatoes. She put five or six into her basket, then selected a red pepper that was pockmarked on one side, and a bunch of wilted green onions, browning at the tips. "That should be enough for tonight."

She climbed back on her bike and then we rode through a maze of public squares, each one surrounded by terraces where people were sipping small beers, eating olives and nuts out of long white dishes. Manu's watch said it was 5:45 p.m., dinnertime for the Spaniards still a long way off. The few times Peter and I had gone out for dinner, we'd been almost alone at the restaurants, always arriving way too early. I'd been excited to try Spanish food for the first time – tapas, paella, jamón ibérico – but the thing I'd liked best was just eating together again after so many weeks apart: having our legs mixed up under the same table and sharing food from each other's plates. I suddenly felt the emptiness on either side of the bicycle and I touched Annika's back to stabilize myself.

"We're almost there," she said. "It's just past Plaça de la Revolució."

We turned a corner and she stopped the bike in front of a three-storey building. The front door was pasted over with a sign that said something in Catalan, something about not going in. From the railing of the second-floor balcony a cloth banner hung down, hand-painted with a symbol I didn't recognize, a circle with a jagged arrow passing through. The banner looked like the flag of a pirate ship.

Through the open balcony doors came the sound of someone playing a guitar in need of tuning. Annika took out her cell phone and dialed a number, then hung up before anyone answered. The guitar playing stopped. "Sylvain will come down and let us in," she said.

The thought of meeting Sylvain and the other squatters suddenly made me nervous. They would probably ask questions – want to talk to me about things that had happened in the past instead of just the present.

"Hey," Annika said, "can you tell me your name again?"

It was only one question. One answer. One word.

"Jane."

"Ah, yes. Now I remember. Jane, do you mind carrying this upstairs?" She removed the basket from her handlebars and passed it to me.

Behind the door we heard a scraping sound like something heavy being moved. Annika surveyed the street, then knocked on the door and it opened.

Sylvain was a muscular man wearing large rectangular glasses that looked like a pair of picture frames hung slightly crooked around his eyes. He reached out for Annika's bike and smiled at me.

"We have a visitor," Annika said. "This is Jane."

"Bonjour!" Sylvain leaned over the handlebars to give me a quick kiss on each cheek, then pulled the bike indoors.

Annika and I stepped inside and she deadbolted the door behind me.

There was just enough light coming in from the front windows to see that we were in a big open space. In the centre of the room, a staircase led to the upper floors.

"Should we put back the barricade?" Annika asked Sylvain. There was a cement block and something like a wooden battering ram lying a few feet from the door.

"No, I think it is probably okay," he said. "The others will be back soon. I will put it in place when everyone is home."

Sylvain started up the stairs and Annika motioned for me to go next.

"Be careful on the fourth step," she said. "It's broken."

On the second floor, there was a doorway on either side of the stairs. Sylvain moved aside a sheet that was covering one of them, and a strip of faded daylight fell into the dark hall.

When I followed him into the squat, I discovered the light was coming from two balconies: the one at the front of the building and another one at the back. Support beams and pillars stood at regular intervals throughout the large open room.

Sylvain took the basket from me and started to unpack the food onto a counter in a sort of kitchen area.

"We got the tomatoes!" Annika told him.

"Excellent!"

She grabbed my arm. "Come on, I'll give you a tour."

She steered me toward a living room area with couches, then a dining area with a long table and chairs. The bathroom was the only room that had any walls. "We use the other apartment for sleeping," Annika said. "The one on the other side of the stairs."

"And what about the third floor?"

"Oh, we don't go up there. It's too dangerous. Holes in the floor, live wires and stuff. Plus, the roof is missing, so even if we cleaned it up, we wouldn't be able to secure the place."

I guessed she meant they wouldn't be able to prevent the police from getting in, but maybe there were other dangers as well – other potential intruders. "Is this floor secure?"

"Yes. Come here, I'll show you." She took me out to the staircase again, and we climbed halfway to the next floor. Beginning just above the landing was a bunch of furniture all crammed into the stairwell and chained in place, preventing anyone from going up or down.

"No one's getting in through there," Annika said. "And we usually barricade the front door downstairs as well. Not all the time, but definitely at night once everyone's home. So no surprises. You don't need to worry about being safe."

She gave me a sympathetic look, and I felt embarrassed. I hadn't wanted her to know I was worried.

"So what's the deal with this building?" I asked.

"You mean, why is it empty?"

"Yeah."

Annika sat down on one of the stairs.

"A development company was going to tear it down to put up a condo, but they ran out of money. Then their building permit expired. That was over a year ago. Sylvain checked all the paperwork at city hall."

"How did you guys get in?"

She pointed up. "Through the top floor. We used a ladder to climb down from the roof of the building next door. Then we changed the lock on the front door downstairs. Superglued the lock on the back door. Put some bars across the windows. That's pretty much it. Fully secure possession."

"And you haven't had any trouble?"

Annika laughed. "Oh my god, we've had lots of trouble. The first two weeks the builders sent around their thugs, and we had to put up extra barricades on all the windows and balcony doors and stay inside for a while. The police came too, on the first and second day, but they didn't have a warrant. They're probably trying to get an eviction order now, but that takes time. We've been here a month already. Sylvain's our spokesperson for dealing with the police. He's really good at it." She smiled.

"He seems sweet."

"He's the best," she said. "Shall we go see if he needs a hand?" She pushed herself to standing.

The smell of weed met us in the stairwell as we descended.

By the time we were ready to sit down for dinner, all the squatters were home: Annika and Sylvain, plus three other men who had returned at various points over the last couple of hours. Annika had introduced them to me like characters from a joke: Pau, a Catalan tattoo artist; John, an Irish bike-taxi driver; and Enzo, an Italian fire-eater. *They all walked into a bar*, I thought, but I had no idea what the punchline would be.

The chairs around the dinner table were surprisingly expensive-looking, like they'd been stolen from a medieval castle.

"Be careful when you sit," Annika warned me.

"Yeah, they're from a film set." Sylvain wiggled in his throne to show how the whole structure could bend and sway. "They're not real."

The table was spread with food and lit with candles. Sylvain had sliced the tomatoes and sprinkled them with salt and shredded basil. There were open jars of olives and tins of anchovies, sliced baguette in a pile and a ceramic pitcher of wine. It was sort of like being at a tapas bar but with mismatched plates and no electricity.

We'd all gotten high before dinner. I'd only smoked a little, but it was enough to blur some of the pain in my body and heighten my other senses. I took an olive from the jar Pau offered me. It tasted salty like tears, and I chewed on it until there was no flavour left and the pit was clean.

"So, where are you from?" Pau asked. He had a gruff voice, was hairy and hobbit-like.

"Canada."

He leaned forward. "From Montréal?"

"No. From Toronto."

"Oh." He seemed disappointed.

"Have you been to Montréal?" I asked.

"No. But people here always talk about Québec. A lot of Catalans also want to separate."

I thought about the independence flags hanging from balconies all over the city. In the weeks since my arrival, the flags seemed to have multiplied.

"I saw there was a protest at Plaça Catalunya a few days ago."

Pau nodded. "The central government is trying to break their promises, so some people are beginning to fight back."

"What about you?" I asked. "Do you think it's a good idea to separate?" Pau was the first Catalan person I'd been able to have a real conversation with.

"Uff," he sighed. "Some of the reasons are good. Some are just capitalist bullshit. The Catalan bourgeoisie are no better than the Spanish bourgeoisie." He rubbed a thumb across the inside of his wrist. On his forearm there was a tattoo of Che Guevara with a red star behind it.

"Nice tattoo," I said.

He chuckled. "Yes, 'nice.' The artist who did it is almost as good as me."

Everyone at the table was listening to our conversation. I hadn't talked much before dinner, and now they seemed to be waiting for an explanation: about who I was, and what I was doing in Barcelona.

Enzo, the fire-eater, finally asked. "So. Why you come to Spain?" His head and eyebrows were shaved which made him look intensely interested in my response. A purple shard of crystal hung from his neck on a leather string.

"Um, it's a bit complicated," I said, trying to figure out where to start.

Pau came to my rescue. "If it's complicated, then it must be a man."

I shrugged.

He reached across the table for a packet of loose tobacco. "Is it a Catalan guy? I heard we're very attractive to foreign women, *no*?"

He had a mullet with a rat-tail on one side, and pale chubby cheeks.

"Pau, what are you talking about?" Annika said. "Catalan men are ugly as shit."

"Hey!" Pau puffed out his chest.

I listened to them argue for a while about which country had the hottest men, their conversation drifting away from English until Annika was speaking entirely in Spanish and Pau was answering her in Catalan. It was a kind of Ping-Pong game, like the one I'd seen earlier in the square. Annika was making a strong case for the men of France. Sylvain lifted his arms in the air, victorious.

I looked over at Enzo to see if he was still waiting for an answer, but he just smiled at me. Apparently, having a complicated romantic situation was explanation enough for being here; I didn't need to go into all the details. "Hey, do you know what day it is?" I asked him.

"Sunday."

"Right. Actually I was wondering –"

"It's the thirtieth of May," John interrupted. He was typing a text into his cell phone, one leg bouncing up and down as if he was pedalling his bike-taxi. His bulging calf looked like it belonged to a superhero.

"Thanks."

John ran a hand back and forth once through his blond mohawk. He didn't look up.

May 30. Under the table, I tapped out the days with my fingers. My cancelled wedding was twelve days away. At the end of June, my court date in Toronto would pass, and after that, I'd have a Failure to Appear charge against me. I'd used a computer at the locutorio one day to look up what that would mean. Nothing would happen immediately, but if I ever got arrested again in Canada, or wanted to cross the US border, or even tried to renew my driver's licence or passport, that's when the charge would be a problem. Some of the legal websites said I could be held in jail without bail until my court date since I hadn't shown up the first time. Hopefully none of that would matter since I wasn't going back. But, in a couple of months when my tourist visa expired, I'd be illegal here too; I'd be illegal everywhere.

I set down the piece of bread I was eating. My ribs were hurting again, and I wished I could lie down somewhere.

Annika broke off her conversation. "Jane, you look tired. Do you want to try to sleep?"

"Would that be okay?" I glanced around the table. Everyone made big-handed gestures, affirmative noises.

Pau was adding a substantial amount of weed to the cigarette he was rolling. "Are you sure you want to go to bed right now?" he asked. "This might help you sleep."

"Thanks," I said. "But I think I'm okay."

Annika stood up and I followed her into the apartment on the other side of the stairwell. It was a mirror image of the main apartment, but with sleeping bags and blankets scattered on the floor, here and there a mattress. The most striking feature of the room was that a quarter of its back wall was missing; a large V-shaped gap surrounded by crumbling bricks dipped down from the ceiling in one corner. Through the gap, I could see the night sky, and across the back alley, another apartment building. In some of its windows, the shapes of normal people were doing normal things.

I walked closer to the gap and noticed there were pointy shards of glass glued onto the bricks like sharp teeth inside a mouth.

"That's just a precaution," Annika said. "We're trying to make sure no one can get in through there. Sylvain's going to patch up the hole soon. He just needs to find the right materials."

I touched a fingertip to one of the shards. It was sharp. From the other apartment, the squatters' voices floated out the back balcony and past me into the night.

"Jane," Annika said, and I turned. "I'm sure Pau will let you borrow one of his blankets, and I'll give you one of ours too. It's starting to warm up now, but it still gets a little cold, especially in the morning."

She walked to a corner of the room where two large tie-dyed scarves hung on a string like curtains. When she disappeared through a crack between them, I caught sight of a fancy canopy bed, the posts tilting slightly in toward the centre like knock knees. It was probably from the film set too.

Annika reappeared and handed me a fuzzy blue blanket. She wandered over to a bumpy piece of yellow foam on the floor. "You can sleep here, if you like. There was another girl staying with us for a while, but I'm pretty sure she's gone now."

I shook out the blanket and laid it over the foam, then eased myself down to sit on the makeshift bed. My entire body felt achy, punctured in places by points of sharper pain.

Annika collected another blanket from the mattress closest to mine and passed it over. It smelled like a campfire and there were cigarette burns along the edge. I felt very small, sitting on the floor with Annika standing tall above me.

"Are you okay?" she asked.

I wasn't sure if she meant okay like I had everything I needed, or okay emotionally. This was the type of tricky question women sometimes asked one another; I was out of practice.

"Yes. I think I'm fine."

"Good."

"Thanks for letting me stay here."

"No problem." She spread her arms. "Welcome to the Ritz-Gracia! I'll see you in the morning."

She went back to the other apartment, and the squatters' muffled conversation dipped briefly toward quiet, then returned to full volume.

I kept my coat on and lay down between the blankets, grateful I wouldn't have to move again for hours. I could hear the squatters' laughter, feel the pull of their higher-functioning lifestyle. I should have tried harder to answer their questions, asked them some questions of my own. If I had made that effort, or maybe if I made it tomorrow, the strangers on the other side of the stairwell might let me stay longer. The squat didn't feel entirely secure, but at least it was an indoor space where I wouldn't have to pay rent. Plus, there was safety in numbers. Tomorrow, I'd answer any questions the squatters asked.

Outside, the crescent moon looked like a thin white scar against the dark sky. Manu and I had never really talked about our pasts. For a second, I missed him so much I could feel his warmth at my side.

I thought about the pastry he'd fed me on the first day we met, and the many other ways he'd tried to look out for me. He might not have left an address or a phone number, but that didn't mean he hadn't cared – or that he wasn't missing me too.

I slipped my fingers into the gap between his watchband and my wrist. I wondered what time it was in Ecuador.

12

When I woke up, a hint of daylight had crept into the room and there was a loud murmur coming through the gap in the wall. I realized it was the sound of people in the building behind us – people who were dressing their children, calling out reminders, making coffee, taking showers. At the construction site in El Raval, it was always the lack of noise that had alerted us it was almost morning. In Gràcia it seemed to be the opposite: all night it had been quiet and now the windows across the alley were filling up with sound.

I sat up and looked around. Annika and Sylvain's socked feet were just visible at the end of their bed. John and Enzo were both wearing Peruvian-style hats with earflaps, and had their sleeping bags zipped up to their chins. Two pigeons in the corner were sleeping as well, their heads tucked into their chests. On the mattress closest to me, Pau was snoring, his tattooed arm bent up under his head.

I got up and went into the other apartment. Alone, I was able to really explore the space. Each of the balcony doors was covered by a cage of wire mesh bolted into the bricks. The same symbol I'd seen on the banner outside was painted on the living room wall:

the circle with a jagged arrow passing through like a lightning bolt. Posters for protests and marches were taped up beside it. On the windowsill, a variety of herbs sprouted from teacups, and beneath the sill, a complicated-looking lineup of containers held food scraps and recycling.

The table was still messy from our dinner the night before. I gathered up the dishes and set them on the kitchen counter. When I turned the taps above the sink, cold water came out of both. I bent my head down and took a drink, then began rinsing the dishes. A small ripped towel hanging from a nail smelled clean enough to dry with. There weren't really any shelves or cupboards, so I just organized the plates and cups into stacks and rows on the counter.

When I was finished, I wasn't sure what else to do while I waited for the squatters to wake up. I wondered what the rules were for deciding who could stay – if you had to be an activist of some kind. The protest posters on the wall were about many issues. The ones for environmental causes I understood, but there were also political posters with screen-printed graphics of fists and barbed wire – posters with words I'd seen before but couldn't exactly define: *xenophobia, disbandment, expropriation.*

I picked up a thick book that was lying on a chair. I was expecting it to be a manifesto of some sort, but instead it was a novel in English, *The Girl with the Dragon Tattoo*. The review on the back began with a quote in large excited-looking type: "Captivating, suspenseful, and complex!" I hadn't held a book in my hands for quite a while, and the idea of reading a novel seemed somehow luxurious. The only things I'd read over the last couple of weeks were cover stories from Yaya's newspapers. I thumbed through the book's pages, stopping occasionally to skim a paragraph.

"Good morning!" Annikà said. She was stretching in the doorway.

"Hey. Good morning."

"Did you sleep well?"

"Great. I slept great." I didn't think I'd even had a nightmare.

"Have you read that?" she asked.

"No. Is it good?"

"Yes, it's really good. It's the first book in a trilogy." She walked over to the kitchen area. "You can read it, if you want, when I'm finished."

"Okay, cool." I wondered how long it would be before she was done, and whether she thought I might still be around.

"Do you want some tea?" Annika asked. "We haven't figured out where we can borrow electricity from yet, but we do have a little camping stove." She poured water from a plastic jug into a small metal pot. "Don't drink the tap water, by the way. We're happy to have it, but we're not sure where it comes from." She looked at the lines and piles I'd made on the counter. "Thanks for cleaning up."

"No problem." The tap water gurgled in my stomach.

"So, listen," Annika said, "I talked to the guys last night, and we decided you can stay for a few more days if you want. Sort of like a trial. You know, see how it goes."

"Really?" I couldn't hide my excitement.

"Yes. We were thinking you could help out with the shopping, maybe the cooking and cleaning too. Also, there has to be at least one person here at all times. So we'll put you on the schedule once you get to know how things work."

"Sure. I can definitely help with all that."

"Good! It'll be nice to have another girl around," Annika said.

My face flushed. Maybe we were going to be friends.

"What kind of work did you do when you lived in Toronto?" she asked.

"I was a graphic designer."

"Cool! Maybe you can design something for us."

"Yeah, sure." I couldn't imagine what sort of design work the squatters might need. I looked at the circle with the jagged arrow on the wall. "What does that symbol mean?"

"Oh, it's the squatter's symbol. Hobos used to use it as a sign for other travellers. It meant, 'Continue on. There's a safe place up ahead.'"

"So, having that banner on the balcony … is that like a sign to tell other squatters they can come here?"

"Not exactly. It's more about letting the community and the police know who we are. That we're not thieves – that we're just people who need a place to live in a city that's full of empty buildings, and so we're occupying this space for justified reasons." She grabbed a pair of mugs from the counter. "Do you want black tea or peppermint?"

"Um, black tea would be nice." I wondered if she knew I was a thief. The disapproving way she'd said the word didn't really make sense; it seemed like the squatters probably stole lots of things.

A pigeon came strutting into the room. "Hey there, Mister," I said. "Where do you think you're going?"

"Ugh." Annika grabbed the towel and ran at the bird, shooing it away.

The intensity of her disgust surprised me.

"They're so filthy," she said. "And they're impossible to keep out." She rummaged through a box on the floor, then handed me a water gun. "Here, you're on pigeon duty. Keep watch while I make us something to eat."

Annika cut a banana into two bowls, then covered the fruit with granola. While we sat eating our breakfast, I confessed to her that I didn't have any money at the moment, but that I could get some if I needed it.

"Money's not a problem," Annika said. "We're actually freegan."

"Freegan. Is that like …" I had no idea.

"It just means we try to live without money. Dumpster diving for food and other things we need. Also, we're pretty much vegan. So, *free-gan*. Although a couple of the guys eat meat if we happen to find some."

By Annika's description, most of the people I'd met on the street were freegans too – they just didn't know it. I'd never heard of anyone living without money by choice though. "You must need money for some things."

She shrugged. "Not really. Here, wait. I'll show you." She left the apartment for a minute, then came back with an armful of clothes and dumped them on the table.

"Whose are those?" I asked.

"Nobody's. We just found them in the garbage and washed them up. Eventually, once we get settled, we're going to open a Free Store so we can give something back to the community."

"A Free Store?"

"Yeah. The squat in Sants has one, the squat in Collserola too. It's basically just a store where everything is free."

That sounded like something that couldn't possibly exist. "Everything is from the garbage?"

"Mostly," Annika said. "Or donated by people we know. There are lots of unwanted things in the world. You just have to match them up with the right person – the person who really wants them."

"We could use a place like that in my old neighbourhood." I was picturing a storefront in Parkdale: a blank white box that could be turned into a Free Store on one side and a gallery on the other.

"Every neighbourhood could use a Free Store." Annika motioned to the clothes on the table. "Go ahead. Take whatever you want."

I started searching through the pile. The clothes all had a slightly herbal smell, like they'd been picked from a garden. I set aside a slate grey tank top, and a thin white blouse to wear over it. A black peasant skirt looked like it might fit me, as well.

"That's it?" Annika shook out a few other pieces and held them up for me. "What about this? Or these?" Everything she suggested was way too colourful.

"No thanks."

Annika pulled off her dress, and I looked away from her nearly naked body as she tried on a floral-print wrap that could have been a tablecloth at a Mexican restaurant.

"What do you think?" she asked.

I didn't know her well enough to tell her the truth. "It's not bad. Maybe try that one instead?" I pointed to a turquoise dress on the pile. When she grabbed it, I spotted a long saffron-coloured scarf that had been hidden underneath – a cheap version of the cashmere scarf I'd tried to shoplift at the department store in Toronto.

I untangled it from the other clothes. It was silky and soft, long enough to wrap several times around my neck. I lifted the scarf to my nose for a moment, then dropped my hand back to the table. My mother had loved the scarf I'd stolen for her when I was twelve. Whenever I saw it on the hook inside the front door of our apartment, it meant she was home. I would bury my face in it and smell the bakery, her shampoo, her cigarettes. Sometimes if she was sleeping, I'd wind the scarf around my body while I watched TV. I didn't even care that she had asked me to steal it for her. If I got caught shoplifting as a minor, I'd just get a slap on the wrist. She knew that because it had happened before. We might not have enough money, but we still deserved to have nice things. That's what my mother always said.

"That scarf is great!" Annika said. She was mostly naked again, slipping the turquoise dress over her head.

"Yeah, I might take it, if that's okay?"

"Of course!"

I glanced at the door to the hall. There was no noise coming from the other apartment, so I stripped out of my clothes and began wrapping the saffron scarf tightly around my ribs to keep them from moving so much.

I thought Annika might ask me what I was doing or how I'd gotten hurt, but she didn't. Instead, she waited until I was dressed in the new outfit I'd chosen, then stepped back to assess the result.

"Fantastic," she said. "And how about this to finish things off?" She held up a jean jacket with loopy gold words painted on it. They seemed to be in Italian.

"No, that's okay. I've got my trench coat." I pointed to where I'd hung it on the back of a chair. The weather was getting too warm for coats, but I still liked to wear mine. It was one of the only things I had left from my old life.

"Well, if *you* don't want this jacket, maybe I'll take it." Annika slipped it on and pulled up the collar, posing with an exaggerated pout. "How does it look?"

"Very chic."

She stuck one arm in the air, and then the other, shouting out the words painted on the sleeves: *"Baci! Amore!"*

One of the sleeping guys from the other apartment groaned. "Shut up!"

Annika stuck out her tongue in the direction of the voice. She pulled off the jacket and tossed it back on the pile.

"Should we go do the shopping now?" she asked.

"Sure."

She went into the kitchen area, then handed me a large cloth bag with other bags inside. I reached for my trench coat.

"I don't think you're going to need that," she said.

I held onto the coat for a moment, then hung it back on the chair. She was right. It was almost summer now. I hurried to catch up with her on the stairs.

13

Even though Annika was a foreigner, a lot of people in the neighbour-hood seemed to know her. The first place we went was a bakery that had set aside a cup of wayward sesame seeds for her. The next place was a tiny supermarket with a carton of expired eggs waiting behind the counter. I noticed Annika was speaking Catalan with some of the shopkeepers.

"People are a lot friendlier if you know some words and phrases," she explained.

As we continued our rounds, she told me that she'd just turned twenty-eight, and that she'd been away from the Netherlands for almost a decade, travelling and living in different places. "I've actually never gone back."

I knew there must be a reason, but I didn't ask why. Annika and I both had places that we'd left behind for good. She probably didn't want to talk about it either.

We dropped off our first load of groceries at the squat, then rode into the city centre on her bike. Even with the scarf wrapped around my ribs, every bump in the road caused my vision to blur for a second.

By the time we stopped behind the Carrefour, I was feeling light-headed. Tylenol was one thing we weren't going to find in the garbage.

Outside the back door of the store, a group of people were waiting: a mix of backpackers, vagrants and elderly locals. Annika knew a couple of the cleaner-looking people, and I knew one of the dirty ones – a junkie from the courtyard. Now that I was relatively clean from showering at the hospital, I noticed there was a difference between the smell of the backpackers and the smell of the people who lived on the street. The backpackers had a two- or three-day smell that could still be washed off; the street people's smell seemed permanent, baked by the sun into their skin and their hair and their clothes.

"The security guards always try to put out the garbage just before the truck comes," Annika told me. "They don't want people picking through it, but sometimes we have a little time." She pointed at the door where two security guards with garbage bags were emerging from the store. They tossed the bags into the dumpster, then one of them stood watch while the other disappeared. A moment later he returned with a large jug of bleach.

Annika sighed, and some of the other people shouted at him as he emptied the contents of the jug into the dumpster. An old woman standing beside us spat on the ground.

"Why did he do that?" I asked Annika.

"His boss probably told him to. They don't want anyone eating the food because it's a liability. So just to cover their asses" – her voice rose sharply so the security guards could hear her – "sometimes they destroy perfectly good food. Food that could feed hungry people."

I was worried the guards might come over, but they ignored her. Annika shook her head. "It's the same reason dumpster diving is illegal – everyone's afraid of being sued."

"How can it be illegal to pick up garbage?"

"Well, it definitely shouldn't be," Annika said. "But technically we're on their property, so in court they could say we were trespassing and that we stole stuff they were planning to use again."

"That's crazy."

"I know. It's obviously stuff they don't want anymore if they're pouring bleach on it, right? But you'd be surprised how hard it is to prove that something's been thrown away – legally, I mean. Sylvain can explain it better sometime, if you're interested. There's this whole 'law of abandonment' thing."

The security guards went back inside, and most of the waiting crowd began to move away.

"Shall we go try the market?" Annika asked.

"Okay." The junkie from the courtyard was inside the dumpster, throwing things over the side. The old woman was using a newspaper to wipe off an apple. She brought it to her nose, frowned, then threw it into the gutter.

Annika followed my gaze. "Yeah, that's the problem," she said. "People make a mess. The first rule of dumpster diving is that you should always leave things the way you found them." She climbed onto her bike and swung her long braid around, almost hitting me in the face.

I hesitated before getting on behind her. No one I'd met on the street had ever mentioned the etiquette of dumpster diving. Annika's rules had been made by people who were less hungry. I kept the thought to myself.

At the back of the market we found a box of overripe plums, and a large basket of lettuce leaves that had been torn off, maybe because they were ugly. After filling our shopping bags, I went into a coffee shop to use the bathroom. When I returned, I handed Annika a roll of toilet paper and some packets of sugar to add to our supplies. It was a habit I'd gotten into when I was staying with Manu. He sometimes liked to eat sugar on bread, and we always needed toilet paper.

"Um, thanks," she said. "But you don't have to do that. To steal things, I mean."

My face went red. "Sorry."

"Oh, don't worry. It's just that there's so much stuff in the garbage. Sylvain and I haven't bought anything for almost two years. And we try never to steal. It's sort of a game for us."

I nodded. I'd been trying to live without buying anything for a while now too, although it didn't feel like a game. "Do you want me to return this stuff?" I asked.

Annika waved away my suggestion. "No, that's a terrible coffee chain. Not a bad place to steal from … if you have to."

Annika was scheduled to be the person who stayed at the squat that afternoon, and we spent a few hours reading magazines and then having a long nap. When Sylvain returned to spell us off, Annika and I went for another walk in Gràcia. This time she pointed out places of interest on almost every block: a library where there were public-access computers, a store that pumped up bicycle tires for free, the tattoo shop where Pau worked and an elevator that led to an underground parking lot.

"There's an old bomb shelter down there," she said. "One of the parking attendants will give you a key if you ever want to take a look."

Walking around with Annika felt totally different than moving through the city with Manu. Instead of trying to be inconspicuous, she seemed to want us to be seen. She had a loud voice, and gestures that were slightly oversized. Many people who passed us took an extra moment to check out her bright clothes and mismatched socks.

In one of the public squares a group of drummers was rehearsing. We sat in the sun to listen. When I glanced over, Annika had her face lifted to the sky, her eyes closed. All day, I'd been expecting her to ask me a bunch of questions, but she hadn't. Maybe it was a Dutch thing not to pry. Whatever the reason, I was happy to just sit with her in silence; even if it felt a little strange. Manu had never asked about my past because he didn't want to talk about his own. With Annika, it felt more like she just wasn't interested.

We returned to the squat at the end of the afternoon to prepare some food for dinner: a salad of multicoloured vegetables, and a soup made with carrots, onion and ginger. I wasn't sure how to help, so Annika gave me instructions, and I did what she said, chopping the vegetables once, and then cutting them again when she suggested I make them smaller.

As we cooked, the other squatters turned up, telling us loud funny stories about their days and emptying their pockets and bags to show us the items they'd collected. At one point, Enzo came running up the stairs to grab Sylvain, then the two of them returned more slowly, lugging an old washing machine into the room.

Pau flirted with me a little over dinner, but I wasn't interested. Even if I had been, I wouldn't have wanted to do anything to put my living situation with the freegans at risk. The squat felt like a perfect place to live for a while: a place where all my basic needs could be met without too much trouble and where I might even have a bit of time to finally explore the city or make some art.

"Hey, what do you guys think about me painting a mural for the Free Store?" I asked. It was a way I could thank them for letting me stay.

"Jane, I love that idea!" Annika said. "We're planning to set up the store on the ground floor. Maybe you could paint a wall of flowers or something?" She made an arc with one arm like she was imagining a rainbow of colourful blooms.

"Yeah, something like that."

The other squatters chimed in, offering suggestions. I didn't want their ideas cluttering up my head, but I smiled and nodded, only half-listening.

After dinner, I rummaged in the recycling bin looking for some paper to draw on. I found a few good scraps and was smoothing them out on the floor when Pau came over and crouched beside me. He passed me a notebook, and I flipped it open. On the first few pages were drawings for simple tattoos: wheels with cogs, ninja throwing stars, molecules.

"You can just rip those out," he said.

"Oh no. I don't want to take your sketchbook." I handed it back. "Don't worry. I'll find one of my own."

"Are you sure?"

"Yes. Thanks though."

He sat down on the floor. "So, what are you going to paint?"

"I don't know yet. I usually paint people."

He looked serious for a moment. "Are you asking me to be your model?" He placed a hand under his chin and gazed off into the distance.

I laughed. "Um, let me think about it. I'll let you know."

The next afternoon my stitches were itching, and I decided to go to the park to see if I could find Yaya and Malik. Annika and I were already done with the shopping and she didn't need my help again until dinner. When I told her I was going out, she tilted her head and gave me a blank look, like I didn't need to tell her what I was doing – like it was no business of hers.

"I should be back in an hour or two," I said.

"Okay."

I hesitated. I hadn't been separated from her yet, and I didn't know how I was going to get back in. "When I come back, should I just knock, or ..."

"Oh, that's right. You don't have a phone." Annika walked over to the door and pulled a phone card from a basket tacked to the wall. There was a piece of tape on the card that had a number written on it in black Magic Marker.

"Here. Just go to the locutorio on your way back and call this number. It's for the mobile that stays here." She pulled a flip phone out of the basket and waggled it in my direction. "If you just let it ring three times and hang up, then you don't have to pay, and whoever's here will come downstairs and let you in."

"And there's always someone here?"

"Yes." Annika smiled. "I'll come down with you now and lock you out."

On the ground floor, she opened the front door, then looked both ways up and down the street. "If a Mosso tries to talk to you when you're coming or going, just say you're a visitor. Don't say that you live here. It'll be better for you that way."

"Okay." I stepped out onto the sidewalk, and she immediately closed the door behind me. As I headed down the street, I reached into the pocket of my skirt to make sure the phone card was safe.

The park was further away than I remembered. I checked Manu's watch, then picked up my pace. It was already 3:25 p.m. and Yaya's crew was usually only there for an hour or so, mid-afternoon while the stores were closed and people were busy eating lunch.

When I arrived, Yaya was sitting on his usual bench, tearing off pieces from a baguette and tossing them to a wide circle of pigeons and wild parrots. The wild parrots were small, but they were bullies. They strutted through the pigeon ranks like compact green dictators, hoarding all the bread crumbs for themselves.

Malik pointed at a patch of grass, and I sat down and turned my face toward him. He opened his pocket knife, then passed the blade back and forth several times through the flame of a lighter. When the blade cooled a bit, he started to work on my face, picking at the stitches with small quick movements. My stomach flipped over, and I held onto the edge of the park bench. Yaya was watching. I'd been telling him about the squat.

"They call themselves freegans," I said. I had to speak slowly, trying not to move too much. "They get their furniture and clothes and food from the garbage. Annika says there's so much waste, you can just live on that."

"Where are these people from?" Yaya asked.

"Um, the Netherlands, France, Italy, Ireland. One guy is from Spain."

Yaya was looking at me like I was missing something.

"I guess they're all European," I added. I felt Malik's fingers bracing against my cheek, and then a tug that reached under my skin, as if something deeply rooted was being coaxed from the ground.

Yaya nodded. "Me, I like capitalism. If everyone was – How do you say? *Freeganiste?* – no one would have any shoes." He stretched his feet in my direction. He was wearing a new pair of sneakers. They looked like they'd be good for running away from the Mossos.

Malik threw a strand of black wiry thread into the dirt, then wiped off the blade of his knife and folded it away. *"C'est tout."*

"Thanks." I wished I had a mirror. Yaya's expression was serious; there was definitely going to be a scar. I lightly touched my cheek, but Malik brushed my hand away.

"Ne touche pas. Nous n'avons pas d'antiseptique."

One of the other purse sellers said something I couldn't understand, and I asked Yaya to translate.

"He said that in his village they also make a scar like this on the face – to show which community they belong to."

All the other purse sellers were staring at me then, and I didn't know what to say. Without thinking, I tried to touch the scar again. Malik flicked me hard on the back of the hand.

In Gràcia, I went to the locutorio like Annika had said, and dialed the freegans' number. After letting the phone ring three times, I left the shop and hurried to the squat, then waited out front for ten minutes. Nobody came downstairs.

I tried calling again, double-checking each digit against the ones printed on the phone card. This time when I returned, there was a cluster of old ladies chatting out front on the sidewalk, but no sign of Annika. I considered yelling up to the balcony, but the squatters had told me to be careful not to disturb the neighbours.

I stood across the street from the front door trying not to panic, but it was suddenly obvious: the squatters had been waiting for a chance to get rid of me. Now they were pretending they weren't home. I was just about to leave when the door opened and Sylvain came out carrying two plastic bags.

"Jane!" he said. He looked at my face. "What's happened?"

"Nothing. I was just calling to get back in."

"Ah, sorry. Annika and I were busy." He smiled. "We don't have too much time alone these days." He pushed the door wide so I could pass. "I'm just taking out the garbage."

"Do you want me to wait and let you back in?"

"No, that's okay. I brought the key. You can leave the deadbolt off. I'll be back in a minute."

Upstairs, Annika was sitting on a chair in a patch of sunlight reading. Barefoot and relaxed, she looked like she was on vacation.

"Hey," she said, getting up. "Were you calling?"

"Yeah, but it's okay. I ran into Sylvain downstairs."

"Let me see your face." She squinted at my cheek. "You know what it looks like? It looks like – what do you call that thing? That thing on the communist flag?" She traced a crescent shape in the air.

"A sickle?"

"A sickle? That's what it's called in English?"

"I think so."

"Huh. I never heard that before. A sickle … Anyway, it kind of looks like that."

Maybe scars were like ink blots or clouds – people would see what they wanted to see.

"Oh, guess what." Annika went back to the chair and picked up her book. "Look what I found!" She turned to show me the cover. "It's the second book in the trilogy. I just finished reading the first one this morning!"

"Wow, that's really lucky," I said.

"I know! It was just sitting in a box on Carrer Verdi. Can you believe it?"

Actually, I could believe it. I had the feeling that lucky things were always happening to Annika. Since running into her, they were starting to happen to me as well. The whole time I was staying with Manu, no one had ever invited us to come indoors.

14

Living with the freegans, my gaze began to shift from open purses downward, travelling along curbs to the piles of unwanted items that accumulated every day next to the overflowing garbage bins. There were dishes, lamps, old computers, books, photographs, clothes. I seemed to have a knack for finding household items we needed for the squat: a cheese grater, a mirror, a bath mat, a laundry basket.

I was also collecting a little pile of found objects beside my bed: a pair of sandals, a ceramic cat, an old encyclopedia, a wooden comb, a painted hand fan. As the pile got bigger, I needed a bag, then a box to put everything into. Each time I added something new I'd lift the box to check its weight. I didn't want it to get too heavy. Before leaving Toronto, I'd filled four closet-sized crates to ship, choosing only the things I'd felt Peter and I couldn't live without. Now I barely remembered what they were.

All of the items in the box beside my bed were things I liked but didn't need, things I could easily leave behind. The squatters had explained what to do if the police ever came back – what to say, what our rights were. To me, it seemed almost certain we'd someday get evicted, although the squatters liked to pretend that wasn't true. It was a strange way to live – working to build a home that could disappear at any moment. Each time I went out, I felt anxious, knowing there might be a padlock on the door when I returned. The others didn't seem to be as worried, and I wondered if they all had backup plans I didn't know about: escape routes, other homes or secret bank accounts.

Whenever we needed money – mostly for wine or weed or gas for the camping stove – Enzo busked, John drove his bike-taxi and Pau gave tattoos at the shop around the corner. Annika and Sylvain didn't have paying jobs; they tried to live completely outside of the conventional economy. In place of traditional work, they provided services for the others in the collective. Annika was in charge of supplying the squat with food and did most of the meal preparation and cleaning. Sylvain fixed things he found in the garbage and tried to make home improvements. He was building a solar panel to heat water for showers, and was also working on converting the old washing machine to bicycle-power. He'd taken over a corner of the living room for the project.

"When I'm finished putting the washer back together," Sylvain said to me one afternoon, "I am going to set it in front of the balcony, facing the mountain. That way the person who is doing the pedalling will have a nice view."

"Maybe that person could be me," I said. I'd been spending most of my days helping Annika like an assistant, and I was getting tired of always doing what she asked. I wanted a job of my own.

"Yes, that would be good," Sylvain agreed. "If it's not too much work for you?"

"No, I don't think so. It doesn't sound like a bad job, really."

"It's true. Me, I would much rather do work like this – " He pushed on the bike pedal and the barrel of the washing machine spun around. "– than to be, for example, a lawyer."

Becky Blake

I was mending a pair of Pau's pants at the table. I pinched together the ripped edges of the hole and made a stitch. "I thought you liked legal stuff." Sylvain had a large collection of pamphlets about freegans' rights and squatters' law, and he was always mentioning examples of cases and verdicts. Yesterday he'd explained the law of abandonment to me in way too much detail.

Sylvain sighed. "I guess it's just what I know. Both my parents are lawyers. Can you imagine? Two of them in one house?" He lifted his hands to his temples and made a gesture like his head was exploding.

I stopped sewing for a moment, my needle straining against the thick cotton. I hadn't pegged Sylvain for a rich kid, but now that I thought about it, it made sense. I pushed the needle a bit harder, and the sharp tip poked through to the other side of the fabric. His parental situation didn't sound bad to me. If I had a lawyer-parent – even one of them – I'd have someone to give me advice on my court case, and how to get a visa to work in Spain, and what would happen if I overstayed without any papers. "Two lawyers, hey?"

"Yes," Sylvain said. "Always lots of stress in our house. But at least I know how to argue because of them. Most of the time, when I'm dealing with the police, this helps me, you know? Although sometimes the situations are impossible. Last year, for example, Annika and me, we were in Berlin and the police wanted to evict us. I tried to explain to them about the law, but they didn't want to listen. So finally, when they came to throw us out, we decided – we have to use the Death Plank."

"What's the Death Plank?"

"It's just a long piece of wood," Sylvain said. "But very thick." He opened his fingers into a wide C to show me the thickness. "We put one end out the window facing west and the other end out the window facing north. On the corner of the building, you know? It

136

was on the third floor, so pretty high up. Then Annika, she goes out one window, and me, I go out the other. Then we just sit. Each on one end."

"Outside of the building?"

"Yes." Sylvain pushed up his glasses. "At first we had to move very slowly – at the exact same moment so we can balance, you know? So we don't fall."

"Wow." I bit off an extra length of thread. "What happened?"

"The police they were all the time yelling, 'Hey! You must come inside! You must leave the building!'" Sylvain laughed. "But we didn't come in. We just sat for a long time and there was nothing they could do. If they tried to grab one of us – Annika or me – then the other one was going to fall." He made a sudden slanting teeter-totter motion with his arm. "You understand?"

"Yes." If living without money was a game to Sylvain and Annika, it was a game they took seriously. "So how long did you stay outside?"

"Mmm ..." Sylvain looked to the ceiling, remembering. "Sixteen hours?"

"Sixteen hours?"

"Yes. The police they were all the time leaving one man inside the building. But in the end they decided, okay, this is enough."

"That sounds terrible."

"No, actually it was all right. We each had a backpack with a long rope, so when we were having a bad moment, we could lower the pack down to the street and our friends would send food or messages back up to us. For me, it was a little bit of fun. Not so much for Annika. She has some fear, you know, of being up high. So when the wind was blowing, sometimes she was feeling really scared." Sylvain wiped his hands on a rag and gave the washing machine a pat. "I think this is almost ready."

I tried to imagine sitting mid-air on the end of a plank, nothing to hold onto on either side. "I don't think I could do that – what you and Annika did."

Sylvain walked over to the table. "Don't worry. We only need two people. If we have to do it again, we choose someone else."

We heard Annika coming up the stairs, and Sylvain went over to the curtained doorway to meet her. When she appeared, she greeted him in a singsong voice. *"Bonjour, mon amour!"* She leaned over the basket she was carrying, and they kissed for a long moment like I wasn't in the room.

I focused on rethreading my needle even though the mending was done.

"Hey, Jane, how's it going?" Annika brought over her basket and plopped it down on the table. A clump of dirt fell from a green frond waving above the rim. "Look what I found in the forest at Park Güell!" She started to pull things from the basket. "Wild rhubarb, mint, raspberries and this – " She held up a large dirty mushroom.

"Cool," I said.

"I know, right?" Her cheeks were flushed.

I'd gone out with her on foraging expeditions a couple of times, but I could never match her enthusiasm. At first, I'd thought this was the reason Annika and I weren't connecting. But after a few days, I'd realized the truth: Annika didn't really want to be friends with me. She'd just been doing her duty – rescuing a stray. It was part of some code she lived by. I was a project, and that project had clear boundaries. Annika was unswerving in her respect of my privacy, and she herself only talked to me about practical things. Maybe moving from place to place had made her like that. She was friendly but detached, as if she wanted me to be as easy to leave behind as a box of belongings beside the bed.

"I'm going to make some soup," she said. "Do you want to help?"

Her question wasn't really a question; as her assistant, she was expecting me to say yes.

"Actually, I was thinking of going downstairs and getting started on the mural."

"Oh." Annika switched gears. "I didn't know you'd found some paint."

"I didn't really – I'm still looking – but there's a bit of cleaning up and planning I can do."

"Okay. That sounds like important work."

I couldn't tell if she was being sarcastic. Ever since I'd mentioned to her that I probably wasn't going to paint a flower garden, she'd been a lot less excited about the project.

"I'll come back to help in a bit." I folded up Pau's pants and went into the sleeping apartment to put them away.

Downstairs, I walked across the empty ground-floor room to the pile of materials I'd been collecting in a corner. The building's owners had left behind a roller, a couple of brushes and some industrial paint: black and a muted yellow that had been used in the stairwells. Pau had brought me a package of markers from the tattoo shop, and I also had some pieces of coloured chalk that I'd found in the garbage. I needed some other colours of paint though, before I could really begin. Some better brushes too. I'd been tempted to steal them, but when I'd tested out the idea on Enzo, he'd been even more disapproving than Annika, giving me a long lecture about how the universe provided everything that people needed. From experience, I knew that wasn't true – at least not for everybody – but I'd decided to play by the squatters' rules for a few more days. Now that I was getting luckier, maybe some supplies would turn up. If not, then I'd take things into my own hands and make a set of acrylic paints "magically" appear.

For today, all I could do was prep-work. I used the paint roller to wash the dirty walls and emptied out bucket after bucket of grimy water into a sink. When I was finished, I stood back a bit, trying to figure out how I was going to use the wall space. It was so much larger than a canvas. Maybe instead of a single piece I'd do several smaller panels.

In the past, a few of my best ideas had come to me after going ahead and making the first mark. I pried open the can of black paint, then dipped in one of the brushes. After a moment, I drew a stripe up from the floor to as far as I could reach. The brush was crunchy with some kind of old varnish that gave the line a rippled effect – a bit like wood grain. I continued the line across at a right angle above my head, then back to join the floor a couple of feet from where I'd started. A final stripe along the baseboard closed the rectangle. It was a frame of sorts, a big one.

At the frame store where I'd worked to pay for design school there'd been an endless stream of limited edition prints to press between museum-grade glass for people who could afford it. In a way, it was because of that job that I was in Barcelona.

I began to paint another rectangle further down the wall, remembering the auction where Peter and I had first met. During the bidding, he'd stared at me from across the room as if I was a piece of art he was trying to guess the value of. He'd assumed I was also a buyer – rather than just some salesgirl sent to hand out business cards – and when we spoke, I hadn't corrected him. After that, it was a crazy couple of weeks: borrowing fancy clothes to wear on dates with him; not lying exactly, but not telling him the truth either – not until after we'd slept together. Sex was the one part of our relationship where we'd always been equals, the one area where, with me being fifteen years younger, I'd even had an advantage.

Memories from a weekend morning came back to me while I painted a third frame: the clinging tangle of Peter's duvet as I climbed out of his bed, his eyes on me as I slipped into one of his dress shirts, the smell of his cologne keeping me company as I poured myself a coffee in his immaculate kitchen – a room where everything was new and functional, and all of the cupboards were full.

A swell of longing rose up in me, then fell back like a half-hearted hand reaching out toward something too far away. I swirled my brush in a bucket of water, watching as the black paint fanned out in threads that got thinner and thinner, until they were too skinny to see. A list was running through my head now, a scrolling tally of everything I'd lost: Peter's hands on my body, the art on his walls, the view from his balcony. All of the promises he'd made to me about a future full of so much beauty.

Our wedding.

Without meaning to I'd been counting down the days until the courthouse ceremony we'd planned, and now there were only two days left. Two more days to wonder what Peter was doing – if he missed me by now, or if he even remembered the date of our wedding at all. He'd promised to take me to Paris for our honeymoon. In two more days, I would finally have been able to visit all the places from the pictures on my old bedroom wall: the Eiffel Tower, the Louvre, the bridge covered in lovers' padlocks along the Seine.

I let out a long breath. Now that I'd started thinking about Peter, I probably wouldn't be able to stop – at least not until the next two days had passed and the countdown was over. After that, I would force myself to start counting up again, slowly climbing away from feeling shitty.

I wrung out the paintbrush with my fingers, squeezing it hard.

"Jane!" Annika called. She was coming down the stairs. "The soup is ready. Do you want to try it?"

"Sure, I'll be right there!" I hurried to meet her, and our paths intersected on the landing.

"Are you making any progress down there?" she asked.

"A little." I steered her back toward the soup. I didn't want her to see what I'd been working on – not before I figured out how I was going to fill in the frames.

15

By the next afternoon, my thoughts about Peter were stuck in an obsessive loop: wondering where he was, who he was with and what he was thinking and feeling. Annika was at the kitchen sink, rinsing out a long line of jars she was planning to use for jam. I grabbed another overripe strawberry from a gigantic pile on the table and sliced off its top.

"How's it going over there?" she asked.

"Fine." Like everything Annika wanted my help with, making jam was boring and took forever. Now that I knew she didn't really want to be friends with me, I was feeling more annoyed each time we hung out, although I was careful to never lose my temper. I didn't want to end up like the girl who had been at the squat before me, the one whose bed I was sleeping in, and who had apparently "not fit in."

"A lot of these strawberries are rotten," I said. "Is that okay?"

"No problem. For jam, it doesn't matter. It'll just make it sweeter."

Rotten jam. The strawberries began to smell fake, like the sugary filling of a jelly roll. The only reliable food in my mother's apartment had been baked goods from her factory job: white bread, doughnuts, cakes and pastries. Except on Sundays. That was her one night off when she cooked dinner on the stove and listened to all the things I'd saved up to tell her during the week. Then she'd met Max, and I'd gone weeks without seeing her. Eventually he'd moved in – him and his little boys – and after that, I'd had to watch her taking care of his kids, how she knew more about them than she'd ever known about me: their favourite colours and foods, the names of their friends at school.

The tips of my fingers were red from the strawberries. I went to the kitchen sink and rinsed off the sticky juice, snagging a packet of rolling papers and a bag of weed from the counter on my way back to the table. It felt like everything bad from my past was mixing together today – too many colours on a palette blending into a muddy brown.

Annika glanced over a few times as I rolled a joint. I thought she might finally ask me a personal question, but she didn't.

"Do you want some of this?" I asked.

"No thanks."

The joint was ready but I didn't light it, unsure now if it was okay for me to be smoking without her in the middle of the day.

"Hey, how come you've never gone back to the Netherlands?" I asked. Maybe I just had to get the conversation started, show her the kinds of things a friend might wonder about.

Annika thought for a moment. "Well, I guess I just figure: Hey, I lived there for eighteen years. I don't want to waste any more time in a place I already know."

"That makes sense." There had to be another reason.

"Plus, I have a really big family," Annika explained. "Six brothers and one sister. So there's not much room in my parents' house."

"Wow. That's a lot of people. I always wanted to have a sibling."

"Yeah, it's pretty great. Once a year, we all meet up someplace different in the world. This fall it's my sister's choice. We're going to Istanbul."

"Nice." I hadn't thought it was possible to feel any more annoyed with Annika, but now that I knew her reasons for not returning home, I couldn't even stand to be in the same room with her. "If you don't need me, I think I'm going to go downstairs for a while." I pocketed the joint. "Is that okay?"

"Sure. What are you painting down there anyway?"

She'd obviously taken a look. "I'm just playing around," I said. "I'll let you know as soon as I figure it out."

On my way down the stairs, I tripped on the broken fourth step and scraped my arm as I tried to catch myself. All the things I might have told Annika if she'd asked me – about Max and my mother, about Peter and the wedding, about Manu and the angry man, all of it – came rushing into the centre of my chest like bits of sharp metal to a magnet, and I couldn't take a full breath with so many cutting edges inside me. I needed to get some paint. I wanted to make something outside of myself, something other people would see and then know things about me that I couldn't say.

In the mural room, I sat on the floor and lit the joint. The smoke entered my lungs, and I held it there for as long as I could before exhaling toward the wall. At first, the stream of smoke retained the tight circle of my lips, then the line turned cursive and slowed down, as if backing away from what I'd begun to paint. It wasn't a row of picture frames after all. It was a long hallway of doors, all of them closed.

On the night Max had locked me out for missing curfew, I'd banged on the door until my hand hurt, yelling to be let in. Rosa was away visiting one of her sons, and all the other doors on our floor stayed shut. The hallway carpet smelled like wet sneakers and kitty litter as I sat waiting for my mom to come home from her shift. I was happy she was finally going to see what an asshole Max was. I waited almost until dawn before I realized: she was already at home on the other side of the deadbolted door. For once she'd taken a night off – to be with her new family, the one I didn't belong to.

Behind the wall of the mural room, the pipes gurgled, as if swallowing up the last bits of my inspiration; the room no longer felt like a place I wanted to be. I yelled up the stairs to Annika that I was going out for a bit, and she came down so she could lock the door behind me.

"Here." She'd brought me the phone card.

"That's okay," I said. "I memorized the number."

I walked over to the tattoo shop to see Pau. I'd been hanging out there a lot because I liked to watch his clients. They were always so determined and spoke their ideas with conviction: I want a butterfly, a Gaelic band, an Aztec sun, they'd say, as if they really believed they wanted that – would always want that. They never seemed to think about the future, or to worry about regretting their decision. Maybe a tattoo was a sort of fuck you to the fact that everything changed, a single stationary point in the otherwise chaotic swirl of a person's life.

In the back of the shop, Pau was working on a lizard design for an upcoming appointment. I watched as he drew two versions for his client to choose from.

"Can I try one?" I asked.

Pau handed me his sketchbook and I flipped to the next page. When I was satisfied with the outline, I added some shading, then a pattern of spots along the lizard's back.

"Hey, that's good," Pau said.

"Thanks."

"Do you want to draw on her body when she comes? For me, it would be better. She is very beautiful, and she wants to have it here." He pointed at the inner crease of his thigh and rolled his eyes. "I am a professional, of course. But I am also a man."

I smiled. People who spoke romance languages always sounded so dramatic in English. "Let's see how it goes."

When the girl arrived, she looked at the designs, taking a moment to trace each one with her finger.

"This one," she finally said, pointing at my design. "It looks like the lizards in Ibiza. Best summer of my life."

Pau pulled a paper sheet down over the length of the table. The girl took off her jeans and lay down. She was wearing tiny hot-pink shorts and had a matching jewel winking from her navel. Pau looked at me across her body and handed over the red marker. The skin of her inner thigh was soft and cool, an unsuspecting canvas.

"Here?" I asked.

"Here." She pointed higher.

I slowly copied my drawing onto her skin. Every mark I made would soon be permanent. When I finished, she stood up to have a look.

"Perfect," she said.

"Are you sure?" Pau asked.

"One hundred percent."

Her certainty was like a car crash; I couldn't look away.

Pau began preparing the ink and sterilizing the tools. The girl lay down again. Then the stylus in Pau's hand was buzzing. I watched as it touched down and he cut the first deep inky groove into her leg. A bright spot of red appeared on each of her cheeks and her pupils were large.

I went and sat in a chair by the door and drew some more sketches: the three-legged dog, a wild parrot, the tall sculpture of rusty cubes from down at the beach. I tried to imagine each image transposed onto my body for all time, but I couldn't. The only thing I was sure of these days was that everything disappeared. I couldn't think of any way to draw that.

After a while, the buzzing stopped. "Time for a break." Pau set down the stylus and massaged his fingers.

The girl sat up and fished in her bag for a cigarette. The outline of the lizard was done. It was crawling toward her crotch, just the way she wanted.

Pau came over and I folded my page of sketches in half.

He grabbed it and opened it to have a look. "Ha! You want a tattoo."

"No. I don't."

He stabbed his finger at the parrot. "That would look good."

I shook my head.

Across the room, the girl tilted her leg, so I could see the progress. "Cool, right?"

"Cool."

"I already want another one." She looked high and happy.

"I think you should wait at least until tomorrow," Pau told her.

The girl laughed, then gave him a flirty smile. It was probably a natural reaction: to be attracted to the guy who'd spent an hour with his hand between her legs and left an indelible mark there.

"I'll see you later," I said to Pau. He gave me a desperate look, but I ignored him.

Back at the squat, Annika had gone out and it was John who came downstairs to let me in. I was relieved to see he was the only person home. He barely spoke to me, and I was fine with that. Living with a group of people was exhausting. There were so many different personalities to deal with, so many conversations involved in making even the simplest decisions.

I lay down to take a nap. It was Big Garbage Night – the day of the week when people could set out larger items like furniture for collection – and Pau had reminded me that we'd all be going out late. We were planning to create some "outdoor homes" to protest the lack of affordable housing in the city. After a long discussion at dinner the previous night, it had been decided we would all participate – that it was safe to leave the squat vacant for a few hours since there hadn't been any sign of the Mossos for over two weeks.

When I woke up, it was already dark. From the other apartment, I heard the squatters arguing about various injustices, their voices climbing up on top of each other, building toward a wobbly pyramid of outrage. I went in to join them at the table.

Pau scowled at me. "Deserter."

"Sorry. Did you get her tattoo finished?"

"Yes. But now she's addicted."

"Oh, poor you. You might have to see her again. You might even have to sleep with her."

"Never," he said. "She's not my type."

Everyone else at the table was talking a little too loudly – they seemed tipsier than usual. Pau poured some wine into a mug and handed it to me. "You need to catch up."

I drained the mug and Pau refilled it. Soon after, we all stomped down the stairs and into the street. As we headed toward the city centre, Sylvain started belting out a cheesy pop song that had been playing everywhere lately. The other squatters joined him on the chorus, looping over and over, making up words and laughing. "I'm yours" got changed to "I'm bored," and "Love, love, love," to "Blah, blah, blah."

Becky Blake

We were blocking the road, walking side by side with our arms linked. Each time a car approached, we broke apart in the middle and then came back together like a magician's trick cigarette.

I didn't have as much energy as the others. I was still sleepy, and trying to figure out the nightmare I'd had while napping. I'd been dreaming that my body was covered in tattoos, words and images that had all been scribbled over or crossed out. Only one tattoo had been left unvandalized. It was simpler than the rest, an outline of a human shape. It looked like the chalk line police draw around a dead body they find on the sidewalk. I'd discovered it hidden in the palm of my hand.

I noticed we were getting close to Plaça Catalunya. "Hey, where are we going?" I asked.

"Gótico," Annika called over.

I missed a step and felt the jolt in my arm. I didn't want to go to the Gothic Quarter and risk running into Peter, especially not on the night before we were supposed to get married.

"There's always lots of good garbage in Gótico," Pau said. He flexed his bicep, squeezing my arm into the crook of his elbow. "People never live there for long."

Less than a week – that's how long I'd lived there. I glanced backward, wishing I could return to Gràcia, but the line of squatters was pulling me forward. It would be hard to explain my sudden need to back out of our plan. I reached over with my free hand and snagged the cap off Pau's head.

"Hey!" Pau frowned.

"Come on, it looks better on me, don't you think?" I liberated my other arm, then twirled my hair up under the cap, pushing it down hard. It was possible Peter wouldn't even recognize me – not in the company of the squatters, not if I kept my head down.

Pau grumbled and passed me the joint that had been moving slowly down the line toward us. I took a long hit, then handed it back.

We turned down a street I'd never been on, and I stopped and pulled away from the group. We were in front of a concert hall – Palau de la Música. It was the building that had been on the postcard I'd sent to my mother. The architecture was even more impressive in person – the arched windows and mosaic pillars, the huge stone balcony wrapped around the second floor. From one corner of the balcony sculptures of impassioned people were reaching out. Leaning out the furthest over the street was a woman in a long dress. She looked unafraid of falling.

Pau came back and pulled me along.

I turned to look over my shoulder. She was so lovely, like a figurehead on the front of a giant glowing ship.

"You're high," Pau said.

I held out my thumb and forefinger a short distance apart.

"More like this." He grabbed my fingers and stretched them wide.

"No way."

"Yes way." Pau did an imitation of me, letting his mouth drop open, then looking up to the sky as if awestruck. I punched him in the arm.

Annika called back to us.

"We're coming!" I shouted.

Pau wiggled a finger in his ear as if I'd deafened him.

We hurried for a few steps, then sunk back to a more leisurely pace. Pau rethreaded his arm through mine to keep me on course.

When we caught up to the others, they were standing in the middle of a wide street, lined on both sides with discarded furniture. Enzo was bouncing from foot to foot like a boxer.

"Is everyone ready?" Annika asked. She looked at Pau and me.

Becky Blake

"We're ready," Pau said. He smacked his hands together.

"Let's go then!" Annika lifted a coffee table and carried it a few feet away, then set it down in front of a ripped leather couch. Enzo ran off down the street with his arms out like an airplane and returned with a tall silver floor lamp. John pulled a dusty carpet from a long box and rolled it out, kicking down the corners with his foot. Sylvain had found a book about antique cars and he laid it open on the table.

Pau and I watched from the sidelines as an entire living room took shape in under two minutes.

"Jane, Pau, come on," Annika said. Little wisps of hair were curling at her temples. "We've got a whole street to decorate." She shooed at us.

I didn't know where to begin – there were so many possibilities. I looked around, imagining different configurations. There was a futon leaning up against a wall.

"Bedroom?" Pau asked.

"Sure." We flopped the futon onto the sidewalk, then added a rickety bedside table, a tasselled pillow and a framed portrait of a family, the five children lined up from largest to smallest like a set of Russian dolls. I stood back and surveyed our work. "I think we need a blanket," I said. "And maybe a light."

"What you need is this." John came over, thumbing through a glossy porn magazine.

"Eww."

"Here." Sylvain handed me a stuffed elephant with a ripped trunk.

I laid the elephant on the futon, and then I felt like we were in the bedroom of one of the children in the photograph – a kid who maybe didn't own a lot of things but was still well looked after.

Down the street, Enzo was yelling, his bald head glistening with sweat. "Hey, *chavales*, where can I hang this?" He was holding up a wicker swing chair. We all looked up, considering the buildings for a moment, then shrugged; he was going to have to figure it out on his own.

The more progress we made with our decorating, the more passersby stopped to watch. A few of them were taking pictures. Sylvain and Annika posed in one of the living rooms as if they were a perfect husband and wife from *Better Homes and Gardens*. Annika lifted a foot into the air behind her and leaned in to kiss Sylvain.

Across the street, John was turning up his Irish charm, explaining what we were doing to a group of giggling British girls in matching tiaras. "Homes for the homeless," he said, sounding like a campaigning politician. One of the young women was wearing a bright yellow sash with the words *Former Slut* written on it in a teasing font. I figured she must be the bachelorette. I looked for the ring on her left hand and there it was: heavy and glittering. Her hand was slightly flexed as if she was afraid the ring might fall off. Suddenly my arms felt tired. I didn't know why we were bothering to haul heavy things over cobblestones when the next day the garbage men would just disassemble our mini-habitats and throw the pieces into their trucks.

I noticed a homeless man in shabby clothes watching us from a short distance away. He was swaying, and his shoes looked too big.

Annika came up beside me. She called over to the man. "Hey! Would you like to come and sit down?" She made a wide sweep with her arm to indicate the most recent living room we'd built. She looked like a game show assistant highlighting a special prize.

The man stared at her but didn't move.

"We built this for you." She pointed at him, talking slowly as if he were a child. "For you. Do you understand?" She tried a couple of languages, but he didn't respond. Instead he turned his back and shuffled off.

Annika shrugged. "He'll come back later. Probably when we're gone."

"I doubt it." The words popped out before I could stop them.

Annika raised an eyebrow at me, and in that instant I was certain: our relationship had an expiry date. A rat ran down the centre of the street and the Former Slut started squealing. John laughed, then moved in to comfort her. He repositioned the sash between her breasts, his hand lingering for a second, and she swatted him away. Someday soon she'd be promising to love one person forever. That would probably be a lie.

I was suddenly sick to death of avoiding Peter's street like it was roped off and belonged to only him. I couldn't believe I'd never passed by in all this time.

"I'm going for a walk," I said to Annika.

"Okay."

"I just want to pass by my old apartment."

This surplus information seemed to push her off balance, and she took a small step back. "Of course." She bent down and began searching through a box of old dishes.

I waved goodbye to the guys from a distance, then hurried off before Pau could catch up with me. Peter's apartment was only two blocks away. I forced myself to walk toward it, past the grocery store that'd briefly been mine, the pizzeria we'd gone to for takeout. The closer I got, the more I was trembling. I didn't know what I would do if any of my things were out on the curb for Big Garbage Night.

I rewound my hair under Pau's cap, then turned onto the street I'd been avoiding for almost a month. Outside Peter's building, I stopped and counted up to his floor. All the windows were dark, but I could see Peter's bicycle on the balcony and beside it a healthy-looking plant. It wasn't right that Peter was comfortably tucked away four floors up while I was down here in the street.

Proof I Was Here

I stood very still beneath my old bedroom window, the unforgiving pavement pulsing up through the soles of my feet. Peter had promised me the world, and then snatched it away. Someday I would steal something of his.

16

When I arrived back at the street where the squatters had been, everyone was gone, and the decorated habitats felt desolate, like a tornado had blown through, ripping the roofs off the rooms we'd built and carrying away the people. Enzo had managed to hang the swinging wicker chair from a street lamp. I tested to see how much weight it could take, then settled in. I was too tired to walk all the way back to the squat. Slowly, I spun around until I fell asleep.

The sound of the cathedral's bell woke me, and I counted how many times it rang out. It was 7:00 a.m. on the day I was supposed to get married. A garbage truck was coming down the street.

I started the long trek back to Gràcia, feeling dirty, and wanting to brush my teeth. Walking up Portal de l'Àngel, I could see the tourists lining up along one side of Plaça Catalunya, waiting to take the bus to the airport for their morning flights. There were a couple of beggars working the line. I heard someone coming up behind me, pulling a suitcase that clicked against the cobblestones. It sounded like a roller coaster straining to climb to the top of a track.

I turned and stepped out of the way as a young man rushed past. A few paces in front of me, he stopped for a second to switch hands on his suitcase. When he started off again, a thin wallet fell from his back pocket, then hit the sidewalk, splaying open, gold and shiny. I walked over and scooped it up.

"Hey," I called out, but the guy didn't hear me. Up ahead, he joined two friends who'd been waiting for him in the middle of the bus line. As I approached they were laughing and pushing at him, teasing him about why he was late. I heard the word *whore*, and I wondered if they were talking about a professional like Fanta, or maybe just some girl they thought was easy.

The guy who'd dropped his wallet turned suddenly toward me. "Piss off," he said.

I looked at him and he stared back coldly, then waved me away. He thought I was one of the beggars.

I moved off down the line, pressing his wallet tight against my leg and hoping no one had seen me pick it up. After a block my shoulders began to relax. No one was following me. I turned the next corner, then stepped into a doorway and opened the wallet: forty-five euros and some change.

I touched Manu's watch. "You always have good luck" – that's what he would have said if I'd told him a wallet had landed at my feet. I wondered if Enzo might say it was an example of the universe providing. If so, then the universe was no better than a pickpocket, randomly choosing whose day it was to win and whose to lose.

I went into a café and ordered a coffee with steamed milk, a piece of egg tortilla, some toast and an orange juice. I took the heavy tray outside and sat alone at a shiny metal table on the sidewalk, eating everything slowly, and feeling my stomach becoming big and round like the sun. It was Day Zero of my countdown and I wanted to feel full. After breakfast, I would buy myself some art supplies. Then I could paint over the door frames and start fresh.

"Welcome back," Annika said, when she opened the front door of the squat to let me in. Her voice didn't sound very welcoming.

"How was the rest of your night?" I asked.

"Good. We built a bunch more homes. I think there's even going to be a picture in the newspaper."

"Cool." I followed her upstairs to the main apartment. On the table, there was a rectangular white cake – the cheap frosted kind from the grocery store – collapsed on one side and smushed up against its clear plastic container. "Where'd that come from?" I asked.

"Someone dropped it outside the Carrefour." Annika was braiding her hair, her elbows pointing at me. "Do you want some?"

"No, thanks." I sat down carefully on one of the wobbly dining-room chairs and pulled off my sandals.

She wrapped a hair elastic tightly around the bottom of her braid. "Are you going to rest for a bit? Or are you ready to go do the shopping?"

I'd noticed that whenever Annika gave me two choices, she always wanted me to pick the second one.

"I think I need to rest," I said. "And then I was planning to work on the mural." I lifted the bag of art supplies I'd bought. "I finally got some paint."

Annika glanced at the bag. I knew she must be curious about where I'd gotten the money, but as usual, she didn't ask. When she finally spoke, it felt like a box of thumbtacks had spilled onto the floor between us. "So, you'd rather not help with the shopping today."

"Yeah, sorry. I think I just need to do my own thing."

"Okay. I guess I'll see you later." She snatched some shopping bags from the counter and headed out the door.

"Should I come down and lock you out?"

"No, I've got the key." Her footsteps were loud on the stairs.

I let out a long breath. I hadn't wanted to piss her off, but I couldn't help myself; she was so annoying. It was something about the way she said things. "We built a bunch more homes." Annika and Sylvain had no idea what it was like to be homeless. If they did, their protesting would be different, less about photo ops and more about providing help: a good meal, a safe place to sleep. They'd given those things to me, but there were other people who needed them more. Instead of making temporary homes on the street, we should be inviting others to stay at the squat. There was a lot more room.

I knew if I suggested this, Sylvain would probably have some reason or rule for why the plan wouldn't work. He was so fixated on the way things *should* be done that sometimes he seemed disconnected from what was really happening. When he'd explained the law of abandonment to me, he hadn't even noticed the effect it was having. He'd just gone on and on about how there were two conditions you had to prove: one, that the item was outside of the owner's possession, and two, that the owner had no intention of reclaiming it. That second bit was the tricky part, he'd said, and I'd nodded, swallowing back tears. Over the years, a couple of neighbours and teachers had managed to prove that my mother had left me briefly unattended, but I'd always covered for her, and she'd had a special knack for reappearing just in time to reclaim me.

The plastic bottom of the cake container stuttered against the table as I pushed it to the edge, and then further. The container cracked as it hit the floor, but didn't pop open. The cake inside was just a little more distressed, its layers coming apart now, exposing its cheap angel food interior. Almost every day, my mom had brought home similar shitty cakes from the factory. I wondered what Annika's mother did. Maybe she was a lawyer like Sylvain's, or maybe a fucking astronaut.

I picked up the cake and replaced it on the table. I hadn't slept much, and I considered going to bed. Instead I grabbed some clean clothes from the sleeping apartment and took a cold shower, then went downstairs and lined up my new paints along the wall. Standing in front of the door frames, I realized I needed to fill them instead of painting over them.

My mind wandered back down the hallway of my mother's building. I'd been eight or nine the first time I'd gone knocking on my neighbours' apartment doors, the first time I'd seen how other families lived. There'd been a fundraiser at school: selling cookies to collect money for a new gym. After that, whenever my apartment got too quiet, I'd taken some of the pastries my mother brought home from the factory and gone through the hallways tapping on doors, pretending to be raising funds again. Inside those squares of light, different combinations of people were eating dinner, vacuuming, petting dogs or drying their hands on dishtowels while kids ran by in pyjamas. Sometimes they invited me in, and for each family or group, I would change myself a little – imagining I was a granddaughter of the Hungarian couple in 412, or the little sister of one of the drug dealers in 719, or an extra child of the large Vietnamese family on the ground floor who all slept in one room.

I lay down on the floor with the long saffron scarf balled up as a pillow under my head. I could feel an idea coming, but it was just out of reach, like a word on the tip of my tongue. I lay there for so long that eventually I couldn't keep my eyes open. All afternoon, I drifted in and out of sleep as Annika and the guys came and went on the stairs, calling to me as they passed. When I finally woke up, my back was stiff, and the idea still hadn't come. Above me, I heard the squatters' voices.

I climbed the stairs, then stood for a moment in the doorway looking in at them: at the home they'd made out of found objects, at the family they'd made out of found people. If I ever wanted to really belong on the inside of this door frame, I had to patch things up with Annika.

Everyone was sitting in a circle around the table, and I joined them. "*Hola*," I said.

The squatters made muted gestures of welcome. There was a baguette on the table and an open jar of strawberry jam. I was hungry again, but I didn't touch the bread. I hadn't helped Annika with the shopping. Maybe that's why everyone seemed pissed.

"Hey," I said to Pau. "Did the lizard girl come back to visit you?"

"No, not yet." He gave me a small smile.

"Jane, there's something we want to talk to you about," Annika said.

"Okay." My stomach dropped. This was some kind of intervention. Maybe they were going to kick me out.

"We live here together like a collective."

I didn't like the condescension in her voice.

"And we all have to do our part to make things run smoothly."

"Sorry. I know I haven't been helping out much for the last couple of days. There was just something going on. And now it's over."

"I have things going on too," said John. "We all have things going on."

Beside him, Enzo nodded.

I looked down at my hands. I felt like I was in the principal's office waiting for a scolding to end.

"I found a man's wallet beside your bed," said Annika. "Where did it come from?"

I didn't answer. I hadn't technically stolen it, but I knew she wouldn't believe me.

She waited for a second and then continued. "Well, I think we all know where it came from."

I looked up. "Do you want me to leave?"

"Jane," Pau said, "that's not what we want. Try to be calm."

Even Pau was being patronizing. I was sick of the squatters acting so superior. They were thieves, just like me; living in a building that wasn't theirs. Annika called squatting "a justified crime," but it was still stealing. All stealing could be justified if you looked hard enough for a reason.

"Jane," Pau said again, and we locked eyes. He took a breath, and I did the same.

"Okay," I said. "I'm being calm. What do you guys want me to do?"

"Well," said Annika. Sylvain was holding her hand. "If you want to stay here we just need you to make a commitment to help out with the cleaning and shopping, and we also need you to stop stealing things. If the police come to evict us and they find stolen goods here, we could all go to jail."

I hadn't thought of that.

"And, if you need money, just tell us," Pau said.

John snorted. "I'm not giving her money."

"Just tell *me*," Pau said.

"Okay." I turned to Annika. "I promise I'll clean up the whole place tomorrow. And do the shopping."

"Good." She nodded.

I looked around the table. The squatters seemed to be waiting for me to say something else. "And I'll stop stealing stuff."

"Great!" said Sylvain. He squeezed Annika's hand.

John was leaning way back in his chair, picking his teeth. I hoped he would fall. "Just make sure you clean up the pigeon shit this time," he said. "It's everywhere, and it's poison if you breathe it in."

"Fine. I'll clean it up tomorrow."

Pau stood and put his hand on my shoulder. "We're very happy you are going to stay."

I knew this might be true for him, but I doubted if everyone felt the same way. I glanced around the table at the others. Together, they seemed to form a unit – one that was complete without me. If I forced myself to stay at the table, maybe the feeling would pass, but at the moment I just couldn't deal with it.

"I actually have to get going," I said. "I'm meeting a friend down-town." I touched Pau's hand and he released me.

Annika gave me a saintly look. "I'll save you some dinner."

"Thanks." I didn't know why she thought her lifestyle was so much better than regular people's. Except for some pigeon shit in the corners, it was almost exactly the same.

In the sleeping apartment across the hall, I changed into a short dress from one of the Free Store boxes: it was the colour of a raspberry Popsicle, or more like the colour a Popsicle would leave on a tongue. I picked out a black purse and hung it over my shoulder so it would look like I had some money – more than just the handful of coins I had left from the wallet.

Downstairs I grabbed some pens and a marker in case I wanted to make some sketches for the mural. At the little sink in the corner, I washed my face and smoothed down my hair. When I was with Peter I'd been pretty – the kind of pretty men followed with their eyes – but I didn't know if I was anymore: not without makeup and needing a haircut, not with wrinkled second-hand clothes. The scar on my cheek was shiny now, a little initial signed in metallic pink.

I went outside and started toward the city centre. It was my cancelled wedding night. I thought I might sleep with Atlas if I could find him.

17

By the time I got to La Rambla, it was dark and most of the human statues had packed up for the day. I went to the Black Sheep to check if Atlas was there and found him sitting with a loud bunch of buskers at a long table.

"Hey, where've you been?" he asked.

"In Gràcia," I said. "Mostly."

"With Manu?"

"No. Manu's gone."

"Here, come and join us." Atlas made space for me to squeeze in beside him on the bench and poured me a glass of beer from a pitcher. "*Salud.*"

"*Salud.*" I moved my glass in a half-circle to include everyone at the table. I recognized the operatic chef busker who juggled kitchen knives, and the woman who dressed up as a giant butterfly. I wasn't sure who the others were. It was impossible to tell without their costumes on.

The buskers were speaking in a lot of different languages, and it was hard to follow their conversations. I drank my beer fast, and Atlas refilled my glass. The bar was noisy, with patrons standing around barrel tables, yelling over '90s rock music. A hot guy across the room looked over at me.

"I think I need a gun," Atlas said.

"What?"

"A gun. Something to scare off the fucking Romanians."

"What's going on with the Romanians?"

"They want my spot. They've been sending their mobster thugs every day and it's scaring off the tourists."

I pictured Atlas and the other statues on La Rambla springing into action, pulling out firearms from under their costumes, tourists screaming. "Can't you just move to a new location?"

"No! Why should I move? I'm not scared of those assholes. It took me over a year to get that spot. It's the best place on the whole strip." Atlas pulled a wad of bills from his pocket and fanned them in my direction. I decided I wasn't going to sleep with him.

The hot guy glanced over again. He was wearing a black T-shirt, and part of a tattoo was visible at the edge of his sleeve.

"Can I get out for a second?" I said to Atlas. "I have to pee."

Walking past the guy's table, I could feel his eyes on me. I waited for a couple of minutes outside the locked door of the women's bathroom, but no one came out. The men's bathroom was open and empty, so I went in. The stall I entered was covered in graffiti: dirty pictures and boastful messages. One guy was bragging about how he'd slept with ten different women who were all in the bar that night.

After leaving the stall and washing up, I found a clear space of wall above the mirror and pulled a marker from my purse. It squeaked as I wrote the letters in bold thick lines.

Just as I finished, the guy with the black T-shirt walked in. He looked at the marker in my hand, then the word on the wall.

"Who's a liar?" he asked in English.

I put the marker back in my purse. "I don't know. Guys?"

He nodded, then walked over to the urinal and turned his back: "I have some spray paint in my bag," he said, "if you want to make it bigger."

I paused on my way to the door. He had nice shoes, good jeans, was fit and solid. "No, that's okay. Thanks though."

He finished peeing, then zipped up and turned around. "Women can be liars too, you know." He went to the sink to wash his hands. We looked at each other in the mirror.

"Maybe," I said. "But not me." That was a lie. I'd spent most of my life pretending to be other people, acting differently from how I really was.

"Okay," he said. "Tell me something true."

I thought for a moment. "I'm a thief."

"Ha. I think you're lying."

"No, I'm not."

Another man walked into the bathroom and frowned at us. I stepped out through the door and the guy in the T-shirt followed me. Atlas raised an eyebrow from across the bar.

"So you're a thief and you write graffiti in men's toilets? That's what you do?"

"More or less," I said. "What do you do?"

"I'm a photographer."

"That's nice."

"I also paint graffiti, but not in men's toilets."

"I think you're lying."

"No, I'm not. I can show you, if you want."

I looked down, studying the composition of beach sand, cigarette butts and toothpicks on the floor. I hadn't really flirted with anyone for two years, and I had to force myself to look up.

"Okay," I said. "You can show me."

Our motorcycle helmets bumped together as we jerked forward into the night, first through the chaotic city centre, then up the curving mountain roads of Tibidabo, the lights of the city receding below us. At each turn, the bike seemed to tilt further to the left or to the right, and I relaxed into the motion until it felt like rocking – until I thought, *This is what my life is like: sitting astride the moment, a single headlight moving through the darkness.* It wasn't all bad. Inside this particular moment, nothing hurt. It was the wishing I could stay like this forever, that's what hurt.

At the top of the mountain, Xavi parked the bike. He was Catalan, and he told me he would rather speak English than Spanish.

"Fine by me," I said. "Unfortunately, I don't speak any Catalan."

"You should learn," he said, "if you're living here." He stooped to pick up a pine cone and placed it in my palm. "*Pinya.*"

"*Pinya.*" It wasn't a very useful word, but it was a start.

I tucked the pine cone into my purse as we followed a series of signs that led down a path to a lookout. When we arrived, Xavi pointed into the distance at some ugly contorted faces spray-painted onto a wall. "You see down there?" he asked.

"Did you paint that?"

He nodded. "I hate the idea that millions of people follow these signs, that they all come to this same point and take the same picture. Why should the city be telling people where to go? And why do people listen? It's like we're just waiting for another dictator to tell us what to do. Like we didn't learn anything the last time."

Pau had told me a few things about Catalan history – how the language and culture had been banned under Franco – but I didn't know enough to say anything intelligent. "So you ruin the view?" I asked.

"Yes. If I put something ugly in their way, it forces people to find a new perspective. Their *own* perspective, you know? Like this one." He pulled me off the path and over some uneven uphill ground. Through a gap in the branches I could see the towers of the Sagrada Família church lit up below us like a sandcastle on fire. He put his hands in front of my face and made a frame. I could feel his breath on my neck.

"It's nice," I said.

He dropped his hands onto my shoulders, then down to my waist. When I turned toward him he kissed me in a way that felt almost like there was love passing between us, but I knew that couldn't be true. I took a step back. It was the first time in two years that I'd kissed someone other than Peter. Maybe the sensation of love was coming from me – maybe I'd forgotten how to kiss someone without it.

Xavi and I looked at each other.

"Do you want to paint something?" he asked.

"Sure."

He flipped open his shoulder bag and pulled out a can of spray paint. After shaking it, he handed it over. "Hold it like this," he said, adjusting the can to a vertical position. "It helps minimize the splatter."

We walked back toward his motorcycle along the main path. Every time we came to a sign with an arrow on it, I added another arrow pointing the other way. Xavi was spray-painting the word *català* over every sign that was in Spanish.

When we put on our helmets again to ride back down the mountain, Xavi reached over and opened my visor. "It's better like this," he said.

I climbed on the back of the bike and squeezed my knees in tight, then wrapped my arms around his waist. I could feel his rib cage moving in and out, the muscles of his stomach tensing and releasing. He flicked up the kickstand and we drove off down the mountain, circling around and around, like a screw tightening into the city below.

At the bottom we idled at a red light.

"Where do you live?" Xavi asked.

I waited for a moment, hoping the light would turn green and we could drive away from the question.

"That's okay," he said. "We can go to my place."

Xavi's apartment turned out to be just a few blocks from the squat. He parked and locked up his motorcycle on the sidewalk, then opened the front door of his building. He had a lot of keys on his key ring.

"I hope you're in good shape," he said. "I live in the attic. It's 113 stairs to the top."

When I stopped partway up to catch my breath, he pressed me against the wall and kissed me for so long that the timed light in the hallway went out and we had to grope our way to the next landing in darkness. The same thing happened twice more as we climbed, and by the time we got to the top we were almost undressed.

We crossed a small stretch of rooftop terrace to get to his front door. Inside his tiny apartment, the sloping walls of the single room were covered in black-and-white photographs. More photos hung clipped to a clothesline that crossed the room. Xavi set the helmets on a shelf and pulled me toward a futon in the corner. His warm skin was sticking to me in places: at my wrist, across my belly, along the inside of my thigh.

After being with only Peter for so long, sex with Xavi was like a new activity, one where every sensation was different: the pressure of his lips, the coarse hair on his chest, the sound of his breathing, his smell, his rhythm, his taste. When we were finished I lay back on the bed, my heart beating fast. It was the kind of sex I hadn't had for a long time: urgent and basic. One-night-stand sex. Something I had thought I would never do again.

I looked over at Xavi, and he laid a hand on my leg, as if he wanted to make sure I didn't get up. We didn't speak. There was nothing to say. We both knew that we were going to do it again in a few minutes. That we were going to do it as many times as we could until one of us fell asleep.

By the time I slid out of the bed it was starting to get light. Several of Xavi's photographs had come unstuck from the walls. I remembered a pair of them slicing down through the air like swooping birds. I started to look for my clothes.

"Are you sure you don't want to sleep a bit?" Xavi asked. "Maybe eat breakfast in a while?"

"No, that's okay. I live near here. I think I'm just going to go home."

"Do you have a phone number?"

I shook my head.

"Do you want to take my number, or ..."

I did want his number. But I knew if I had it, I'd just want to see him again and again until, eventually, I'd start to depend on him for feeling good and then he'd disappear.

"I'm sure we'll run into each other," I said. Probably we wouldn't.

I slipped the raspberry-coloured dress over my head and pulled it into place. Most of the photographs hanging around the room were pictures of rough-looking elderly people, their eyes gleaming with a hard wisdom. "You're good," I said. "The photos."

"Thanks." He glanced at the photos, then back at me. "Are you really going to leave?"

"Yeah. I have to go."

"Okay. Should I be checking your pockets? Your purse?"

I reached into my purse. "I was planning to take this with me, but I guess you caught me." I set the pine cone on his bedside table.

At the door, I bent down to adjust my shoe and pulled a can of paint with a red lid from his bag, then slipped it into my purse with exaggerated stealth. I stood up and glanced over at Xavi to see if he'd been watching me. He definitely had, and his smile nearly drew me back to the bed.

"Thanks for taking me up the mountain," I said. "It was really fun."

I let myself out, then paused on the other side of his door, remembering how good it had felt to hold on to Xavi as we drove up Tibidabo – to be two people sharing the same headlight for a moment. But I couldn't hold on to him forever. One good night was one good night – no more, no less.

I crossed the rooftop terrace, then started down the dim-lit stairs, counting softly as I went. At the bottom, I pushed open the front door and stepped out into the morning. There were 113 stairs. Just like he'd said.

PART THREE

18

The city seemed to have layers that became saturated with detail once I noticed them. First, it had been street people, filling the corners like swept-up piles of trampled flowers. Then half-open purses and bags had appeared, their most valuable contents rising to the top like cream. Treasure in the garbage had popped up next, and now, as I walked back to the squat from Xavi's, the neighbourhood was overflowing with graffiti: colourful tags and stencilled images, quotes and slogans, declarations of love. The styles of different artists wove through the streets leaving trails I could follow.

In Plaça de la Revolució, the biggest piece of graffiti was a giant Catalan flag. Passing it, I wondered how long it had been there, and how long it would last. Some graffiti seemed to become an accepted part of the landscape, but most was considered an eyesore, an unwelcome annoyance that had to be scrubbed away. Suddenly I had a bad feeling – that maybe the squat had been raided during the night. I hurried toward a pay phone in front of the metro and was relieved when Pau answered. "*Hola.*" He sounded half-asleep.

"I'm sorry it's so early," I said. "Can you come down and let me in?"

Five minutes later, he opened the door, sizing me up. "Good night?" he asked.

I blushed. "I just had to let off some steam."

"Steam. I see." He shoved the squat's mobile phone into his pocket, then pushed the door wide so I could pass. He must have been keeping the phone beside him in case I called.

"Thanks for watching out for me."

He grumbled something about needing more sleep, then started up the stairs. When I didn't follow, he looked back. "Not coming?"

I shook my head. "I'm just going to stay down here for a while."

I watched him go, then wandered around the ground floor, shaking the can of red spray paint I'd taken from Xavi's. In front of a blank wall, I stopped and removed the cap. The first line I painted was thick and drippy. I moved my hand further away from the wall, then painted a bunch more lines, experimenting with different angles and speeds. Unlike drawing, or painting with a brush, there was no physical connection between the surface and me. The can felt untethered in my hand, free and light.

I tried out different tags: *Jane* in bubble letters, *Jane* like lightning. One time I wrote *Niki*, then stood back, watching the thin letters drip down the wall before covering them up with a big red square.

The Jane tag that looked the best was an uninterrupted line. I practised it until I could paint it with confidence, until my arm was tired, and the can was sputtering, then empty. It felt good to fill a space where nothing had been. Addictive too. I was already imagining trying to paint a graffiti portrait. But maybe I should start with something simpler, a stencilled image like the ones I'd seen in the street. To try making a stencil, I would need to find a sharp knife and some heavy paper, another can of paint and maybe some gloves. I examined the pattern of tiny speckles clustered around my right thumb and first two fingers – the fingers that had been closest to the nozzle. The speckles would be a dead giveaway if I ever risked painting in public and got caught. The odour too – a sweet chemical smell that lingered on my skin.

Behind the wall, the pipes clanked; one of the squatters was awake upstairs and trying to use the water. In a way, squatters were like graffiti. We didn't know when we would be removed, but on a day like this, when I was feeling touch-drunk from sleeping with Xavi and inspired to paint, the possibility of eviction seemed less like a threat and more like a reminder: to treat each day we spent here as a kind of lucky break, as something we'd stolen and gotten away with.

I spent the rest of the morning and part of the afternoon cleaning up the squat the way I'd promised. When I was done, I went to the tattoo shop and sat in the corner sketching some ideas for stencils while I waited for Pau to finish with a client. It was Day One of my counting up – my cancelled wedding was finally behind me – and I'd thought of a way to mark the occasion.

Pau pointed his cigarette at one of the drawings. "That would look cool."

"These aren't for tattoos."

He rolled his eyes. "You know you want one."

"You're right. I do."

"Ha! I knew it."

"Yeah, but you're going to think it's stupid."

"Nothing is stupid, *carinyo*. What do you want? Tell me."

I drew a circle the size of a dime in the centre of my left palm.

Becky Blake

"That's it?"

"Yes." An *O* for *open*, that's what I would tell people, but it was also a ring, one that was impossible to grasp, one that would disappear when I closed my hand.

"If that's what you want, that's what you get," Pau said. "But I have to tell you: that area hurts a lot. Also, tattoos on the inside of the hand don't last forever. Over time, it will fade unless you keep going over it again and again."

"Are you serious?" I asked.

"I'm afraid I am."

I couldn't believe I'd somehow chosen the only kind of tattoo that could disappear. In a way, it was perfect. "Fine, let's do it."

"Are you sure?"

I nodded. Pau had kind eyes for a guy whose profession was causing pain. I closed his sketchbook and laid my hand on the table between us.

Pau wiped my palm with antiseptic, then ripped open a packet of needles and fit them into the stylus. "Ready?"

"I think so."

When he turned on the tool and cut into my palm it hurt so much it was hard to keep my hand open.

Pau stopped. "Are you all right?"

"Yeah, great. Holy fuck."

He smiled and went back to work.

After a few minutes, the pain reached its summit. There was a vista at the top, a landscape of thought that was clear and sharp with detail. Even if I found a way to get along with Annika, and even if the squat never got raided, I still couldn't stay there much longer. I didn't want to be a freegan forever, didn't want to live within the grid of dumpster diving rules and squatters' law. The squatters had chosen a lifestyle with a built-in reset button, and although, on a good day, that could make each moment feel sort of heightened, my life had been reset enough times already. I didn't want to be kicked out of anywhere ever again; I needed to live in a place where I had my own key.

When he was finished, Pau cleared away the excess ink and little drops of blood with a tissue, then sat staring into my palm as if he could read the future. The circle he'd drawn was either a hole you could fall into or a ledge you could hold onto. It was everything and its reverse if you looked at it for long enough.

"You're still thinking of leaving," he said. It was a statement and a question.

"Maybe. But not any time soon. I still have to paint a mural for you guys."

Pau placed a little gauze pad over the tattoo and gently taped it in place. "Well, wherever you end up, you're going to need me to touch up your tattoo from time to time."

"Obviously."

"And to buy you weed."

I laughed.

He reached over and pulled a thin joint from a jar of pens and markers.

We went out back and stood in the sunshine together, smoking. Under the little bandage, my hand was hot and stinging. I didn't know if I would get the tattoo touched up or not when it began to fade. Maybe by then everything would be different.

I decided I needed a backup plan – a way to earn some money of my own so I'd be able to leave the squat whenever I wanted and not have to worry about Annika or the police evicting me. To get started, I borrowed some money from Pau and used it to buy a large sketch-book, so I could try to sell portraits down at the beach.

The next afternoon, I went from towel to towel offering to draw people for ten euros. After many hours, I was sunburned, and I only had thirty euros to show for my work. Each of the portraits I'd done had taken way too long, and one woman had refused to pay because she said I made her hair look greasy.

That night, I paid back Pau and bought some sunscreen. I had six euros left over and I stored them in the pocket of my trench coat, which was hanging from a nail in the mural room. If I kept working at the beach and learned to draw faster, then I should be able to save up a good amount of money within a couple of weeks. I also wanted to start contributing a little cash to the squat. That way I'd no longer be a charity case.

My days became really busy: helping Annika in the morning, and then spending all afternoon at the beach. In the evenings, instead of hanging out, I went to the locutorio to search job sites for design work and to draft a resumé on the computer. I was especially looking for jobs that might sponsor me for a work visa so I could legally stay in Barcelona beyond three months. Pau said I could use his cell phone as my contact number whenever I was ready to start applying.

No matter what I was doing, one thought kept returning: I wanted to paint more graffiti. Everywhere I went I studied the street art, imagining the different types of stencils I could make. In the pile of Free Store clothes, I found a courier bag and began filling it up with cans of paint. I allowed myself to buy one colour per day.

On several occasions, I was tempted to pass by Xavi's, but I kept reminding myself it was a bad idea. Even so, I couldn't stop flashing back to the hours we'd spent in his bed, single moments returning to me in sensory snapshots: his warm breath against my neck, his square fingertips at my hip bones, one of his photographs falling and grazing my shoulder like a kiss.

At the locutorio on Saturday night, I was working on my resumé, trying to choose a font for the header. I had been staring at my name floating at the top of the page for a long time when I suddenly knew what I wanted to paint for the mural. I logged off the computer and paid, then telephoned the squat and let it ring three times. I was crossing Plaça de la Revolució when someone touched my shoulder.

"Jane," Xavi said, "I was calling you."

"Oh hey! Sorry, I didn't hear you." Either that, or the name hadn't registered. The resumé I'd been working on had my real name at the top.

Xavi kissed me on both cheeks. "It's good to see you."

"It's good to see you too." Neither of us took a step back, and the narrow space between us began to fill with heat.

"Come over and join us." He pointed to a terrace where his friends were sitting.

I hesitated. In a minute, someone would be waiting downstairs at the squat to let me in.

"Come on. I'll buy you a drink." Xavi touched my arm, and his fingers were slow to move away.

Whoever was waiting for me at the squat wouldn't wait too long – five minutes tops. I could call again in a while. "Okay, maybe just one." We walked together across the square.

When we reached the terrace, Xavi pulled out a chair for me, saying something to his friends in Catalan. I heard the word *Jane*.

The three guys nodded in greeting, then went back to their conversation. Two of them had beards; the third guy was cleaner cut and seemed out of place with his dress shirt and shiny shoes.

Becky Blake

Xavi ordered me a beer from the waiter, then asked me how my week had been.

I smiled. It was such a normal question – the type of question he'd ask a person who had a job and an apartment, a gym membership maybe. "It was good."

"Did you steal anything interesting?"

I glanced at his friends, but they weren't paying attention. "Actually no. But I did buy myself something." I opened the top of my bag so he could see inside.

"*Déu meu.*" Xavi ran his fingers along the tops of the coloured lids. Then he moved his hand to my thigh under the table. It was the same gesture he'd made when we'd been lying together in his bed, a movement that felt like he was claiming me, at least for the moment.

"I want to paint something," I said.

"I can see that." He squeezed my leg. Then he said something to his friends, again in Catalan, and they all stopped talking and looked at me. One of the bearded guys had wooden disks the size of golf balls stretching his earlobes; the other was a rapid blinker, his eyelashes tapping out feathery Morse code messages.

"What's going on?" I asked Xavi.

"I just told them you want to paint with us sometime. With the crew."

The crew. I noticed then that there were heavy-looking bags on the backs of their chairs, gloves on the table. They were all wearing dark clothes. Painting with Xavi's crew might be risky – depending on what they painted and where – but it would be worth it if I got to learn some tricks.

The blinking guy asked a question, and Xavi answered him in a soothing tone. A long discussion followed. Either they didn't speak English, or they didn't want me to understand. The waiter brought my beer and began to clear the table of bottles, empty chip bags and plates puddled with olive oil. One plate had a few cubes of white cheese remaining on it. I was tempted to grab them, but I didn't want Xavi to know I was hungry.

Finally, he turned back to me. "Can I tell them what you do?"

"What I do?"

"You know ... stealing things."

"Oh. Sure, I guess so. I'm not like a professional or anything."

"I know. But they're worried about you going to the police. I think they'll feel better if I tell them." He said a few words to his friends. I watched their reactions, a slight shift in their postures. Having them know I was a thief embarrassed me, made me want to explain, although I wasn't sure what I would say. Maybe that stealing things was something I didn't really do anymore. I wondered if that was true.

A new round of conversation started up. "Look," I said after a few minutes, "I don't want to cause any problems. If they don't want me to go, it's no big deal."

"It's not a problem," Xavi said. "They're just asking about an initiation. But I told them we already did one up on Tibidabo last week. That you did very well."

His friends were staring at me, and I tried to look relaxed.

"So, I think it's settled." Xavi raised his glass of beer, and one by one the others joined. They were serious men, but there was something very alive about them too. A small surge of electricity passed through me as I added my glass to the circle.

"*Visca Catalunya*," the clean-cut guy said, and then we drank.

Xavi smiled at me. I noticed he had dimples underneath the scruff on his cheeks. I really wanted to make some art with him and then go back to his place. "Are we going to paint now?" I asked.

"No. We already went out tonight." Xavi slipped his hand under my hair to the back of my neck. "But don't worry. We'll go out again soon. And next time you can come. We'll paint something big, I promise."

"Okay. I have a lot of ideas."

"Really?"

"Yeah. I'm not sure if your friends will like them though."

"Well, let's see how it goes."

"When?"

"Soon," he said. "How about Monday?"

"Okay." I stood up. "So I'll meet you at your place on Monday. When it gets dark?"

"Sure. But wait, where are you going now?" He grabbed my hand, and I winced. My tattoo was covered with gauze, but underneath it was still scabby and tender.

"I'm just going to practise. There's something I want to paint tonight."

Xavi pushed out his bottom lip. I knew what he was thinking. It was tempting, but I'd made up my mind.

"I'll see you Monday." I gave a semi-salute to the men in black, then turned back to Xavi. "Hey, how do you say 'I'll see you Monday' in Catalan?"

"Ens veiem el dilluns."

I tried to repeat the words in the direction of his friends, but I was pretty sure I'd failed.

Xavi laughed. "Don't worry. They all speak English."

"Good to know." That meant they'd been excluding me from their conversation on purpose.

The clean-cut guy raised his glass in my direction. "Until Monday."

"Yes." I shouldered my bag and walked across the square, imagining the guys watching me, probably teasing Xavi and saying macho things. I didn't care. In two days' time, I was going to paint some-thing big – something outside, in a place that could be seen.

When I got back to the squat after phoning again, John was waiting downstairs to let me in.

"I'm not your personal doorman," he said.

I apologized for calling twice, then told him I was going to stay on the ground floor to work on the mural. When he was gone, I smoked half of a tiny joint I'd left on the windowsill, then stood for a few moments in front of the wall, visualizing how the finished mural would look. Typing my real name on my resumé had given me the idea – I wanted to paint the people who knew me as Jane before I went back to being Niki.

I moved aside my acrylic paints and replaced them with the cans of spray paint from my bag. I didn't know if I had the skill to pull off what I was thinking, but the walls were already pretty messed up; it wouldn't hurt to try. Mentally, I divided the first door frame into quadrants, then made a sketch with chalk, stopping now and then to erase and adjust a line with my fingertip.

It was hard to see clearly with just the light coming in from the street lamps, so I went over to the hook by the front door and grabbed the camping headlamp that we used for getting up and down the stairs in the dark. Wearing it, I felt like I was on Xavi's motorcycle again: attached to a light that moved with me, cutting a brighter path in the direction of my gaze.

When I was satisfied with my sketch, I tied the saffron scarf across my nose and mouth, then shook a can of blue paint. The first line I made was a curve, light and soft like a caress. After that, I didn't think. I just worked for a long time, switching colours, and using the tail end of the scarf to wipe away any drips. When the portrait was finished, I stepped back. It wasn't perfect – the outlines were a bit wobbly and the perspective was off – but overall it was lifelike enough: Manu in his ratty blue T-shirt. Behind him, an older man who could be his father.

I smoked the rest of the joint, then started on the next door frame, sketching, then painting Fanta and the little boy from the photograph she carried. As I worked, I thought about going back to El Raval some day to see if I could find her – ask her what she and Manu had been doing on the night I was attacked. Now that some time had passed, I no longer thought that Fanta had set me up. It was more likely she'd seen an opportunity – a chance to break out of her debt – and had taken a risk. She probably hadn't planned for the consequences to land on me. Or even if she had, I couldn't really blame her. There was only so much bad luck a person could take before she was forced to shift a portion of it onto someone else.

Whatever Fanta had done, I was pretty sure she'd done it for her son. I added a few more touches to his face, brightening his expression a little to make him look happier. He might never entirely forgive his mother for not being around, but hopefully one day he'd realize that she'd been trying to get back to him – trying to make as much money as possible to give him a better life.

The headlamp's battery died, but I didn't need it anymore. Outside, it was starting to get light as I began to make a sketch in the third frame: Yaya holding a piece of chalk in the air, as if he was explaining something to a group of students. By the time I finished painting him, my head was hurting, and my arm was sore. I lay down on the floor, exhausted, facing the wall. These were some of the doors I'd looked through in Barcelona. The people I'd met were spilling out of the frames.

When I woke up, Annika and Pau were standing over me.

"Ah, here she is," Pau said. "The artist at work."

I sat up and coughed. My throat felt raw, and my hands and arms were freckled with multicoloured dots.

Annika pointed at the wall. "Is that the guy you used to stay with?"

"Manu. Yeah."

"The mural looks good." She sounded impressed.

"Thanks."

She glanced over at the other side of the room where the wall was full of tags: a frenzied collection of *Jane*s crowded around the dark red square that was covering *Niki* up. All week I'd been expecting her to lecture me about making such a mess.

"Don't worry," I said. "I'll paint over that."

"I think you should leave it," Pau said. "We can all add our names." He rummaged through my cans of paint. When he found one that wasn't empty, he walked over to the tagged wall and painted bright green letters that spelled out PAU WAS HERE.

For some reason, the statement made me sad. We all stood looking at it in silence for a moment. Then I snatched the paint can from Pau, walked over to the wall and crossed out the word *WAS*. Above it I wrote the word *IS*.

I offered the can to Annika. "Your turn."

She looked uncertain.

"You can choose a different colour if you want." I pointed to the other cans on the floor.

"I don't know what to write."

"Just paint your name. Or maybe draw something?"

"Let me think about it."

"Sure. Hey, did you guys already eat breakfast?"

"About three hours ago," Annika said. "But there's food for you on the table."

This felt like a peace offering. Maybe food was Annika's way of connecting with people. I imagined painting her in the next door frame. She could be holding a basket full of foraged food. I would even add some flowers if she wanted.

She pointed at the middle panel of the mural. "Who's that?"

"Fanta. I met her in El Raval when I was living with Manu."

"What kind of name is Fanta?" Annika asked.

"I don't know. A nickname, I guess." Or maybe it was an alias like mine. I'd never thought to ask Fanta for her real name. It was another reason to go back to El Raval and find her.

19

On Monday morning, everyone at the squat was sleeping when two Mossos arrived to deliver an eviction notice. They banged on the door until we all went downstairs. Through a window, Sylvain told them that they didn't have the right to remove us, that squatting wasn't illegal – only unlawful, a civil dispute. Before leaving, the Mossos pasted their notice to the front of the building and said they'd be back in twenty-four hours. If we hadn't left by then, they would forcibly remove us.

Sylvain turned to where we were all standing and listening. "We have twenty-four hours to mobilize."

I was the last one to follow him up the stairs. I remembered the panic I'd felt at the police station in Toronto, the total lack of control. Being arrested in another country, in another language: things could be even worse. I wondered if the Mossos would be able to see that I had a charge against me in Canada.

Upstairs, we pulled chairs around the dining-room table, and Annika began to boil some water for tea. I was feeling more and more uncomfortable – like I'd racked up a debt to the squatters I couldn't pay.

"I doubt they'll even come back," Pau said. "At least not this week. There's a holiday for Sant Joan. They're probably just trying to scare us."

"That's true," Annika agreed. "In Berlin, it was at least three months before we ever saw them again. But still, we should be ready."

"I think we should make a safe room," Sylvain said. "The bathroom would be a good choice. There's no window, and the lock on the door is very strong. I can add some extra bolts. Then two people can lock themselves inside and the Mossos won't be able to close up the building."

All the squatters seemed to be in favour of this plan.

"If the Mossos return," Sylvain continued, "I will go outside to talk to them. That way I can also speak to the community. I think we have some support from our neighbours. Pau, maybe you can come with me. Talk to the people in Catalan."

"Sure." Pau gave me a guilty look, as if accepting a job that would separate us was breaking a rule.

"And if some of us have to get arrested," Sylvain continued, "it's important to show that we are resisting peacefully. Annika and Enzo, I think you have the most experience. You know what to say, and what not to say."

The two of them nodded.

That left me and John to be locked in the bathroom. We looked at each other.

"Don't worry," Sylvain said. "We'll put lots of supplies in there for you. And at least it's not the Death Plank." He smiled at me.

"I think we should also set up some traps," John said. "Cut a couple holes in the floor over by the door. Cover them up with a carpet or a sheet. Let the Mossos fall through."

Annika shook her head. "It's always worse when the police get injured. We don't want anyone here being charged with a serious offence."

"Or getting hurt," Pau added. "The Mossos love to get violent if they have an excuse."

Sylvain turned to me. "Are you legal here?"

"Yes, for another month and a half."

"If you get arrested, you'll need to have ID. Do you have some?"

I considered using my lack of ID as an excuse to leave. Another option was to just go – disappear like the girl who'd come before me. "I can probably get some," I said.

"Good. I think you should work on that today, just in case."

"Okay. Should I go try to get it now? It might take some time."

Annika set a cup of tea in front of me. "Drink this first."

"Thanks." I wrapped my hands around the hot mug and left them there until my tattoo hurt too much, and I had to let go.

After breakfast, I went into the sleeping apartment and stuffed my sketchbook and a change of clothes into my courier bag, then pulled on the white sneakers Manu had given me. They were pretty scuffed up now.

The squatters were arguing in the other apartment, still figuring out the exact details of their plan. I paused outside their door for a moment before heading down the stairs. I'd already told them I was going out. There was no reason to say goodbye again.

On the ground floor I stood in front of my mural, wondering what would become of it – who would see it before it was someday painted over, and what would they think. I grabbed my last cans of spray paint and loaded them into my bag. My trench coat was hanging on the wall and I went to retrieve the money I'd been storing in its pocket. When I checked the other pockets to be sure they were empty, I discovered the red paint chip. It was scuffed up a bit like my sneakers, but the colour was still vibrant, pulsing almost, as if wanting to be freed from its little square. I glanced over at the opposite wall, at the explosion of red tags covering its surface. My red wall had turned out very differently than I'd imagined.

I tucked the paint chip back in the pocket of my coat, then opened the front door and looked both ways up and down the street. There were no Mossos around, and not many people. I set my bag just outside, then closed the door again and called up the stairs for one of the squatters to come and lock me out. I guessed it would be Pau, and I was right.

"Are you going now?" he asked.

"Yes."

He gave me a long look. "Are you worried about what's going to happen with the police?"

"A little. Do you think they could send me back to Canada?"

"No, I don't think that's possible."

That was easy for him to say. All the squatters had European passports; they could choose any country in Europe to live in for as long as they liked, and they wouldn't ever be kicked out.

"Anyway," Pau said, "the police might not even come back."

"But what if they do? Where are you guys going to go?"

"If we get evicted, we'll just find somewhere else. And, of course, you're coming too. You're one of us now, *carinyo*."

He gave me a hug. "I mean it," he said. "Don't worry about Annika. She is always tough at first, but I can tell she likes you. We all do."

I pulled away and gave him a steady smile. "Okay, I should get going."

"I'll see you when you get back."
"See you soon." I opened the door and stepped outside.
Behind me, Pau slid the deadbolt into place.

I walked around Gràcia for a long time, trying to figure out what to do. Pau's words had gotten to me a bit, and I wondered if I was being too hasty. Maybe I should go to Peter's and try to get my ID. He was probably at work, but on the off chance I succeeded, then I could go back to the squat and take a stand alongside the others. The squatters' passion to protect their home was contagious. It almost made me want to stay and fight.

I sat for a while in one of the squares. When Annika had given me a tour of Gràcia she'd mentioned a bomb shelter that tourists could visit in an underground parking lot, and I realized I was sitting across from the elevator. I took it down one floor and walked across the humid, stuffy garage to a toll booth. The parking attendant was grumpy that I'd disturbed his lunch, but he handed me a key and told me to go down to the bottom floor. Four floors down, I used the key to open a gate with metal bars. Behind it stretched a dark, damp cavern with a low ceiling and curved walls. I felt inside the gate for the light switch the attendant had mentioned and flicked it on. The illuminated space had a long bench running along one side. I sat on it and imagined all the families who must have been packed together down here, waiting for the danger outside to end.

Living at the squat had always felt a bit like staying with Brigid and her parents – like I was a welcome guest, but would never be part of the family. I didn't want to be locked in a bathroom with John, sharing his oxygen as the Mossos kicked our home to pieces on the other side of the door. I also didn't want to end up in a jail cell. I pictured the metal gate swinging closed and locking me in. A shelter and a prison – the two spaces were surprisingly similar. The only real difference was who was able to open the door. Suddenly, I couldn't breathe. I turned off the light, then hurried back to the attendant to drop off the key.

Outside, I took several large breaths, letting the fresh air fill my lungs until I started to feel better. I wasn't going back to the squat – that was decided. The squatters would think I was a coward, and maybe I was. But in a few days, I could go to the tattoo shop and explain what had happened. I knew at least Pau would understand.

Xavi and I were meeting up later to go paint with his crew, but this afternoon, I was suddenly free of any plans. I thought about going to the locutorio to continue my job search, but maybe for just one afternoon I would try not to worry about the future. With money in my pocket, I could have a normal day – the sort of day a person with a tourist visa was supposed to have.

I went to the movie theatre on Carrer Verdi and bought a ticket for a matinee that was just beginning. I'd assumed the "version original" movie would be in English, but it turned out to be in French with Spanish subtitles. The two languages combined and made my brain feel blurry like I was looking at an optical illusion and seeing several possibilities at once. I let the visuals wash over me, guessing at a storyline. The basics were familiar – two attractive people falling in love – but the film was clearly European; it had more sex scenes than North American movies, and the story didn't seem to have a happy ending.

After the film let out, it was still too early to go to Xavi's, so I spent a half hour walking uphill to Park Güell – a major attraction I hadn't yet had a chance to visit. At the front gate, long buses were idling, and it seemed like hundreds of people were waiting to have their picture taken beside a mosaic lizard statue. I wove through the crowd, then entered the park and began to wander, following the winding paths and trying to spot the wild parrots that were screeching from their nests in the palm trees high above. The park was massive, and it turned out to be the best place I'd ever gotten lost. Each detour brought me to a new tower, garden or pavilion. Each wrong turn led me to a wider panoramic view of the city.

When Manu's watch said 7:00 p.m., I started the walk back to Xavi's, grateful that it was at least downhill. Outside his building, I rang the buzzer for the attic apartment, but he wasn't home. I was too exhausted to go anywhere else, so I waited out front for him, sitting on the curb.

Finally, just after 8:30 p.m., he came around the corner and I stood up. My legs were numb.

"Hey," he said. "Sorry. I thought we were going to meet a little later."

"I know. I'm a bit early. Do you want me to come back?"

"No, definitely not." Xavi put his arms around me. His neck was warm against my nose.

After a moment he let go. "Are you okay?" he asked.

I tried to give him a brief synopsis of my day, but instead a whole flood of things came out. I told him about living at the squat, and about the eviction notice from the police, and how I felt terrible about not wanting to go back, but that it really didn't seem like a place where I belonged.

Xavi listened, his keys cradled in his hand. "Do you want to come upstairs? You've seen my apartment. It isn't much, but ..."

Four walls, electricity, keys; he had no idea.

He opened his front door and we started up the stairs. After a few minutes of steady climbing, he looked back and smiled. "Almost there."

Inside his apartment, he took my bag, and we sat down on his futon. He moved a strand of hair behind my ear.

"Maybe we should go out with the crew another night," he said.

"Yeah, maybe." I really wanted to paint something, but it was also tempting to stay alone with Xavi.

He gave me a long kiss, and his hand slipped under the bottom edge of my shirt, his fingers brushing against my skin. After a moment, he pulled away. "Do you want some tea or wine? Or something to eat?"

I shook my head, pressing myself back into his hand.

"Okay, just give me a minute," he said. "I should call one of the guys."

Xavi's pillow was very soft. I lay back on his futon and closed my eyes, listening as he talked on the phone. Without subtitles, he could be saying anything. I let myself slip into the plot of the European film I was imagining: an attractive photographer making secret plans while his lover lay waiting. Their story might not have a happy ending, but there would definitely be some sex.

When I opened my eyes again it was light outside, and it felt like a lot of time had passed. Xavi was coming in the door.

"How are you doing?" he asked.

I pushed myself to sitting and checked Manu's watch. It was almost noon. "Oh my god. I'm so sorry I fell asleep."

"That's okay." Xavi smiled. "You must have been really tired." He set his helmet on the counter and kicked off his shoes. There was a greasy-looking paper bag in his hand. "Are you hungry?"

"Yes." I felt light-headed.

Xavi came over and sat on the edge of the futon. He pulled a small pot of chocolate from the bag, then a long twisted pastry.

"*Xurros.*" He dipped the pastry in the chocolate and handed it to me. It was warm. A shower of fine sugar sprinkled down my arm.

I didn't want to be ungrateful, but I couldn't do it. "Sorry," I said, handing it back. "I don't actually like sweet things."

Xavi looked amazed. "How is that possible?"

I shrugged.

"Please. Just try one bite. This is my very favourite thing. I promise you'll like it."

"No, I won't."

He broke off a small piece and moved it toward my mouth. "Please."

I sighed. "One bite."

He watched me chew and swallow. "It's good, right?"

It was slightly better than I'd imagined, but only because he'd fed it to me. "It's not terrible."

"You see?"

"Definitely messy." I pointed at a smear of chocolate on the front of my shirt.

He set aside the bag, motioned for me to lift up my arms, then pulled the shirt up over my head. His eyes travelled down to my breasts then back to my face. I leaned over and kissed him. He tasted like the outside world, like life in Barcelona. I wanted that taste to fill me up until I felt rooted – like I was in the right place and belonged to someone again. I pulled him toward me and tugged at the tangle of his clothes, tossing them into a pile beside the bed. Then I pressed him down onto his back and climbed on top. The air coming in from the window was hot. I lifted my hair and tied it into a loose bun that immediately fell out again. Through the window, I could see Barcelona shimmering in the heat. Having sex with Xavi felt like grabbing on to everything I loved about the city.

By the time we were finished, the churros were cold and the chocolate had a thin skin on top. I broke through it with the tip of my finger, then drew a chocolate tag across Xavi's bicep. "Could we paint tonight?" I asked.

"Sure."

I pointed to the other tag on his arm, his tattoo. "Why do you have this?"

"Ah, it's a bit silly. I got it a long time ago."

"Is it a donkey?"

"Yes," he said. "A *Catalan* donkey."

I looked at it more closely.

"The Spaniards have their bull. We have our donkey. It's kind of a joke."

It seemed like an odd symbol to choose. Loud, unintelligent. "Why a donkey?"

He shrugged. "I guess it's because a donkey is small, but strong. He carries a lot of weight. Sometimes he has to carry the weight for the whole country because everyone else is too lazy."

The charged feeling of electricity I'd noticed with his friends was back, a momentary crackling.

"Did you know the people in Catalunya pay the most taxes?" Xavi asked.

I shook my head.

"It's true. And what do we get in return? No new highways, no new trains. Instead, all our money goes to Madrid. And then they expect us to speak Castilian, to say 'Gracias' for giving us nothing." He studied my face, searching for signs of outrage.

"That sounds like a bad deal."

"Yes." Xavi let out a long breath. He reached across my body and turned on an oscillating fan that began to move back and forth. "Sorry. I know you're not from here – you probably don't care too much about these things."

The fan turned to face me, as if curious how I'd respond.

"I do care," I said. "I just don't know too much about what's going on."

Xavi propped his head on his hand. "Well, it's basically like a bad marriage. It's obvious that Catalunya and Spain are not a good match, but the Spanish state won't let us go. Every day they tell us we won't be able to manage without them, but of course we will. And once we're free?" He rolled onto his back and stared up at the slope of the ceiling. "Imagine having the chance to build a whole new country from the ground up. That's what we're fighting for. The chance to make our own decisions – to be who we really are."

"What would you do first?" I asked.

"That's a good question." Xavi thought for a moment. "To begin, we would of course take down all of the Spanish flags and signs. Then we would have to figure out a lot of things: how to defend ourselves, what currency to use, who would make the rules."

I shifted closer to him and touched his tattoo again.

Xavi took my hand and held it for a moment, then turned it over. The ring tattoo on my palm looked childish and unconsidered compared with the detailed work on his arm. "Why do you have this?" he asked.

I looked at the red swollen skin around the circle. It wasn't healing well. "It's just an *O*."

"An *O*?"

"Yeah, for *open*. Like keeping an open hand?" This was supposed to be a simple answer – pseudo-Buddhistic and final – but Xavi was waiting for me to continue. "I guess I just wanted to remind myself that you can't hold onto things."

Xavi studied his own hands, as if checking for holes. After a minute, he reached down and picked up some photos that had fallen onto the floor. He shuffled through them, then stopped at a black-and-white close-up of a young woman's face. She was peering up at the camera from behind a curtain of long hair. She seemed like she was just about to say something, to make a joke maybe.

"That's a nice picture," I said. "Who is she?"

Xavi didn't answer right away, and I assumed he was searching for her name.

"She's my wife," he said.

I dug my fingernails into my tattoo and felt a rush of pain. "She's pretty."

Xavi looked at me, flustered. "Yes." He set the photographs on the bedside table. "Sorry. I should explain."

"No, you don't have to explain." I grabbed my shirt from beside the bed and worked to turn it the right way out.

"Jane." Xavi squeezed my shoulder. "She's not my wife anymore. She died last year."

I stopped with my arms in the sleeves of the shirt, halfway between one state and another. The tight ball of anger in my stomach began to release.

Xavi examined his hands again as if they didn't belong to him. "You're the first person I've been with … It just feels a bit strange."

"I know. It feels strange for me too."

Xavi glanced up, wanting to know what I meant. Then I felt like an asshole. Peter wasn't dead. I could go to his apartment and ring the buzzer any time – be face to face with him in less than an hour. "I'm sorry," I said. "About your wife."

"I guess I should put the pictures away." Xavi looked at the photos on the bedside table but didn't move to touch them. We lay down beside each other, and he curled around my back, his fingers moving slowly up and down my arm like he was searching for something beneath my skin.

"I was supposed to get married a couple of weeks ago," I said.

Xavi's fingertips paused, idling at the inside of my elbow. "What happened?"

I was about to tell him that Peter had fallen out of love with me, but that answer suddenly felt too simple. "I don't know. Maybe we weren't a good match."

Xavi laid his hand flat against my skin and I could feel a growing warmth between us, tiny pulses of heat that coloured me in from my edges to my centre.

He squeezed my arm. "You want to paint tonight?"

"Yes."

"Okay." He sat up. "I'll call the others."

"Wait. Can't we just go by ourselves?"

Xavi poked me with his toe. "No way! After all the negotiating I had to do? What's the problem? Are you scared?"

"No."

"Good." He grabbed his cell phone from the floor beside the bed. "Because you're going to have to be brave if you want to paint with MGIC."

20

La Milícia del Graffiti per la Independència de Catalunya. As soon as Xavi told me the name of the crew, I realized I'd seen the MGIC tag in a number of places throughout the city, usually beside a striped independence flag somewhere high up. All week, I'd been wondering how graffiti along the rooflines was done, and maybe tonight I'd find out. The highest graffiti always seemed to be about love or politics, as if those were the only subjects worth the risk.

Xavi had arranged to meet his friends at one of the biggest squares in Gràcia: Plaça del Sol. I hoped we wouldn't run into any of the squatters. Tomorrow I'd go see Pau at the tattoo shop and explain some of the reasons I'd decided to leave. Maybe he could smooth things over with the others.

While Xavi and I were waiting for the rest of his crew to arrive, he crossed the square to buy us a can of beer from one of the beer sellers on the corner. I sat down on a wooden bench and ran my fingers across the hearts and names scratched on its surface. There were small groups of people all around, talking and laughing. I closed my eyes and listened to the sound. It was the lively hum of people who spent a lot of time outdoors and stayed up late. I felt a strange wave of homesickness for Barcelona, even though I was smack in the middle of the square, in the middle of the city. Maybe wishing a place was your home was a different kind of homesickness.

Xavi came back and wiped off the top of the beer with a corner of his T-shirt, then opened the can and handed it to me.

"I think I'm in love with Barcelona," I said.

Xavi smirked. "People who aren't from here always talk about Barcelona like it's a person. It's not a person. It's just a city."

"It's a very good city," I said.

Xavi's two bearded friends were walking toward us, motorcycle helmets swinging from their hands. Xavi gave them kisses on the cheeks and slaps on the back. It was one of the things I loved about Barcelona: people being physical together, little sparks of affection visible between them.

"Jane, you haven't been properly introduced." Xavi pointed to the bigger guy, the one with the disks in his earlobes. "This is Os." Then he turned to the rapid blinker. "And this is Conill."

I stood up and gave them awkward cheek-kisses in greeting. "It's nice to see you guys again."

The two men agreed in broken English. Then Os mimed drinking from a can and they both walked off toward one of the beer sellers.

"Sorry for the fake names," Xavi said.

"Oh. That's okay." I hadn't even noticed.

"They just thought it would be safer if you only knew their code names."

"Os and . . ."

"Conill. Bear and Rabbit. That's what they mean in English."

"Really?" They sounded like characters in a children's book. "Are they like best friends who do everything together?"

"Sort of. They're brothers."

"So what's your code name?"

He patted his bicep, the donkey tattoo. "Ruc."

"Aha . . ."

"You should have one too, you know." He squinted at me. "Maybe Blondie? *Xurro?*"

I kicked his foot. "How about Niki?" The name hovered for a second in the air between us.

"Niki? Why Niki?"

I took a sip of beer. It felt strange to hear him say my name. "I don't know. Maybe not. Give me a minute. I'll think of something else."

The clean-cut guy was suddenly behind us. He grabbed Xavi by the shoulders. "*Hola!*"

Xavi turned to greet him. "*Hola!* Jane, this is the Doctor."

The Doctor kissed the air on either side of my face. "How are you doing today?" he asked.

"Good."

He looked at Xavi. "You too?"

"Very good." Xavi glanced at me, and I blushed.

The Bear and the Rabbit returned, and we all headed toward the centre of the square to find a place to sit. Xavi and I lagged a little behind the others.

"Why is he called the Doctor?" I asked.

Xavi smiled. "Because he's a doctor."

"That's not very creative."

Xavi grabbed me around the waist, and I squirmed away from his tickling fingers. He pulled me back, his mouth close to my ear. "I'm happy you're here." His words buzzed through me with a different kind of tickle.

Ahead of us, Xavi's friends were settling into a semicircle on the ground, placing their heavy bags and knapsacks in the middle. When we joined them, they each shifted back a bit to make more space, and

I felt like I was disturbing the normal circumference of their group. I really wished Xavi and I could have just gone out alone.

It was a humid night, and the crew's action plan seemed to be wilting in the heavy air. I tried to be patient as they talked about a movie I hadn't seen, then a girl the Bear wanted to sleep with. They were all attempting to speak English for my benefit, so I tried to be encouraging, nodding and asking simple questions. The Doctor was almost as fluent in English as Xavi, but the Bear and the Rabbit were struggling. Eventually, they both fell silent, then slipped back into Catalan, looking over from time to time to see if I could understand. I couldn't really. Just a word here or there that sounded close enough to Spanish for me to guess at.

I noticed the Doctor studying me. He was wearing a pair of designer glasses that made him look older than the others.

"You're from Canada?" he asked.

"Yes."

"From Québec?"

"No, from Ontario. Toronto."

"I see. Have you been to Québec?"

"Once, on a school trip."

"It must be very different there: the language, the culture."

"Yeah, it's pretty different."

"And the people there, they also want to have their independence, *no?*"

I glanced at Xavi, wishing he would join our conversation, but he was talking to the brothers. He seemed like a slightly different man in his own language: someone goofier with more bravado. I looked back at the Doctor. "There are definitely separatists in Québec, although I don't think there are as many as here."

The Doctor took off his glasses and wiped them on a corner of his shirt. "We prefer to call ourselves independentists," he said. "We don't *want* to separate, but if that's the only way for us to gain our independence, then that's what we'll do."

I thought about this distinction. At first, the two terms seemed like sides of the same coin – but no, they were different coins.

"Someday soon," the Doctor continued, "we are going to have a referendum, just like the one in Québec." He replaced his glasses on his nose. "Everyone will have the chance to vote – to stand up and be counted. To finally be heard."

His words made me picture a courtroom. Maybe because in a week's time a clerk would call my name, and no one would stand up to answer. If the security guard from the department store was there, he'd get to tell a bunch of lies about me – describing the spoiled woman he thought I was.

A car alarm went off and the Bear and the Rabbit hid their beers under their legs.

"Mossos," explained the Rabbit, his eyelashes fluttering in the direction of my beer.

I looked around. There had been three or four beer sellers and now they were gone. Instead, Mossos edged the square. Someone must have set off the alarm as a warning. I handed my beer to Xavi and he tucked it under the flap of his bag.

"So." The Doctor rubbed his hands together. "The Spanish team is playing again on Friday."

"*Traïdors de merda*," said the Bear. This sounded like a curse. He belched, then said something else in Catalan and the others laughed. "I hope to lose," he explained to me.

"He hopes *they* lose," Xavi said. "They're talking about the World Cup."

"Right." Recently, I'd seen a lot of drunk people wearing Spanish soccer jerseys and waving flags, especially in the tourist part of the city.

The Doctor reached for his bag. "They're going to be showing the game on a big screen at Plaça Espanya. Thousands of people will go there to watch."

The guys discreetly finished their beers, then stood up. My comprehension was on time-delay. "Where are we going?" I asked Xavi.

He handed me a motorcycle helmet. "We're going to paint something big."

At Plaça Espanya, an imposing bronze-and-marble monument several storeys high sat anchored in the middle of a gigantic roundabout. The traffic around the monument was fast and heavy, all the major thoroughfares of the city converging into a hectic centrifuge. We parked the motorcycles in an alley behind a large circular building with lots of broken windows. I looked through one of them at the rubble inside.

"What is this place?" I asked Xavi.

"It's called Les Arenes. It used to be a bullfighting ring. But Catalans don't approve of bullfighting, so we shut it down. I was hoping they might turn it into a concert space, or an art gallery, but unfortunately it's going to be a shopping centre."

The five of us walked around the building to the front. The tone of the group had begun to shift, a tense energy bouncing between the men. I felt it jump to me, but I wasn't able to absorb it. I still didn't fully understand what we were doing, or why.

Past the monument, across the busy multi-lane traffic, two tall thin towers stood on either side of a long carless avenue. "That's where the screen will be." The Doctor pointed across the road, then turned and looked up. Above us there was a large construction company billboard affixed to the top of the bullfighting ring. "We should be able to get up there."

We crossed at the light so we could see the billboard from the other side of the road, from where the spectators would be gathering to watch the game.

"Yes, I think that will be perfect," the Doctor said. "We can go up the construction fence and in through that top window. There should be a ladder on the back."

My palms were damp with sweat and it was stinging my tattoo.

The others were silent, assessing.

"I think three should go up, and two should stand guard down here," the Doctor said. He was looking at Xavi and me.

"Sure, we can keep watch," Xavi said.

I felt both annoyed and relieved. Mostly annoyed. I'd been waiting around all night and now they weren't even going to let me paint.

"Just tell Jane the signals," the Doctor said.

"Okay." Xavi nodded. "But she doesn't have a cell phone."

"Here. You can use mine." The Doctor handed me his phone. He scrolled down to show me a number in his contacts listed under the name *Rubèn*. He glanced at the Bear.

"Call this number if we need to run. Xavi can help you choose a good place to stand." He motioned to the brothers, and the three of them left Xavi and me alone.

Xavi pointed to the centre of the roundabout. "Over there would be good. You just have to watch for police cars, police on foot or anyone else who seems to be angry, or making a call. I'll go around to the other side." He grabbed my hand. "Hey, I know you wanted to paint tonight but it's going to take some time for them to trust you." He gave me a quick kiss. "If anything happens I'll meet you back at home."

Home. The word sat like oil on water. I'd never felt more like a tourist. This was just another group I didn't belong to.

When Xavi headed off, I crossed the lanes of traffic to the monument and stood on the far side where I had a view of the billboard and three of the wide streets that were feeding the roundabout. I perched on the edge of the monument, pretending to be texting on the Doctor's phone. When I glanced up, the three members of MGIC were already climbing the construction scaffolding. In their dark clothes they looked like ninjas. There was a trickle of people going into the metro, but they were busy and far away. The drivers of the cars, cabs and motorcycles were all zipping by too fast to notice.

The guys vanished through a window, then a minute later they appeared on the catwalk in front of the billboard. A police car drove by, and I snapped to attention, but the car whipped past on the roundabout and headed off in another direction. I pulled up the number the Doctor had shown me on his phone and readied my finger on the call button.

The MGIC crew was painting the billboard now, one of them working to cover·the construction logo under messy swathes of white paint, while another added a flag: alternating stripes of red and yellow with a star on one end. The third guy traced out large capital letters that slowly formed the words *CATALONIA IS NOT SPAIN*. I was surprised he was writing in English, but maybe it was for the benefit of the tourists who would be watching the game. Or maybe English was just the universal language of complaint.

When they were finished, the three men disappeared behind the billboard, and I made my way back to the motorcycles. In the alley, I discovered the others' bikes were already gone and Xavi was waiting for me with a tense look on his face. I hurried to get on his motorcycle, passing him the Doctor's phone.

"I guess we're not going to be coming here to watch the game," I joked.

"Definitely not." Xavi handed me a helmet and started his bike. "I don't care if Spain wins or loses. And besides, there are a bunch of other things I'd rather do with you."

I held on tight as we roared out of the alleyway and onto the roundabout.

21

MACBA, the contemporary art gallery where Xavi took me the next afternoon, was on the outskirts of El Raval. As we approached the building, we passed a mural that showed the word *raval* conjugated as if it was a verb. When I asked Xavi for a translation, he said it was a made-up word that could mean whatever I wanted. To me, El Raval would always mean walking around with Manu.

Xavi bought us gallery tickets, and we spent a couple hours visiting a photo exhibit he wanted to show me, then wandering through the permanent collection. The gallery was spacious and modern with lots of natural light. The front of the building was glass, and as we moved between the floors via ramps, I looked down at the square below. A bunch of skateboarders were practising their jumps on the front steps.

After we were finished in the gallery, Xavi and I headed back to Gràcia to collect the things we would need to celebrate Festa de Sant Joan that night. There was specially ordered coca bread to pick up, cava to chill and a picnic to pack. We waited in a long line to buy fireworks. Sant Joan was a celebration of the summer solstice, and Xavi said the entire city stayed up until dawn.

We spent the evening down at the beach, drinking and dancing amidst the noisy chaos. Sant Joan seemed like a dangerous festival: children throwing fireworks at people who were swimming in the sea, men in flammable-looking devil costumes juggling fire. I was ready to leave around 4:00 a.m., but Xavi said there was no point in going home; the fireworks would be too loud for us to sleep until after the sun came up.

Everyone in the city had the next day off work, so we slept late, then watched movies on Xavi's computer all afternoon, nursing our hangovers. I guessed he might need some space after spending so much time together, but when I suggested I could move to a hostel, he said I could stay as long as I wanted – until I figured out what I was going to do next. I told him I was looking for a design job, and he offered to talk to a friend who might need some help; it would be freelance only, but it would be a start. That night we went out with the crew again – this time to spray-paint the word *català* over any Spanish text we saw on local posters or signs. The crew was also putting up posters for an upcoming protest. The Doctor said it was going to be the biggest one yet.

On Friday morning Xavi had to go to work at the university where he taught photography. Before leaving, he pulled a bunch of books from his shelf. "Just in case you get bored." He smiled. They were books about the Spanish Civil War, about Catalan nationalism, about photography and art.

"Cool. Thanks."

"Here's an extra set of keys," he said, dropping them on the kitchen counter. "And if you need something else to wear –" he pointed at the closet "– I think you're more or less the same size as Laia."

Laia. The discovery of his wife's name added a burst of colour to her photograph, which was still on the bedside table.

"I know I probably should have gotten rid of her clothes by now." His words were slowing down. "I just … I haven't had the opportunity."

I joined him at the kitchen counter where he was packing a lunch. "I'm sure you'll find a good place to take them when you're ready."

"Yes."

I tried to think of something to distract him. "Hey. I have a question. How do you say 'You have to eat' in Catalan?"

"Has de menjar. Why?"

"I have an idea for a stencil."

"Here. I'll write it down for you." Xavi printed the phrase on a fresh page of the little notebook he'd given me to keep track of the Catalan I was learning. To get me started he'd written translations for some basic phrases, and also some romantic words, including *kiss* and *love.* Since then, I'd copied down a few words from signs in the neighbourhood: *xocolata* (chocolate), *caixa* (bank), *rebaixa* (sale). Catalan was full of *X*s. They seemed to cross out the *CH*s and *J*s from their Spanish equivalents, replacing the missing letters with a shushing sound.

Xavi handed me back the notebook, then gave me a kiss. "I'll see you tonight."

"Yes. I'll see you." There was a slight pause before he moved to the door. Each day we had several of these awkward moments, little gaps that could have been filled with sweeter words, but so far had remained empty. We were doing our best to take care of each other, but the harder we tried, the more obvious it was that neither of us was ready for anything serious. The previous afternoon, I'd found Xavi sitting outside on his rooftop terrace, and when he turned to look at me, it was like he hadn't recognized me, or worse, that he'd been expecting someone else.

When the door closed behind him, I lay back on his bed, enjoying the quiet. After dozing a bit, I picked up Manu's watch from the bedside table to check the time, but the hands were frozen in place. I shook the watch and held it to my ear, wondering why it had stopped today – if something bad might have happened to Manu. Some of his superstition had obviously rubbed off on me. The only reason the watch had stopped was because its cheap dollar-store battery had run out. It didn't mean anything else.

I took a long shower, the warm water and citrus-scented shampoo still feeling a bit miraculous after so many weeks of cold, trickling taps at the beach and the squat. I dried off with a large towel, then wrapped it around me and walked over to the closet. Coming from the back corner was a faint smell of perfume, which was likely why Xavi had kept her clothes. Or maybe there just never seemed to be a good day for throwing them away – no day yet that he'd woken up and really believed she was gone. Xavi would probably miss his wife forever.

I pulled a bunch of hangers from the closet and fanned the clothes out on the bed. She'd had good taste, a bright playful style. I tried on a sleeveless peach dress with a clingy skirt. The neckline was too low, but otherwise it fit. I swapped it for a navy-blue sundress with off-the-shoulder sleeves. The dress made me feel like I might be able to pass for a local – or at least someone who'd been in Barcelona for a while and knew how things worked.

My arm felt bare without Manu's watch. I slipped it over my wrist and let it slide into its regular position. Even though it had stopped, it was still doing something important: reminding me of Manu and all that had happened since we'd met. Manu was someone who I might miss forever.

I washed the clothes I'd been wearing for the last few days, then hung them out on the terrace to dry so I could change again before Xavi came home. I didn't think it would be good for him to see me in Laia's dress. Maybe I'd suggest that he donate her things to the Free Store; I could take him to the squat and show him my mural, if the squatters hadn't been evicted yet, and if they didn't hate me too much. The first thing I wanted to do today was go talk to Pau and find out where things stood.

Outside, it felt like the hottest day yet. I held the door open with my foot until I'd double-checked the inside pocket of my courier bag, making sure that my money and Xavi's keys were safely stowed away. It was strange to have things to protect again. I decided to walk by the squat before going to the tattoo shop, just to see if anything looked different. I tried to keep within the stripes of shade closest to the buildings, but crossing Plaça de la Revolució, there was no shade at all.

When I turned onto the squatters' street, their building looked more abandoned than usual, like it had been drained of all life. The windows were boarded up and the front door was padlocked. The banner was gone from the balcony.

I sat on the curb across the street for a long time, looking at the building. I'd known there was a good chance the squatters would be gone, but even so, I couldn't quite believe it. Or maybe what I couldn't believe was that they'd ever been there. It was almost eerie how quickly the Mossos had been able to erase all signs of the building's last inhabitants. I stood up and began searching the ground for some trace – a piece of splintered furniture, a broken dish – but there was nothing.

When the tears came, I didn't know exactly why I was crying. Maybe because I'd never be able to show Xavi my mural, or because the squatters had lost their home. Or maybe just because a thing could be destroyed with so little effort, and there was no real way to resist.

I imagined the Mossos breaking down the door, streaming into the apartment in riot gear, dragging Annika down the stairs in her bare feet while John punched anyone in sight, and the others yelled until their voices went hoarse. I should have been yelling with them. Even if that's all I'd been able to do, it would have been better than being silent.

I walked to the tattoo shop to see if Pau was working. I wanted to apologize, at least to him, and find out where the squatters had moved.

Inside the shop, a woman with bright pink hair was sitting at the front desk.

"Is Pau here?" I asked.

She glanced up from the fetish magazine she was reading. She had a silver barbell through the bridge of her nose, connecting the dark dots of her heavily made-up eyes. "Pau doesn't work here anymore."

"What? I just saw him a few days ago."

The woman shrugged.

"Do you know where he went?" I shifted to one side, peeking around her into the backroom to see if anyone I recognized was working.

"No." She rolled backward in her chair and pulled a curtain shut between the rooms.

We looked at each other. For some reason, she was being purposely unhelpful.

"Okay," I said. "I guess I'll go then."

A French bulldog emerged from under her desk and waddled toward me, its toenails clicking against the wooden floor. It followed me as I walked to the door.

"Don't let him out," the woman said.

I raised an eyebrow in her direction, my hand on the doorknob.

She sighed. "Pau said he was moving home for a while – to some little village where his parents live." She flipped a page of her magazine.

"Thank you." I held the dog back with my foot, then stepped out onto the narrow sidewalk – a sidewalk that would no longer lead me to Pau.

I started to walk down Gran de Gràcia. It was just before siesta time and all the shopkeepers were rolling down metal doors over their storefronts. It made me feel dizzy, like my life was being erased behind me as I went. I stopped and turned, then stood for a moment, looking back at where I'd come from. Everything was still there – the long uphill street lined on both sides with parked motorcycles, the art nouveau buildings with their iron balconies and hanging bird-cages. Even so, I couldn't shake the sensation that I was on the edge of something; everyone I met in Barcelona seemed to disappear. I thought about Pau's kind eyes, and the cigarette burns in the blanket he'd loaned me. I shouldn't have waited so long to go back.

I wrapped my fingers around Manu's watch. "Don't look back" – that's what he'd always said. And it was good advice if you were running away. But I didn't want to keep running, always moving forward through a world I didn't quite belong in, everything slipping away behind me.

I decided to go to La Rambla and look for Atlas. With his unusual job of standing perfectly still, there was a good chance he'd be where

I was expecting. When I found him in his regular spot, I joined the small group of tourists who were watching and taking his picture. After they walked off, Atlas jumped down from his crate.

"How are you doing?" he asked.

"I'm okay. How it's going with the Romanians?"

"Bah. Bunch of bludgers. I think they've moved on."

We sat down on his crate. His gold paint smell was familiar to me now. It was the same smell I tried to scrub off my hands at night.

"How's it going with your new Catalan friends?" Atlas asked.

"Pretty good."

"Huh." He seemed doubtful. "It's not easy to make friends with Catalan people. Usually, they're very closed." He brought his hands together like a pair of sliding doors.

I thought about something Xavi had told me – that there was a fortress on Montjuïc where a lot of Catalans had been imprisoned while Franco was in power. "Maybe they're closed for a reason."

Atlas looked at me strangely.

"You know, oppression, torture. That sort of thing."

"Jay-sus!" Atlas laughed. "What have they done to you?"

I tried not to smile. Testing out new knowledge was embarrassing, sort of like showing up to a party with a new haircut – people needed time to adjust.

"It's not really funny," I said.

"Right." Atlas pulled an exaggeratedly solemn face. Some passing tourists stopped in front of us as if we were performing. Atlas shooed them away. "Fuck. It's not easy being gold."

I picked up his globe. "Do you ever think about going home?" First Manu had gone home and now Pau.

"You mean to Australia?"

I nodded.

"Nah. Sometimes I think about going someplace else."

Someplace else. I hadn't considered that. Maybe after my tourist visa ran out, or if Xavi and I got sick of each other, I could do that too – travel around from place to place drawing portraits of people and staying for as long as I could, then moving on. Travelling forever would be exhausting – something like Atlas holding up his globe and never being able to set it down – but at least I'd get to see the world up close.

"Do you think you'll leave soon?" I asked.

"No way. Do you know how many tourists pass by me every day?"

I certainly did; he told me every time I saw him. "A hundred thousand?"

Atlas shook his head. "It's way more than that. At least a hundred and fifty. Probably more."

After we said goodbye, I walked back up La Rambla. On one side was El Raval, on the other side the Gothic Quarter. I considered turning in one of those directions – either going to look for Fanta on the street behind the hotel, or stopping by Peter's to see if I could get my wallet. Those were two places I needed to go back to, but I'd waited so long that the required actions seemed almost impossible: to walk around the perimeter of the construction site after all this time, or to finally go and ring Peter's buzzer. I decided that for today, I would just keep to the centre of La Rambla: pick up some art supplies, then head back to Xavi's to sit in front of the fan and make my stencils.

I continued north, weaving through the groups of tourists clustered around their open maps. As I was crossing Plaça Catalunya a pair of hands landed on my shoulders and made me jump. It was Yaya.

"Jane."

"Hey! You scared me." Yaya looked tired, and he smelled like he'd been working hard for a long time in the sun. "How are you doing?" I asked.

He sighed. "These days have been bad."

I looked around for his crew, but I couldn't see them. "What's going on?"

"Malik was *arrêté* ..." He searched for the word in English. "Stopped."

"Oh my god. When?"

"Yesterday. Probably he's in the CIE now." The CIE was the detention centre for people who were caught without papers. Yaya always said the prisoners there were treated like dogs.

"I'm so sorry. Do you have time to go sit down for a few minutes? Maybe have a coffee or some lunch? It's my treat – I've got some money."

Yaya's expression softened. "You do owe me lunch."

"I do? Oh yeah! That's right!" Manu and I had promised to buy him lunch if the Everybody Laughs scam was a success.

I pointed toward a busy tourist café on the edge of the square. Yaya and I walked over and wove through the outside tables looking for a spot to sit. The table we chose was covered in baskets filled with half-eaten sandwiches. I gathered the baskets up, then took them inside to the garbage. Yaya watched me return.

"Someone's been feeding you, *non?*" he said.

I blushed as I sat down. "Yes, I guess that's true."

"It's good," said Yaya. "You have to eat."

I smiled. He must have read Manu's note.

Yaya's sack of knock-off purses didn't quite fit under the table. The waiter eyed it as he took our order: coffees only; Yaya said he wasn't hungry after all, and I couldn't persuade him to change his mind.

"So, have you heard something from Manu?" he asked.

"No." I laid my hand over Manu's watch, then turned its motionless face to the inside of my wrist. "I hope he's okay."

"Probably, he's fine," Yaya said. "At least he's with his family."

There was a long pause. Yaya and I had never sat on a restaurant terrace before, and our conversation felt a bit stilted, like we were interviewing each other for jobs we didn't really want. A young couple sitting nearby got up to leave and we watched them go. A pair of pigeons landed almost immediately on their table and began fighting each other for the crumbs.

The waiter returned with our coffees, then shooed at the pigeons with his tray as he walked off.

"So what's going to happen to Malik?" I asked.

Yaya sighed. "I think he will be in the CIE for a long time. It will be hard for him. Every day he is in there, he is not here, and he is also not home. Being in the CIE is like being nowhere."

"But eventually they'll send him back?"

"Probably, yes." Yaya looked almost wistful. I knew his greatest fear was being deported, but still – he must miss his home a lot.

"Do you think you'll ever get to go home for a visit?"

"Maybe someday."

For Yaya to go back to Senegal and not get stuck there, he'd need to have paid off his debt, become a resident and gotten a passport. He'd need to have accomplished all that without being "stopped" like Malik.

Yaya took a sip of his coffee. The espresso cup and saucer looked like doll dishes in his hands. "First I need to make a lot of money," he said. "My family, they are expecting a return on their investment."

I nodded. He had a lot of people counting on him. I could see it in the slope of his shoulders.

Yaya turned his head to watch a glamorous woman walk by, her hands full of shopping bags. "When I go back," he said, "I'm going to bring a lot of presents, *tu sais?* Football shirts, iPads, running shoes."

"You're going to be popular."

"Yes."

"Do you talk to them? To your family?"

"Sometimes. I will talk to them more when I am a success." Yaya set down his empty cup, then looked at his gold watch – it was a knock-off, of course. "I'm sorry. I have to go." He unfolded his long body from the chair. "Thank you for the coffee." He took my hand and shook it formally. A family at the next table was watching us.

Yaya retrieved his sack of purses and swung it up over his shoulder. For a second, he looked like a tall skinny Santa Claus, and I pictured him returning home with his bag full of gifts, everyone so happy to see him. I really hoped that would happen for him, but he would need a lot of luck to pull it off.

I watched him move off up Passeig de Gràcia until he disappeared into the crowd. Then I sat at the table for a long time with the sun on my face, feeling almost as still as Atlas, like there was a pin holding time in place. At first it was just an insignificant moment – enjoying the last of my coffee on the edge of Plaça Catalunya – but then it grew into something larger: a sudden certainty that Manu had been right. I was a lucky person. I could go home and come back whenever I wanted. I didn't have any debt to pay off, and I had no one to worry about except myself.

I walked to a locutorio and wrote Peter an email: *I need to come and get my things. Please let me know when you'll be home.* I wasn't sure where the next weeks or months would take me, but whatever I decided to do, I would need my wallet and passport.

I clicked Send, and immediately an auto-response appeared in my inbox. The message said Peter was on vacation in Paris for the rest of the week – that he would reply to any emails when he got back. He'd probably taken someone else on our honeymoon. I let out a loud breath, feeling as if his email had punctured me somewhere. I checked the date of his return. It was the day after my court date, so now it was official: I wouldn't be able to make it back in time, even if I wanted to.

I hadn't realized I'd even been considering returning for my court date — it was only five days away — but now that I knew I couldn't, I felt anxious. I went into one of the phone booths and shut the door, so I could be by myself to think. If Peter had left the kitchen window open, I might be able to climb in from the stairwell. But no — that was crazy; there was no way to break into his apartment. I'd have to wait until he came back from his trip. Even from a distance, Peter had stolen something else from me: the opportunity to defend myself. I thought of the lying security guard, and how he was probably terrorizing other people. I should have gone back to stand up to him.

My borrowed sundress was damp with sweat, and my legs were sticking to the chair. I pushed open the door of the phone booth with my toe to get some air. In front of the locutorio, four Mossos had congregated, and every few seconds they looked through the window. The owner of the shop seemed stressed. I stood up as the Mossos entered. The last one locked the door behind him.

The locutorio was full of Latin Americans and other newcomers to Spain: people who had the need to call faraway relatives or wire money back home. Three of the Mossos started to make the rounds between the computers, asking for papers or identification. In the back of the shop, a woman with honey-coloured skin was starting to cry. She was holding a baby, and the Mossos in their black-and-yellow jackets hovered over her like wasps.

The fourth policeman was standing in front of the door. He motioned for me to come forward.

"*Muéstrame tu pasaporte,*" he said.

"*Lo siento. No lo tengo.*"

Becky Blake

The policeman furrowed his brow as if my Spanish was terrible. "Passport," he said, in English. "Show me."

I opened out my hands.

He made a beckoning motion with his fingers. "ID."

"I don't have any with me."

"You need to have ID. Always."

"I'm sorry. I didn't know."

He rolled his eyes. "*Guiri*," he muttered. "When are you leaving?"

If he thought I was a tourist, I wasn't going to set him straight. "I'm going home in a couple of days."

"Wait here." He went to talk to another policeman in the back of the shop. I tried to look as relaxed as possible, naive and entitled, checking out the notices and flyers on the bulletin board by the door. As usual, there was a bunch of advertising for locksmiths.

"I'm going home in a couple of days." Suddenly, I knew there was a chance for that to be true if I wanted – a way I might be able to get into Peter's apartment.

The policeman returned. "You can go." He unlocked the door and stepped aside so I could exit. I glanced at the back of the shop where the other Mossos were dividing the remaining people into two groups. The ones against the back wall all looked terrified. If Yaya had been with me, he would have been against the wall, and there wouldn't have been anything I could do to help.

I walked for a few blocks feeling like the policeman had been right to call me a *guiri*. All these weeks, I'd had access to ID that allowed me to go wherever I wanted in the world. It was time to get it back.

As I walked in the direction of the Gothic Quarter, I pulled a marker from my bag. When I spotted a street lamp covered in little coloured stickers, I stopped and copied two of the locksmiths' numbers onto my hand.

22

Outside of Peter's apartment building, I took a breath and rang his buzzer. His email had said he was away, but I needed to be certain. When nobody answered, I stood a little way off, pacing back and forth and watching the front door, waiting for someone to leave or come home. I checked the plastic bag I was carrying, making sure that Xavi's keys were hidden under the vegetables I'd bought. My money was in my bra now, and my courier bag was stashed in a garbage bin around the corner. Hopefully, it would still be there when I returned.

After a half hour or so, one of the building's tenants approached: a matronly woman walking a chihuahua in a pink collar. This was good luck. I remembered Senyora Bellet – she lived across the hall from Peter, and he'd introduced us on the day I arrived.

"Excuse me," I said, intercepting her as she got close. "Senyora Bellet? I don't know if you remember me. I live across the hall with Peter. In 4-1?"

Senyora Bellet stopped, clicking the lock on her extendable leash and reigning in her little dog. The chihuahua looked back at me with a put-out expression. Senyora Bellet was silent for so long that

I started to worry she knew I'd moved out. Or maybe someone else had moved in.

"*Sí, què va passar?*" she finally asked.

"I'm really sorry to bother you, but I don't know what to do. I just got robbed at the market and –" I lifted my plastic shopping bag of vegetables. "I was buying these, and I set my purse down for a second."

Senyora Bellet looked disapproving. "No," she said. "Never do this."

"I know! It was so stupid! I'm *so* mad at myself." Hurt, incredulous, lost – that's how the woman with the blue purse had seemed. "And now I'm locked out of the apartment, and Peter is in Paris, and I don't have my phone or my wallet or my keys."

The chihuahua was pulling on its leash, and the three of us began to walk toward the front door. I showed Senyora Bellet the locksmith numbers written on my hand. "Do you think I could use your phone to call a *cerrajero?*"

She unlocked the front door. "Come upstairs and you can call."

"Thanks! That's so nice of you." I followed her into the building, and for a second, everything shifted backward. The first time I'd been in the lobby, Peter had been pulling my suitcase. I'd been so excited to see the apartment he'd found for us: the high ceilings, the guest room, the Juliet balconies he'd described. That seemed like another person's life now.

As we passed the mailboxes, I noticed that Peter's had a newly printed slip of paper in the name slot; he'd removed the slip that showed both of our names, and replaced it with one that showed only his. That could be a problem if the locksmith saw it.

Senyora Bellet and her chihuahua were getting into the elevator. I squeezed in beside them. The elevator whirred to life like the insides of a clock. For no apparent reason, her dog began to bark at me.

"She doesn't like es-strangers," Senyora Bellet said. The elevator jolted to a stop.

On the landing, I glanced at Peter's front door as I waited for Senyora Bellet to open hers. Inside, her apartment smelled like stale cigarette smoke. The walls were covered in gold paisley-patterned wallpaper. From further down the dim hallway a weak voice called out.

"My father," Senyora Bellet said. The dog scampered down the hall toward the voice, dragging its leash.

I waited in the front hall as Senyora Bellet went to get her cordless phone. When she returned, I dialed one of the numbers on my hand. A man answered, and I tried to explain that I'd been robbed and lost my keys. It was harder for me to have a conversation in Spanish over the phone than in person, and I was making a mess of things. Senyora Bellet took the phone from me and explained the situation in Catalan. She ended with a short question – maybe about the price – then spoke in a loud burst of words, her voice rising sharply. After a minute she covered the phone. "Forty euros. You have?"

I nodded. I had twenty euros, and Peter had kept some money in the kitchen drawer for when we ordered food. If there wasn't any there, I'd have to improvise.

Senyora Bellet hung up the phone. "He comes in thirty minutes," she said.

"Thank you so much."

"You want that I put the vegetables at the fridge?"

"Oh, no. That's fine." I didn't want her peeking in the bag and maybe seeing Xavi's keys.

Her father was calling her from down the hall.

Senyora Bellet pointed to a velvet couch in the living room. "Sit."

"No, no. I'll just go wait downstairs." I needed to get rid of the slip of paper from the mailbox.

Senyora Bellet motioned more forcefully to the couch. "Please."

I didn't want her to get suspicious. "Okay, thanks. Just for a few minutes."

She took the bag of vegetables from me despite my protest, and left to go talk to her father. I perched on the edge of the couch. On one wall there was a poster from a Batman movie, on another wall a picture of Jesus. A huge china cabinet with etched glass doors was filled with teapots, plates and sherry glasses. I bit at the inside of my cheek and watched a little gold clock on the end table tick forward. Thirty minutes was way too much time to sit in a stranger's apartment – way too much time for her to think about my story and begin to doubt it.

When Senyora Bellet returned she offered me a plate of cookies. "Oh, no thank you," I said. "I'm not very hungry."

She set the cookies on the table, then sat down across from me on a hard-looking chair.

I didn't know much about either Batman or Jesus. I couldn't think of anything to say.

"You want you call your husband?" she asked.

Of course she assumed Peter and I were married. I pretended to think for a moment. "No, he's working. I don't want to bother him."

She seemed to find this strange.

"The truth is –" I leaned forward, speaking slowly so she could understand. "He thinks I can't take care of myself – that I need him to do everything. Today, I just want to show him that I can do things on my own. Do you know what I mean?"

She gave a small nod. She wasn't wearing a wedding ring, which meant she'd probably never been married, or else she was a widow. I didn't think she'd be divorced. There were pictures of children on the end table, but they were very old pictures. Maybe one of them was her, forty or fifty years ago. The intercom buzzed.

Senyora Bellet hefted herself off the chair, then walked over and shouted into the speaker. A moment later we heard the elevator humming, then coming to a stop. I hadn't had time to go downstairs to the mailbox. If the locksmith asked me about why my name wasn't on it, I'd tell him that I'd only been in Barcelona a few weeks and we hadn't had a chance to make the change.

The locksmith was a heavy-set man with a tool box and a large ring of keys on his belt. I showed him the door, and explained to him that my purse had been stolen, and that Peter was away – that I could show him some ID once I got inside the apartment.

"Don't worry," he said. *"No tienes pinta de ser ladrón."* He winked. He didn't think I looked like a thief.

"So you're going to be able to get in?" I asked.

"Claro. First, we will try the easy way." He rapped hard on the door with his knuckles.

I held my breath as we waited – it was possible that Peter had a guest, someone who hadn't wanted to answer when I'd buzzed up from the street – but there was no sound from the apartment and the door stayed closed.

"And now the hard way." The locksmith opened his tool box.

As he worked on the top lock, jiggling two skinny metal tools that looked like dental instruments, he told me some ways I could protect myself from pickpockets in future. His tips were pretty good: to be suspicious if anyone approached or bumped into me, to be extra careful on the metro at rush hour, to lock the door behind me at bank ATMs when I was taking out money at night. He also cautioned me about burglars. Apparently, there were some thieves who leapt from one building's roof to another and could jump down onto balconies.

"If you want, I can put some extra locks on your balcony doors," the locksmith said. He was drumming up business.

"Maybe. I'll have to talk to my husband first."

Senyora Bellet was hovering behind us, listening.

"Senyora, you don't need to wait," I said. "I'm sure you have a lot of things to do. I'll knock if we need you." I mimed knocking on her door.

She nodded and went back into her apartment, but I suspected she was still watching through the peephole.

The locksmith got the top lock open and began working on the bottom one.

"Hey, why are there so many locksmiths in Barcelona?" I asked. "Those little coloured stickers are everywhere."

"Stickers? Oh, *las pegatinas*. Yes. You have to be careful." The locksmith stopped to wipe the sweat off his face. "Some of those *cerrajeros* are not real. They're burglars too."

"Really?" I looked at him more closely.

"Yes, it's true. If you and your friends need help like this, you should always call me. The others, sometimes they make a copy of the key, or they are just there to look inside your apartment and see what you have." He stuffed his handkerchief back in his pocket. He seemed too lethargic to be a thief, but I couldn't be sure. Maybe it was an act.

He pressed down on one tool, while carefully threading the other in and out of the lock. Finally there was a clicking sound. He opened the door, and I could see down the hall.

"*Bueno*," he said. "Do you have another set of keys inside, or do you need me to change the lock for a new one?"

I thought about Peter coming home and trying unsuccessfully to open his front door. "How much to change the lock?"

"Uff. Maybe 150?"

I didn't have that much. "No, it's fine. I have a spare set of keys inside. Let me go get you some money."

I stepped into the apartment and went straight to the kitchen. There was a fishy smell seeping in through the drains. I rifled through the drawers and found a bunch of change in one, and my wallet, sitting on top of my sketchbook, in another. I checked over my shoulder to make sure the locksmith hadn't followed me, then pulled out the twenty euros from my bra, another ten from my wallet and scraped together eight euros in change from the drawer. I put my wallet back, then returned to the front door.

"I only have thirty-eight," I said.

Senyora Bellet was in the hallway again. She pulled a change purse from her pocket and opened it, handing me a two-euro coin.

"Thank you," I said. "Thank you both so much." I wanted to be by myself now, but the locksmith asked if he could have a glass of water, and Senyora Bellet went to her fridge to get my vegetables. They both seemed to be moving in slow motion. I wondered if the locksmith was casing the apartment. Finally, he said goodbye.

I closed the front door and stood for a long moment looking down Peter's hallway. Even though he was away, there were still things here that could hurt me. A picture of us that I'd hung by the coat rack was gone. All that was left were the little holes where the nails had been – a constellation gone dark.

I went into the kitchen and opened the fridge door to let the cool air dry the sweat on my face. Inside was a lemon, a takeout container of wilted salad and a half-empty bottle of vodka. Peter had cleared out the food I'd bought at the market. Probably it had all gone to waste.

I took a swig of the vodka, then grabbed my wallet from the drawer again and flipped it open. My credit card and bank card were still in there. I set the wallet beside my bag of vegetables and went down the hall to find my passport.

The door of the spare bedroom was closed. I knocked softly and waited for a moment, then turned the handle. Inside, the wooden blinds were shut. Thin stripes of sunshine crawled weakly across the floor. Half the room was filled with boxes, and I could smell the cedar from the packing crates. I checked the desk drawer where I thought I'd left my passport, but it wasn't there. I walked over to the boxes. Each one was labelled in my own optimistic handwriting, our Barcelona address copied over and over in deeply felt block letters. I'd been so proud when the rough men from the shipping company had come to pick up the boxes in Toronto. "Barcelona?" one of them had asked, impressed, running his thick fingers across a label.

I traced one of the labels' ragged borders now, trying to stick it back in place. *Barcelona*. The word had seemed like magic, like a golden ticket to a happy life. I considered getting a knife, cutting open the boxes, and releasing my things that were trapped inside, but all of them were intermingled with Peter's, and when I thought about sorting through them, I realized there was nothing I really needed, nothing that couldn't be replaced.

I opened the wooden blinds and unlatched the balcony door, then stepped outside. The view was just as I remembered – the Gothic cathedral in the foreground, and then the wide avenue that led to the mountains in the distance. It was a lovely view, but I'd found several better ones since. The best had been from the top of one of those mountains. I stepped back inside and closed the door behind me.

Out in the living room Peter had set up some new shelves – the kind of modern angular furniture he liked. I walked over to a potted plant in the corner. It didn't seem like the type of plant Peter would choose – in fact, I didn't think he would buy a plant at all and now there were two of them: one in the corner and one on the balcony. I touched the leaves; they were healthy. I looked for a card, but there wasn't one. I sniffed the couch cushions for perfume, then went into the bathroom to look for an extra towel or a woman's shampoo. Nothing. If there *was* another woman, then she hadn't left her mark on his apartment yet. For a second, I felt sorry for her. No matter how serious things got between them, she would probably never leave a trace. The living room would be painted gallery white, the way Peter preferred, and the art on the walls would always be chosen by him. I took hold of the leaves of the healthy plant in the corner and squeezed them one by one.

In the bedroom, a new painting was hanging above the bed. It was Miró-inspired, thick black lines suggesting the shape of surrealist people and animals against a dark blue sky. The painting was skilful, and it had an expensive frame. Stealing it would leave an absence above Peter's bed that he would see for a long time. I climbed up and lifted the painting off the wall, then stood looking down at it. Taking it wasn't going to stopper the little puncture hole that Peter's email had made; if anything, it would just draw my attention to it – make it harder for the wound to close.

I rehung the painting and stepped down off the bed. I just needed to find my passport and then I could go. It wasn't in the bedside table's drawer, or on any of the shelves in the living room. I went back into the kitchen and checked the top of the fridge. Peter was organized – he would have wanted to keep my things together. I opened the drawer where I'd found my wallet and pulled out my sketchbook. My passport was inside the front cover and so was a lilac-coloured envelope addressed to me.

I recognized her handwriting immediately. She'd written our address in the same childish printing I remembered from the notes she'd left on the kitchen counter, her letters veering down and to the right like she was running out of steam. When I'd sent her my postcard, I'd hesitated before including our return address, but I'd wanted to show off the name of our street: Carrer de Paradís. It had looked so much like *paradise*.

The letter was still sealed and I didn't open it. Whatever words it contained, I didn't want to be in Peter's apartment when I read them. I put the envelope into the plastic bag with my wallet and sketchbook. The set of keys I'd thrown at Peter were also in the drawer, and I decided to take them with me. I wouldn't be coming back, but Senyora Bellet might watch me leave, and it was better if I could lock the door behind me.

When I let myself out of the apartment, I made a show of using the keys before moving down the stairs. In the lobby, I stood for a moment in front of the mailboxes, staring at Peter's name on the little slip of paper. Peter with no Niki – that was probably for the best. I dropped Peter's keys in the mailbox and pushed out through the front door.

Outside, the intensity of the heat had been blunted a little. A group of teenage girls was walking home from school in their uniforms, laughing together, their braces glinting in the sun. Further along, a man was lounging against a solemn medieval building, a newborn baby sleeping in his arms. From an open window, I could hear someone practising her English, repeating the instructor's words: "How much does it cost for a ticket? What time is the train?"

I returned to where I'd hidden my courier bag in the garbage bin, and thankfully it was still there. Everything felt like a sign today, and this one seemed to confirm that some things might be waiting where I left them, if I ever chose to go back.

23

When I got to Xavi's, I undressed on his terrace: changing out of Laia's sundress and into my own clothes that were still a little warm from their day in the sun. Inside the apartment, the light was on, but when I went in, Xavi wasn't there. I set my bag of vegetables on the kitchen counter, then slid the heavy paper I'd bought behind the bookshelf so it wouldn't get bent.

Sitting on the bed, I dumped the contents of my courier bag onto the floor. I lifted my mother's letter to my nose, but it didn't smell like her. I still wasn't ready to open it. Someday I might be, or maybe I would wait until I could see her face to face and respond to whatever she'd written in real time. I didn't know what I was more afraid of: what the letter might say or what it might not say. I tucked it into my sketchbook, then opened my wallet. As I flipped through the cards inside, I remembered the security guard tossing all my ID and found photos onto the table, thinking he knew what they added up to, but doing the math all wrong. In the back of my passport was the thin blue Promise to Appear notice with my court date on it. There was no longer anything preventing me from keeping that promise.

I heard Xavi turning his key in the door.

"You're home," he said when he walked in. "I was hoping you would be."

I went over and kissed him.

"Are you hungry?" he asked, peeking into the bag I'd set on his counter.

"Yes."

"I was going to make pasta," he said. "But since you bought all these vegetables, do you want to learn how to make a fideuà?"

"What's a fideuà?"

"It's sort of like a paella but a Catalan version. With noodles. It's much better." He started to wash the vegetables in the sink.

I peered over his shoulder. "That sounds yummy."

"If I show you, you have to promise not to tell anyone my secret."

"Okay." I laughed.

"I'm serious," Xavi said, spinning around to face me. "Every man in this city thinks he makes the best fideuà. But I actually do make the best fideuà. So it's important I can trust you."

"You can trust me."

"Good." He handed me a wedge of tomato and I popped it into my mouth.

While we were cooking, I told Xavi about seeing Yaya, and about the squat being boarded up, and that I'd walked all the way downtown and back. I didn't tell him about breaking into Peter's.

"Did you steal anything today?" Xavi asked.

"Nope." I remembered how Peter's painting had felt in my hands. "I think I might be done with stealing."

"Huh. Do you remember the first thing you ever stole?"

"I don't know. Maybe a box of macaroni and cheese?"

"Maybe that means you're going to be a chef."

"A chef? Why?"

"I have a theory." Xavi leaned against the counter. "That the first thing a person steals is a clue to what they're going to be."

"What's the first thing you stole?" I asked.

"A magazine. With a picture I liked inside. It was a gorgeous shot of the mountains, plus the girl in the picture was really hot." Xavi reached for my waist and pulled me toward him.

"Okay. But I don't think I'm going to be a chef. I'm pretty much the worst cook in the world." Our mouths were too close not to kiss, but after a moment, I turned my face to the side; I needed a second to think.

"Maybe for me it's the last thing I stole."

"What was that?" Xavi asked.

"Remember when I was leaving that first morning?"

I pointed to his cans of spray paint in the corner.

After we ate, we sat on the bed picking out photographs for an exhibit Xavi was hanging the next day at the university. Most of his photos were portraits of farmers who lived in rural places working the land – a disappearing way of life.

"I'd like to take a picture of you," Xavi said.

"I don't think so." Pictures pretended at forever. They were little snatches of time, locked unnaturally in place. In Peter's apartment, our photos were sealed away in boxes, thin slivers of the past separated now from all feeling and sense.

"Come on. It'll be fun." Xavi picked up his camera from the bedside table. It was fancy and expensive, like the ones thieves loved to steal from tourists.

"What kind of picture?"

"Just a regular picture. A portrait." He took the cap off the lens.

"I don't like getting my photo taken."

"That's okay." Xavi lifted my chin and turned my face toward him. "Nobody does." He snapped a picture.

"You should call that one *Uncomfortable*," I said. "Why do you want a photo anyway? Is it for a souvenir?" Maybe he thought our way of life was also disappearing. If so, it would be easier to tell him I was leaving.

"What do you mean?" He shot several more pictures.

Xavi and I were being lovely to each other, but that wasn't the same as being in love with each other; it couldn't last. "You know, something to remember me by?"

He lowered the camera. "Why? Are you going somewhere?"

"Maybe. I might have to go back to Canada for a while."

Xavi held my gaze. "Just for a while?"

"Hopefully."

"When would you go?"

"Soon."

He lifted the camera again and I couldn't see his expression. "Then I'm going to need a really good picture," he said. "So I can remember you until you come back. Move over a little toward the light."

He took a bunch more pictures, then sat beside me on the bed, reviewing the images.

"This one is good," he said. "Look. Look how beautiful you are."

I took the heavy camera from him. The picture was black and white, and I almost didn't recognize myself. I looked somehow both old and young, both tough and vulnerable. It was an image that seemed to move back and forth between two extremes. For a second I thought I saw a third thing in the middle: a wavering centre point trying to come to rest. "You think this is beautiful?"

"Yes." Xavi leaned over and kissed me, his warm hands on either side of my face. It felt like he was holding me in place, and I wondered if maybe I was wrong about our future, if the outline of loveliness between us might fill in over time, become something solid and lasting.

"Hey," I said. "Say something nice."

He moved my hair behind my ear. "Something nice," he whispered. Then he kissed down my neck, and I was glad I had taken so many drinks from the old fountain on La Rambla. If anyone was guaranteed to return to Barcelona, it was me.

As soon as the sun came up I crept out of bed and slid the heavy paper out from behind the bookshelf. Xavi's snoring made me smile as I drew and then cut out shapes: a grocery cart, a house with a jagged arrow passing through and a pair of heart-shaped lips pursed into a kiss. Food, shelter and love: three things a person needed to have in place before they could care about anything else.

My plan was to paint the stencils in unexpected places, locations that would make passersby snap into the present and feel something: connection, confusion, annoyance – it didn't matter what. I wanted to stencil the grocery cart onto dumpsters, the house onto abandoned buildings and the lips as a repeating image around El Raval, especially on the street where Fanta worked. Hopefully, I'd run into her while I was there.

When Xavi woke up, I showed him the stencils.

"Those are cool. Maybe we can paint them tonight? When I get back from hanging the exhibit?"

"I think I'm going to paint some today," I said.

"Okay." Xavi gave me a warm sleepy hug, then headed to the shower.

I went in to join him, even though I knew it would probably make him late.

The first place I went back to was the squat. I wanted to paint my house stencil on the boarded-up door. The regular squatter's symbol –

the circle with the jagged arrow passing through – was a sort of secret password, something only comprehensible to those in the know. My alternative symbol was meant to be more inclusive, its message more obvious to anyone who might need a place to stay: *there are homes inside this building if you can get in.* It was also a message for the builders and police who had evicted my friends: *people need places to live and this building is sitting empty because of you.*

A few people slowed to watch as I pulled the stencil away. The image left behind was a photonegative of the paint-stained cardboard in my hand: the outline of a house with an arrow inside. It was an image that might be there for a moment, or possibly for years. There was no way to know how long it would last, but in a way, that's what made it so powerful.

The next place I went was the Boqueria. I walked down the market's main aisle, smiling at the vendors who called out to me as I passed. The others were busy with the frenetic exchange of money and food – there were so many hands reaching back and forth across the stalls. Outside the rear exit, I crouched down by one of the dumpsters and stencilled a string of grocery carts along one side. Above them I painted the Catalan words for *you have to eat. Has de menjar.* The graffiti seemed to have changed the dumpster's purpose, to have given it a voice. I imagined the grocery carts rippling out in photographs around the world. As Atlas always reminded me: more than a hundred thousand tourists passed by here every day.

I took my final stencil to El Raval. The closer I got to the construction site, the shakier I felt. I passed by a group of men standing in front of the butcher shop, then ducked into a narrow alleyway that was tight like a throat. From both sides, men and women stepped forward. Some of them were selling things, others had nothing but need humming through their veins or hammering in their empty stomachs. I'd walked down this alley many times with Manu but now it felt more dangerous, maybe because I had something to lose again.

At the end of the alley I came out at the hotel construction site. I remembered the sharp ring cutting into my face, and the footprint-shaped bruises across my ribs. Lying on these cobblestones, I'd made a promise to myself that I hadn't yet kept: that if I managed to get up and get away, then I would be willing to go back as far as it took to make a clean start.

I let out a long breath, then walked around the site's perimeter looking for Fanta, but I didn't see her. I hoped maybe she'd managed to sell the stolen drugs and get out of the business, but more likely she was off somewhere with a client. I knew she took her customers to a dark doorway down the block. I slowed as I neared it. There were two men standing close. I saw a small package changing hands, then they moved off.

If I couldn't find Fanta, I could at least leave her a message, paint her something optimistic like the decals she always had on her fingernails. The doorway seemed to require something bigger than the stencil of the kissing lips I'd made. I thought for a moment, then selected a can of paint with a red lid. Free-form, I drew a life-sized outline of a person on the door – the same shape I'd once dreamt about finding in the palm of my hand. Beside it I wrote the word *love* in English, then Spanish, then Catalan: *LOVE, EL AMOR, L'AMOR*. When I tagged *Niki* at the bottom, the words looked like a goodbye, the end of an international love letter.

I stepped back to assess my work. Now any man who went with Fanta into that dark piss-smelling doorway would have to stand against the cut-out image, would have to think about the word *LOVE* while he received its facsimile. And as for any pedestrians passing by – for some, the empty shape might look like a love that'd gone missing, for others, a love that was still to be found.

Something on the ground caught my eye. It was a little white square – an upside-down photograph. For a second I froze. Then I turned it over like a playing card, but it wasn't the photo I'd feared. Instead of Fanta's little boy, it was a picture of a whole family. Not Fanta's loss, but someone else's.

A pair of Mossos were walking toward me. I scooped up the photograph and without thinking I started to run: back past the construction site, up the alley, along the street with the old hospital courtyard to La Rambla, then across into the Gothic Quarter and up Portal de l'Àngel. Not once did I look back – not until I'd made it through the sliding doors of the giant department store on Plaça Catalunya and stepped onto the escalator. When I finally turned, there was no one behind me.

I rode the zigzagging escalators up through women's fashions, then men's fashions, bridal wear, home furnishings, travel needs and baby goods: everything a person required to have a perfect department store life. At the top, on the ninth floor, was a cafeteria. I sat at one of the tables to catch my breath, staring over at the wall of windows. Through them, I could see all the way to the horizon, the hazy line of undulating mountains cradling the city. The view was so wide that both Peter and Xavi's neighbourhoods were included, and all the distance in between. I put the picture I'd found in El Raval into one of the photo slots of my wallet. Then I walked over to the window.

I stayed very still for a long time looking out. I knew that as soon as I started to move, time would go quickly. In one hour, I'd be back at Xavi's. In one day, I'd be on a plane. In four days, in a courtroom. After that, I didn't know. Maybe I would go to Brigid's wedding. I might even return to the apartment building where I'd grown up – at least to see Rosa. There would be tears probably. Then a blank white room somewhere that needed to be filled.

Far away, on the top of Tibidabo mountain, I could just make out the shape of a Ferris wheel against the sky. Maybe when I returned I would go to that amusement park, buy a ticket and ride to the very top, then look back at the spot where I was standing now. I placed my hands on the glass and leaned in with my full weight. I could see everything.

Acknowledgements

This book has been raised with the help of a village so large it's really a country – or two countries, to be exact. For support in Spain, I would like to say mil gracias to chosen sisters Aaron Crisp, Lourdes Adela Enamorado Alvarenga, Yesenia Patricia Garcia McKinnon, Virginie Lörtscher, Annie Pujkiewicz and Elke Van Ael for accompanying me on research adventures into the darker corners of Barcelona. Thanks also to Juan Ansó for cooking for me, and to Luis Castel and Cesc Martínez for being my go-to guys on all things Catalan. (To Cesc also for a careful reading of the book.) My stay at the Jiwar Creation Residence provided an inspiring place to reconnect with this story.

In Canada, as part of the Creative Writing MFA program at the University of Guelph, I benefitted from early feedback from my classmates, as well as from Kathryn Kuitenbrouwer, Pasha Malla and Russell Smith. Crucial writing and research grants came from the Toronto Arts Council, Access Copyright, the Ontario Arts Council, the Porcupine's Quill (through the OAC Writers' Reserve Program) and the Canada Council. I am grateful for my time at the Banff Centre, and for the opportunity to workshop the manuscript with Shyam Selvadurai during the Diaspora Dialogues Long Form Mentorship program. Amanda Lewis and Barbara Berson offered excellent advice at critical moments. Alissa York provided insightful late-game guidance during the writing program at Sage Hill.

I have greatly appreciated the input of my wonderful agent, Stephanie Sinclair, and astute reader Deanna Roney from Transatlantic. My editor, Paul Vermeersch, has kindly cared for this novel over the last two years. Ashley Hisson's thoughtful copy edits helped so much to polish this work, as did Elisabet Ràfols' final review of the Catalan in the book.

A big thank you to Officer Dave G., John Lefebvre, Sean Marks and Carlos Suárez for conversing with me about crime and punishment. And to Jeffrey Fair for introducing me to freeganism.

The following chosen sisters need to be thanked as early readers and/or literary cheerleaders: Sylvia Arthur, Rachel Deutsch, Rebecca Fisseha, Severn Thompson, Christine Lynett, Nancy Jo Cullen, Eufemia Fantetti, Erina Harris, Leesa Dean, my Cinnamon Karma ladies and the Shark-tailed Grouse Gang. Ayelet Tsabari, Kathy Friedman and Kilby Smith-McGregor each gave essential feedback on this novel at different stages. Kilby also created the beautiful design for this book.

Warmest thanks to: my parents, Pat and Bill, and my sisters, Kara and Julie, for their unwavering support; my old colleagues at ESM for always believing I would eventually have another job; and Sarah Curley for being a truly amazing friend.

Becky Blake is a two-time winner of the CBC Literary Prize (for Nonfiction in 2017 and Short Story in 2013). Her fiction and essays have appeared in publications across Canada. She holds an MFA from the University of Guelph, and teaches creative writing at the University of Toronto's School of Continuing Education. Becky currently lives in Toronto where she's working on a second novel and a memoir-in-essays.